W9-AFC-802

At least once in her life a woman wonders...

Where Is He Now?

Christina Northeast
LLC
Liberty Center, OH 43532

"If either of us wanted to know if there was still a strong spark, I do believe we just found out."

Those soft eyes of Jeanne's didn't deny it, but her frown was becoming deeper. "A spark is one thing. Jumping headfirst into a fire is another. I didn't come here looking for this, Nate."

He could see the power of their embrace had scared her. And told himself that he should be scared, too.

She'd turned into everything he'd dreamed she would. She looked exactly like the million-dollar success she was—and there was that guy in her picture. He'd have to be crazy to forget that guy.

Which all added up to trouble. To know there was still a powder keg of emotion between them made absolutely nothing easier. What was that old saying? *The things we fear the most have already happened to us.* Well, he'd let Jeanne Claire Cassiday free once, and almost hadn't survived it.

He couldn't afford to lose her a second time.

Avon Contemporary Romances by
Jennifer Greene

WHERE IS HE NOW?
THE WOMAN MOST LIKELY TO . . .

JENNIFER GREENE

Where Is He Now?

AVON BOOKS

An Imprint of HarperCollinsPublishers

This is a work of fiction. Names, characters, places, and incidents are products of the author's imagination or are used fictitiously and are not to be construed as real. Any resemblance to actual events, locales, organizations, or persons, living or dead, is entirely coincidental.

AVON BOOKS
An Imprint of HarperCollins*Publishers*
10 East 53rd Street
New York, New York 10022-5299

chapter 1

She was the sexiest thing to pop up in his driveway in a long, *looonnggg* time.

Nate Donneli stopped short in front of the window, a mug of cold coffee halfway to his mouth. He'd come to work in a snarly Monday mood. Lately he couldn't sleep because of a building personal crisis—which he was doing his best to deny by charging into work before dawn. Unfortunately, that lack of sleep had added up. He had a shark of a headache. The weather was as precarious as his temper; Ann Arbor kept promising spring, but the wind out there was bitter and mean. Still. Even a hard-core workaholic had to lighten up for something like this.

1

Man. Lately he felt as if he'd lived ninety hard years instead of thirty-three, but one look at the view out the window made him remember the kick of adolescent hormones, the sizzle of pure hungry lust, that brief, wicked time in a guy's life when he'd have happily died for sex. At least when the sex was worth it.

He didn't know exactly what she was worth, but right then he didn't care about the cost. Just for the opportunity to look at her, his heart started thumping and his pulse did a boogie-woogie. Charlie even stood to attention, and Charlie had been too bogged down by life problems lately to even think about getting a hard-on.

Aw, to hell with work. Nate plunked down his coffee mug, grabbed a jacket against the freezing March morning, and hiked outside to get a closer look at her.

A businessman was standing at her side, dressed in a wool business coat and briefcase, but Nate didn't waste time on the guy.

She was even sexier close up. Oooh, baby. Not everyone could wear that pale, creamy yellow, but on her it was a layer of elegance on a creature who was already in a class of her own. His eyes did more than admire. His eyes . . . caressed . . . with abandon.

Her rump was a perfect smooth slope, her hips exquisitely rounded. Even though she was standing still, you just knew how she'd move—fast and smooth, as if she owned the world. As if she knew there wasn't a man in the universe who could ignore her. As if she could bring any male to his knees without half trying.

Nate circled her, slowly, not caring if the whole damn world saw his tongue hanging out or how close he was to drooling.

He'd always been a breast man, and her headlights were exquisite. Not too big, not too small, just show-off just right, absolutely perfect for her build and size. Come to think of it, he'd probably always been a bumper man, too, because he couldn't stop himself from wandering back for another view of her ass . . . and it was breathtaking. No top. He barely had to angle his head to see all that naked leather trim, which was especially striking next to all that soft, creamy yellow. There were some dazzling spikes on her wheels, but not so much jewelry that it took away from the original body—and it was an original body.

Nate might have been celibate for a while, but he still knew when a body had been bumped up and rehabbed. This one was the real McCoy, sleek and classy from stem to stern, no fakery or flim-flam of any kind.

"I'm in love," he said to the suit, who laughed.

"Stand in line."

"She looks virgin."

"She is."

3

"Where in God's name did you find her?"

"An old man's estate in Scotland. She was hiding in a back room. Been pampered and protected her whole life in every way."

"I can see that. I can't believe you're here to sell her—"

"I'm not. But as I'm sure you already noticed, she's missing her hood ornament. She's so close to perfect that it really bugs me, and I was told that you're the man. From East Coast to West Coast, there's supposed to be no other antique car man even close to your reputation. Think you can come through for me?"

"If your hood ornament exists on the planet, I'll get it for you." Nate wasn't concerned with the job, not yet. He met the stranger's eyes. "Would you mind if I touched her?" When the suit didn't immediately agree, he said, "Trust me, I'd shoot myself before hurting her. In fact, I'll volunteer to kill any guy who put a fingerprint on her."

The stranger relaxed. "Yeah. I can see you've got the right kind of respect. Open the hood."

He did. Reverently. Getting his fingers that close to her private parts was better than being fifteen and touching his first girlfriend's breast—even if it had been in a trainer bra stuffed with Kleenex. There was no padding anywhere on this baby. She was pure, beautifully made sports car. "A 1936 Model Sprite, isn't she?"

"Yup. And damn. You're the first one who actually knew the year."

Nate ignored the compliment. He wasn't showing off. He was savoring. "Right before the Nuffield takeover. That's when Riley was making these sports cars. Who'd have thought the Brits had this much passion in them? I'll bet she purrs when she's lubed just right."

"She'll do anything for you," the stranger affirmed.

The loudspeaker suddenly boomed, *"Mr. Donneli! Telephone! Line 34!"*

Hell. The vacation moment was over. Line 34 was his private line, which meant it could be his daughter, Caitlin—which could mean WWIII. He *had* to take the call. Nate carefully lowered the hood. "Come on inside. Let's get your baby put up in a protected bay, get you set up with the paperwork. You live in the Detroit or Ann Arbor area?"

He steered the suit inside, barking orders through the lobby as he went. Fifteen years ago—in his father's time—Donneli Motors had been a half-assed garage with a mediocre reputation. Now the front lobby had red carpeting and red leather seats, suitable for the clientele who could afford him. Beyond the lobby, of course, was the real business. Smells and sounds and sights bombarded him from every direction. He roared at Daniel to get off his butt, barked at Martha about the call to Austria, poked his head in the first two bays to see how those rehab jobs were doing, and still kept up a running conversation with the suit as they hiked through.

"Okay now. I should be able to tell you by tonight if I can locate her hood ornament or not, although the cost—or how much time it'll take to get it here—those questions could be iffy for longer than that. Some sources are more reliable than others. In the meantime, Martha'll take down your address . . ."

He charged past, grabbing the cold mug of coffee he'd left on the windowsill, about to wing into his private office for the telephone, when the fresh-faced girl manning the phones today said earnestly, "I took the call, Mr. Donneli. It's Jeanne Claire Cassiday."

He stopped sharply, feeling as if someone had slammed a fist in his heart. "Who?"

The girl looked stricken, started wringing her hands and swallowing hard. Everybody knew he could be—just a tiny bit—demanding now and then, but hell, he'd never yelled at a kid. "I meant . . . what? I know I misheard you. I thought you said the caller was—"

"Jeanne Claire Cassiday. That's what the lady said. Honest." Again, the kid clutched her hands, a streak of panicked color chasing across her cheeks.

But he couldn't take the time to mollify the kid then. He hurtled into the office and grabbed the phone—only to hear a dial tone. Whoever had been on the line had hung up.

Still, there seemed to be something suddenly stuck in his throat the size of a boulder. It took several moments before his heart rate slowed down. There was no one on the line. Certainly not Jeanne Claire Cassiday.

And no matter who'd been calling, it couldn't have been Jeanne. He hadn't heard that name in close to fifteen years. He hadn't even let himself *think* that name in fifteen years.

It couldn't possibly have been Jeanne.

Monday, March 29
9:17 P.M.

Jeanne heard the knock on her apartment door. She just ignored it, the way she'd ignored the door and the phone and the pager for several hours now.

She hadn't been completely irresponsible. She'd listened to the messages—two were from her dad. Two from Donald. And the last three were from Martha—the afternoon receptionist at Oz Enterprises—confirming some event arrangements for later that week. Since she lived in a suite on the third floor of the conference center, the entire staff considered her available 24/7. But she was ducking all contact with Donald, and as far as business . . . well, Oz Enterprises was just going to have to do without their Good Witch of the North for a few hours.

Curled up in a corner of the couch in the dark, she took another sip of wine—directly from the bottle—and marveled. Why hadn't she ever done this before? Hidden from her problems. Practiced denial. Shut out reality.

She swallowed the nice, warm gulp of Merlot, thinking that if a woman's life was unraveling at the seams at the ripe old age of thirty-three, she might as well enjoy it. Irresponsibility didn't seem to take any learning curve. She'd gotten into it with no sweat at all. It was easy. Stressless. In fact, it was mighty tempting to just hide out here in the dark and never show up for life again.

The upstart knocked on her door again. Only this time the knock sounded more like a relentless fist-thumping pound. "Jeanne Claire! It's me! Tam! You *have* to be in there. Open up!"

She jolted at the familiar voice. She'd been so sure there was no one in the entire universe she wanted to see . . . but then, how could she possibly have expected Tamara Whitley to show up?

She and Tam went way back—all the way to second grade, to be precise, when they'd tussled on the playground of St. Sebastian Elementary School over the second grade heartthrob. The heartthrob had walked off. Neither even remembered his name. But they'd both emerged from the encounter bruised and muddy and vowed friends forever. Tamara had always been a bad influence, a quality that Jeanne especially appreciated in a friend.

She quickly pushed herself off the couch, but then had to negotiate the unexpectedly complicated path to the door. The doorknob was another dizzying challenge, and then the blinding-bright hall light made her squint.

"You have no idea how glad I am to see you," Jeanne said fervently.

"Oh, yeah, I do. I'd have come over before, but I didn't see the mail until I got home from work, so I didn't see the high school reunion invitation until a few minutes ago. Hell. You started drinking ahead of me. Let me get my coat off and catch up before we start talking about you-know-what. And for heaven's sake, who are those crazy people down in the lobby?"

Jeanne locked the door, switched on a lamp, and sank back on the couch. Her head felt fine—as long as she was holding it. And Tam knew the way to the cupboard and glasses without any help. "It's quite a group. You know the Oz Enterprises motto—Whatever Your Heart Desires. Well . . . sometimes that's a real challenge. This party happens to be the second annual gathering of the College Graduate Ex-Strippers Club."

"Get out." Tamara shivered off her rabbit jacket,

pushed off her red lizard boots, and as expected, aimed for the cupboards and refrigerator. "They all looked well over sixty."

"I'd guess that, too. It's a small but distinctly select group," Jeanne said wryly. She watched her friend uncork a fresh bottle of wine and scoop up a glass. "What can I tell you? It's not easy to book events on a Monday night at the end of March."

"I'll bet not, but what on earth do they *do* when they get together?" Tamara flipped on more lights, making herself at home, before settling on the opposite end of the peach jacquard couch.

"Um. I believe they strip to college fight songs for old time's sake. But truthfully, once I've set them up—and they've paid the bill—I just try to stay out of their way. I don't want to know. They might be a little eccentric, but they're having fun, and I don't care what they're doing as long as it's legal and their check clears." Both of them, Jeanne thought, were doing a fine job of not looking down. With all the lamps turned on, the photographs on the coffee table were hard to ignore, but they managed.

They chattered nonstop for several minutes, catching up on the irrelevant stuff, ignoring the rough-water subjects. Although they hadn't seen each other for weeks, a time lag never seemed to make any difference. Jeanne had always seemed to sense when Tamara was upset and vice versa.

They'd always had a Mutt and Jeff friendship—
a complete mismatch in personalities—yet somehow they'd jelled. Jeanne had always figured it
was the loneliness thing. Back in high school,
Jeanne had been the prom queen, the darling of
the senior class, won the Most Popular tag in the
yearbook hands down. Yet on the inside, she'd
never felt she fit in anywhere.

Tamara was also someone who never looked
lonely—but was. Even today, she dressed like an
irrepressible free spirit. Her rowdy-print top and
skinny pants were a shock of color in the subdued
cream and coral living room. She hadn't been in
the room five minutes before her boots were
thrown here, her jacket there. Her shoulder-length
red hair was flying every which way; her granny
glasses always seemed a little askew, and makeup
never did a thing for her face.

If they hadn't been friends, Jeanne would have
been jealous of her. Standing next to Tamara,
she'd always felt like a pale pastel next to a vivid
rainbow. Even though she'd crashed in a funk
hours before, her red heels were tucked neatly
next to the door, her clothes tidily hung out of
sight. Today she'd worn a Donna Karan black suit,
a white blouse from Ann Taylor, a perky red and
black scarf from the Museum of Boston. Her
clothes were tasteful and classy and she loved
them. But that was the problem. She'd been raised

from birth to be tasteful and classy. Someone great at image but, damn, with Tamara, you always knew there was substance.

"Hey," Tam said suddenly. "Quit with the glum face."

"I'm not glum. In fact . . . I was remembering all those years at St. Sebastian's. You were so smart, so talented—"

Tamara snorted. "I couldn't keep my foot out of my mouth to save my life. I was probably the only student in the history of Catholic school who got all A's and spent half her high school years in detention. You, on the other hand, were the one everyone loved. The beautiful one everyone wanted to be."

Jeanne shook her head. "That was never true. You were the one who had spirit. So much life. You dreamed big dreams, went after everything you wanted. You had guts."

"Yeah, well, because I had guts, I lost everything." Typically, Tamara said the truth bluntly, the same way she plunked down her glass. Wine spattered on her pants. She didn't notice or care. "We all had big dreams in high school."

"Yeah, we did," Jeanne echoed.

"We all had so much hope."

"Yeah, we did."

"We all believed we could do anything. Be anyone we wanted to be. We all thought we had the power to change the world."

It slipped out before Jeanne could stop it. "I didn't want to change the world. I just wanted my guy. I was so in love I couldn't see straight."

Tamara said a rough, sympathetic swear word under her breath, and then suddenly they were both looking down at their high school yearbook. A copy of the same letter they'd both received that day was open on the coffee table. A spray of photographs had obviously spilled out of the yearbook when Jeanne had opened it earlier.

There were at least a dozen of Tamara. The class had voted her Best Musician. If there'd been a category for Worst Smart-Ass, she could have won that title just as easily. She'd probably come out of the womb copping an attitude, and by high school, she'd perfected the defiant look. Her parents had been wealthy, so she'd also had the wildest car, the wildest parties, and God knew, she'd always been drawn to the wildest boys. In every picture, her hair had different colored streaks and her eye makeup looked troweled on.

The yearbook had just as many pictures of Jeanne Claire—which Tamara kept pausing to look at. Jeanne had been voted Most Popular and Most Beautiful. She'd worn her long, blond hair simple and straight in those days, had a figure that could make even the dreaded St. Sebastian uniform look classy. There was no picture in which she wasn't smiling.

"I don't know why we were friends. I should

have hated you. You were so damn breathtaking, it's disgusting."

"It was all fake."

"There's nothing about you that was ever fake," Tamara said fiercely, and Jeanne sighed.

She'd had enough wine to float a yacht. It wasn't enough. There wasn't enough wine in the country to block the memories spilling through her. Pain had sneaked through to the surface like a ripped-off scar—one she'd assumed was long healed.

It wasn't healed. The high school reunion letter had been written by Arnold Grafton. There was no shortage of pictures of him in the yearbook, either. He'd been the class nerd, the guy who couldn't tuck his shirt in, who stumbled into walls when a girl was around, who was smart—but one of those pedantic scholars who drove everyone crazy when he answered a question. He had no life . . . except for following Tamara around with adoring-puppy eyes.

"God, I treated him so badly," Tam said gruffly.

She had, so Jeanne didn't argue. Her gaze zoned on the letter again. Arnold was the head of the fifteen-year reunion committee. Neither had heard from him in all this time. No reason they should have. But a hundred years ago—or fifteen, to be precise—she and Tamara had agreed to be on the committee with him.

At the time, right after high school, forming the

three-person committee had seemed logical. Arnold always volunteered for the jobs no one else wanted, so there'd been no other contenders to head the committee. Jeanne was the most popular kid in the class—she knew everyone and could cheerlead any group into getting together—so she was another obvious choice for the committee. And Tamara was by far the best musician in the class, on her way to fame and fortune, everyone thought—so she'd seemed an ideal person to put together the entertainment for their reunion.

That's how it seemed then. It just didn't seem that way now.

"I can't do this, Jeanne," Tamara said flatly, "I just can't. It's not that I'm not willing to do the work. It's that I can't go. I can't face them. I really can't."

Jeanne gave up trying to drink any more wine. It's not as if it were helping. She knew Tamara's nightmare. But she also knew her own.

On the last page of the yearbook was a picture of Nate Donneli—voted unanimously by the class as the Guy Most Likely to Succeed. Most kids at St. Sebastian's came from wealthy families—they had to be, to afford the exorbitant tuition. Nate's family was straight blue-collar. He'd won the high school scholarship because his family was strongly Catholic and they could prove a big financial need.

But no one ever felt sorry for Nate. Between the thick dark hair, the slow slide of a grin, and the liquid brown eyes, there wasn't a girl in the class who hadn't lusted after him. Jean's pulse could start thumping just from looking at the old pictures. He'd never been ultra tall, but he was broad-shouldered and tight-muscled. He moved, always, with a cockiness and sexiness that riveted attention. He'd worked his way to the top of everything—top grades, president of the class, lettered athlete. And he'd been good to people. Kind.

Damn, but she'd thought of him as a real-life hero when she was seventeen.

Because he was.

She swallowed down a lump in her throat.

"I tried to call Nate's father today."

"Yeah?" Tamara looked up, happy to quit thinking of her own memories and focus on Jeanne's.

"Yeah." It was so ironic. She'd known there was no way to avoid contacting Nate again. Years ago, they hadn't planned much about the reunion except to form a committee, simply because there was no reason to. Even then, though, they'd all assumed that their natural choice for a keynote speaker would be the guy voted Most Likely to Succeed—which meant Nate. And Nate would be easy to find because by then, the whole class believed, Jeanne would be married to him.

Yeah, right. What a joke.

"When I first got the reunion letter, I thought . . . well, I knew I'd be stuck getting ahold of him. So before I had to face him, I thought I'd get prepared, find out where he is now, what he's doing, what his story is. But the only address I ever had on him was his parents . . . only it seems they'd moved from the place they lived when we were in school, and there's no current listing for them in Ypsilanti. So then I looked up his dad's business. You know. Donneli's Garage."

"Okay. So what happened?"

"Some girl answered the phone. Said it hadn't been called Donneli's Garage in years, that it was called Donneli Motors now. Like I cared what the name was." Jeanne pushed up from the couch, unable to sit still any longer. "His dad was always nice to me. So I thought it wouldn't be so hard to just ask where was Nate, could he give me his address and phone."

"And did he?"

"I don't know. The girl put me on hold, and while I was waiting I lost my nerve. Hung up." She paced over to the window and pulled the drapes. The wrought-iron balcony was drenched with diamonds—rain catching a jewel shine from the convention center parking lights. "Then I started thinking."

"That's been my problem since opening this reunion letter," Tamara said wryly. "Thinking. Remembering. All those dreams we had. All the plans."

Jeanne nodded. "That's exactly what's been

bugging me all afternoon, all night. How did I get from there . . . to here? I'm working for my dad, because he needs me. And that's fine. But somehow I'm doing work I never wanted to do. And I leaped into a marriage that I never should have. And when I moved back home from Philadelphia after the divorce, somehow I ended up living here, instead of in a place of my own. And—"

"And you're involved with Donald the-wannabe-Trump."

She pivoted. "Tam, don't call him that."

"I don't like him."

"I know you don't, but—"

"But nothing." Tamara stood up, too. "It all goes back to Donneli for you, doesn't it? You never got over him."

She couldn't deny it. "Everybody gets rejected. But when a relationship doesn't work out, it's normally because one of the two people are unhappy. And that was always the stunner for me. As far as I knew, we were both totally happy, both wildly, completely in love—and then suddenly he dumped me like I was last night's newspaper. A million zillion times, I've told myself that I should have put it all behind me. And that's true. But the problem is—"

"The problem is, that's the point when your life went on stall, when it all started turning down a different direction than you planned." Tamara said flatly, "I think you need to see him."

Jeanne snugged her arms under her chest. "I couldn't even manage to talk to his father, so how am I going to manage talking to him? But when I hung up, I just wanted to smack myself upside the head. I've let that man be unfinished business for me all these years."

Tamara never needed a dose of courage, but the wine had definitely boosted her stubbornness. "So you've got the excuse of the reunion to contact him. So it'll be hard. So it'll be tough. But don't you think it's time you put a period on the end of that sentence?"

"He's probably married. With a gaggle of kids. Living some great life. When he got that scholarship to Princeton, I know he'd planned to be an architect, build things . . . but I always thought he'd end up in business. Be some kind of multimillionaire tycoon by now."

"So maybe he is."

"He probably wouldn't even remember me."

"So maybe he won't."

"And if he does, maybe it'd be an embarrassment if I showed up."

"Maybe it would be."

"I couldn't even face talking to his father," she repeated.

"So it has to be twice as hard, facing him. But wouldn't you like to know, after all this time? What really happened? Why he hurt you?"

"What, you think I could just walk up to him after all this time, say, 'For God's sake, Donneli, I loved you more than my life. And you gave me the impression that you loved me. So why in God's name did you suddenly throw me out as if I were yesterday's garbage?' "

Tamara said firmly, "That's exactly what I think you should say. Get right in his face. Ask the question. Get it out there. I don't know how he'll answer, but at least you'll *have* an answer. And he can't possibly hurt you any more than he already has."

"I don't know." All Jeanne knew was that the wave of loss inside was as fresh as it had been fifteen years ago. And that was so aggravating that she could spit.

She'd actually let that man ransom the rest of her life with his rejection. She'd. Let. Him. That was her fault, not Donneli's. But her reality was still the same: no man had come close to him. No man had come close to touching her the same way. Yearning, lust, longing, laughter, secrets, that rush of a thrill she'd always felt with him . . .

She didn't give a damn about Donnelli.

But she wanted the right to feel it with someone else.

And after the recent debacle with her almost-fiance, she'd come face up with the truth. Her life had dribbled down the wrong track for so long that she didn't know how to make it right anymore. She just knew she couldn't keep going the way she was.

She'd lost herself.

There had to be some way, somehow, to find out who Jeanne Claire Cassiday was . . . and to make something of her life. Before any more years passed. Before any more chances were thrown away.

chapter 2

Right after his wife died, Arnold Grafton could barely cook a meal, much less play both the mom and dad roles for their son. But two years had passed. Howie was now eight. And Arnold was a pro at the morning breakfast ritual.

Meticulously he shook in the exact amount of Cheerios in the bowl with the Spider-Man logo. Then sliced the exact amount of strawberries and bananas on top. Then poured the exact amount of milk. Then came the toast. He spread the exact amount of grape jelly stretched to the very edges of the bread.

"So . . . Billy coming over to play after school today?"

"Yeah. Can he stay for dinner? If his mom says okay?"

"Sure, why not?" The housekeeper was due any minute. Mrs. Hernandez was a live-in, but when she wanted time off, Arnold just adjusted. She loved his son; he loved her. They all agreed on the same set of rules. The idea was to live in a house, not make a shrine of it . . . to give the kid an environment where he could play and work safely, not where there was a giant list of off-limits places . . . to make healthy food available, but not force schedules or types of foods on anyone.

Howie looked as he had at that age. Five hundred cowlicks. Glasses that slid down his nose. Freckles.

But unlike Arnold's, Howie's childhood was happy. Howie was a brain and a nerd, just as he'd been . . . but the squirt didn't realize that being a nerd was bad, because no one had ever told him.

"What are we gonna do this weekend, Dad?"

"I don't know. What do you want to do?"

"Can we build a boat?"

"Sure." Arnold never got tired of it. The simple pleasure. The joy. The power. To be able to say, "Sure" to his kid. He glanced at his watch. Seven-forty. He had another five minutes to snap open his paper and soak in another coffee.

On the black kitchen counter, next to the coffee maker, was the mail—unfortunately. A copy of the letter he'd sent out to the St. Sebastian Reunion Committee had been sitting there for days, unfiled, untouched, as if allowing it to gather dust would make him worry less about it.

Neither Jeanne Claire Cassiday nor Tamara Whitley had responded to the letter yet. He hadn't seen either of them in fifteen years—and had never expected to. Until a few weeks ago, he'd forgotten all about volunteering to head this reunion committee when he'd been a snot-nosed senior in high school.

He hadn't forgotten much else about his years at St. Sebastian's, though. No one had liked him. He hadn't fit in anywhere. Jeanne Claire was the darling of the class, the beauty, the girl every guy drooled over. She'd never been unkind to him, but she'd never bothered to volunteer a conversation with him, either. Still, since he'd never aspired to be friends with anyone as far removed from him as Jeanne Claire, she was really a no-sweat.

Tamara was the way tougher—and way more personal—problem. She came from big money, always had a splashy sense of style, wore wild makeup and walked with a sexy swish, dared anything. Unfortunately, he'd been so foolish as to develop a crush on her. It was hard to remember—much less face—how stupid he'd been as a teenage boy. He'd spent months working up the courage to ask her out. And finally had. Only to have her make fun of him.

When he looked back now—hell, if he were Tamara, he'd have made fun of him, too. Couldn't tuck in his shirt. Probably spit a little when he talked. Shuffled when he walked. His haircut was wrong; his clothes were wrong; everything about him was wrong. All he had going for him was brains.

But what he was years ago wasn't the point. The point was that Tamara had broken his fragile teenager's heart. He'd died from the humiliation. Was it totally her fault? No. Did she have any way of knowing that his entire sense of self-esteem had been invested in the five-million-to-one shot that she'd have gone out with him? No. He wasn't *blaming* her.

He just didn't want to see her again.

Ever.

He sighed and wandered to the glass doors of the breakfast nook with his coffee mug in his hand. Outside, the wraparound deck spooled down to a long slope of lawn. This time of year, the lake still looked icy blue, and the mini nine-hole personal golf course he'd put in three years ago was still too marshy and mushy to play. Still, the trees were budding and the sun glistened on the dew-drenched grass.

The view was beautiful. And like all beautiful views, it cost a ton. He had the ton, these days. For whole stretches of time, he forgot his rotten growing-up years, his rotten time in high school.

But it was funny. He'd really thought that money would make a difference—and it did. But it still didn't erase the squirming memories of the Arnold Grafton he used to be.

Well. He'd set up a meeting in the St. Sebastian High School library for the second of April. The location was obviously familiar to everyone, and either the women showed or they didn't. If they didn't, he'd find someone on his staff who could take it on—get a mailing list from the school, organize some kind of party this fall.

The truth was, he didn't mind doing this reunion thing. In fact, once it had been his dream to achieve success, to be able to go back to the old high school crowd and show them that he'd become someone. That dream just seemed so paltry now. He'd made a good life. He *was* successful—but he didn't care about showing off. He actually wanted to know what had become of all his old classmates, just from curiosity and interest. He didn't care anymore what anyone thought of him.

Except for Tamara.

After all these years, it seemed he was still afraid of humiliating himself with her again.

Jeanne never ventured near the hotel's shipping and receiving area if she could help it. The big, yawning space with cement floors and semi truck docks and forklifts and storage areas looked innocuous enough—but she knew better. It was a place that destroyed white blouses, stockings, and fingernails, no matter how careful you were. The worst problem this morning, though, was the fresh air blasting in through the open docking doors.

Balmy sunshine, way too bright for the end of March, pooled in puddles of warmth and light. Just outside, the hotel landscape was all coming to life. Crocuses stood up perkily; daffodils were thrusting their first green shoots from the ground, and every tree and bush was softened with buds. It was even in the air. That whole, hopeless spring thing—that whiff of magic, that addictive scent of yearning.

It was enough to make her want to scream, which was just plain unfair. Her head was already suffering from a train wreck of a headache.

"Jeanne Claire! I've been looking all over for you, princess!" The freight elevator opened, and her dad strode toward her, looking—as always—charming and handsome. His navy blue suit was impeccably cut. Every morning, he had a nip at the barber so his hair was never unkempt. He smelled like fresh soap and expensive aftershave and something that women hopelessly wanted to hug. Some said that John Sedgwick Cassiday could charm the skin off a snake—not that he'd ever touch one.

"What's this I hear about our housing a zoo?" he asked boisterously.

He bussed her cheek, and she snuggled closer to claim her morning hug. "Well, it's hard to believe, but we're actually staging a party out here on the loading docks this Saturday."

"Here?"

"Uh huh." It was one of the things Jeanne had long realized was a major character flaw. She couldn't say no, even when people told her something was impossible. "There's a little boy named Bobby—he's seven years old. And deaf. And his parents wanted to give him a party he'd never forget, so naturally—"

"They came to Oz Enterprises," her dad said with pride.

"Exactly. Somehow we're supposed to make his wildest dreams come true, and in this case, Bobby's dream was to have a party where all of his friends could go on rides. Animal rides. We're talking a whole class of special needs kids. So. That wasn't exactly going to work inside the hotel. And some of the kids aren't sturdy or strong enough to handle something outside, especially if it's a cold day. So—"

"So you're having it in here."

"Yup. I've got some ponies and a goat and a llama and a Newfoundland lined up, all of whom can pull little carts. And we're creating makeshift stalls for the critters. And we're draping the cement walls with blue and gold fabric—University of Michigan colors, obviously—to take away from the warehouse atmosphere out here. And—"

"That sounds wonderful." Her dad cut her off. He never liked to get into the nitty-gritty of the work. "You're so creative."

"I still need an elephant."

"Well, if anyone can come up with one, it'd be you, princess." Her dad blessed her with another blindingly warm smile.

The princess tag grated, but Jeanne told herself that it was PMS giving her a case of cranks. A few yards away, the maintenance guys were hammering away at the makeshift animal stalls. She still had to figure out what to do with the poop. Her job invariably required creativity and flexibility—but how to cope with a volume of animal poop was a new problem for her—as well as how to keep the food and present areas sanitized and separate from the critters. But those were problems that her father wouldn't want to hear about or discuss. He didn't like hearing about arrangements that weren't on the elegant side.

He chatted on for a few minutes, not about anything in particular, just sharing stories about guests that he'd encountered that morning. He almost always checked in with her at least once a day.

She tucked her arm in his as they wandered around. He was the worst businessman she'd ever met, but so impossible not to love.

Jeanne had never been part of the creation of Oz Enterprises. It had been her mom's dream, her mom who thought up the idea, found the financing, put the business plan together. And the convention center had a great startup, but it was still in its infancy—carrying a big mortgage—when Claire Cassiday had been hit by a kamikaze drunk driver on 1–94. The coma had lasted for months—maybe because God knew neither Jeanne nor her dad could possibly stand losing her and needed some time to get used to the idea. Then, after Claire died, the bills started coming in.

John Cassiday had been born to money. He knew how to spend it; he knew how to play with it; he just couldn't seem to hold on to it. John could make a wallflower feel as desirable as Gwyneth Paltrow, could soften up the meanest bitch, could shoulder-slap and talk tough business when he was with a shoulder-slapping, tough-business man.

But brother. He couldn't add up a balance sheet. Capital gains, depreciation schedules, overhead— he always listened intently and sincerely when Jeanne tried to explain things to him. But nothing got through. It wasn't that he didn't try or didn't care. Give him a personnel problem, and he'd dig in to fix it, no shirking. But numbers just weren't his thing.

Jeanne had been freshly divorced when her mom died, but she'd still been living in Philadelphia. She'd forever associate poor Philly with the four years of a tumultuously bad marriage—but the point was, she'd lost almost all ties to Ann Arbor in those years, lost track of friends, and certainly had no idea what a financial mess her dad was in until he'd suddenly begged her to move home and come on board. She'd never wanted to do that kind of work, but she'd immediately said yes and come home. What other choice did she have? Obviously she couldn't just leave her dad to flounder.

After several years, though, it seemed they were still only a pinch away from Chapter Eleven. Every single time the balance sheets sneaked into the black, her father found some grand way to shovel more money out the door. Always, of course, her dad had great reasons for trying some new scheme. He was always so enthusiastic, so sure the new grandiose plan would be the key to exotic riches.

And Jeanne kept telling herself that she could walk away—but she didn't believe it. No matter how personally stifled she felt at Oz, she really feared he couldn't cope alone—and she just couldn't forget how terribly despondent he'd been after her mom died.

This morning, though, he was happy and chipper, and at least temporarily the financial worries of Oz Enterprises were on a back burner. Or she hoped they were.

"Do you have time for lunch with your old man?" her dad asked her.

"I always have time for you." She smooched that soft cheek, smiled. "But honestly, I'm on the run today."

John steered her away from the dust and hammering. "I hope you're going out with Donald again. He's such a good man."

"Actually, Dad . . ." She sucked in a breath, exercised a new kind of smile. "I'm probably not going to be seeing him as often."

"I thought you two were getting on so well!"

Yeah, well, her dad had wanted to think that. She'd met Donald when her father had dragged her into a meeting of potential investors. She understood numbers the way her dad didn't, so she'd been called in to translate. The first time the group broke for coffee, Donald had asked her out. She'd assumed he wanted to talk business. Instead, he'd never brought up Oz Enterprises in any way.

"Dad, you saw the insurance people—Ralph, Jim—?"

John nodded enthusiastically. "I'm positive I set that up for next week."

"And you sat down with Rhoda over the second quarter's projected earnings—"

"Now, princess, I don't want you worried all the time about money. This is just a business. It's not our life. Although, Lord, I don't know what I'd do without you."

"You'd do just fine!" But he wouldn't, Jeanne thought despairingly. And she really knew it. She loved her dad and she wanted to be there for him, but damnation, sometimes she felt so trapped she couldn't breathe.

Trapped.

Once the word popped into her mind, she couldn't get it out.

For fifteen years, that was exactly how she'd felt. Cornered. Doing all kinds of things—but never the things she'd planned. Achieving some great things and failing at others—but none of what she'd done had ever been on her list of dreams.

How had it happened? How had her life become so drastically sidetracked from where she'd wanted to go as a young girl? How had every dream gotten sabotaged?

But of course, she knew that answer. Somehow she had allowed her entire life to go on stall from the day Nate Donneli dumped her.

To blame him wasn't totally fair. She could sure as hell blame him for crushing her—but not for how or why she'd become a sponge for other people's needs over the last fifteen years. She was the one who had to whip her life back around. But the reasons, the tools, the keys all seemed to lead back to Nate.

Maybe Tamara was right. Whether it hurt or not, she needed to finally get an answer to why he'd hurt her so badly. Even if the answer proved to be some terrible thing she'd done—or some terrible flaw in her—at least she'd *know*.

Nate walked with the phone glued to one ear. He'd never been able to sit still when he talked. The guy on the other end was in Paris. If push came to shove, Nate could make himself understood okay in Italian, but French was a total impossibility. Unfortunately, it was a Frenchman who had the part for the Lamborghini 350 GT that Nate wanted.

If they could get around to understanding each other, both of them just might end up happy with the deal.

Nate ambled back to his office, the phone still plugged in his ear, and passed by Martha—who waved a handful of messages in his face. He ignored her. Martha was always waving messages in his face. Sooner or later she'd catch up with him. No one escaped Martha, least of all him, but he could outrun her for a short while.

At the far end of the hall, past Martha's office, was Jason's. His twenty-four-year-old brother hadn't passed his CPA test yet, but he'd graduated from the University of Michigan two winters ago with top grades. He'd been doing the company books for several years now. Knowing Jason hadn't wanted to join the family business, Nate had started him out right off the bat with a bigger, prettier office than his own as an enticement.

Nate didn't give a damn about pretty, and he'd wanted his brother to feel important, happy. The job was a good deal—a great deal—if Jason would just see it that way.

And now, not that Nate tended to check up on everybody, but he twisted his head around the door—and failed to spot Jason. Of course it was lunchtime. "Yeah, yeah," he said into the phone, "we're talking the V–12 engine, the six horizontal Weber carburetors . . ."

The French guy knew that. So far they hadn't found a common language except for cars. Carburetors seemed to be a universal word. So did terms like V–6 and V–12. Such terms transcended all cultures.

It just confused women, but who could talk to them anyway?

"Okay, that's it, that's it . . ."

Sort of accidentally, he passed by the windows to the bays in the garage. If people were going to be goofing off, it'd be there. More to the point, that was where the money was made—unlike in his father's time.

There happened to be a racing-green '65 Ford Mustang in the first bay. Unlike all the beauties in Nate's inventory, this one looked rode hard and put up wet. Everything on her needed work. The owner didn't care if it was an original restoration, thank God, but he did want her brought up to snuff—especially since she was a high-performance 289 instead of one of the basic 'Stangs of that day.

He expected to see two butts leaned over the raised hood. Instead he saw three. All three fannies were in grease-stained coveralls. One was notably Daniel's. Daniel, at twenty-eight, had caused him more trouble than all five siblings put together, but he was still the best mechanic ever born— surpassing Nate's skill, and a dozen times past their father's in his day. Daniel couldn't keep a dime in his pocket, couldn't seem to turn down a woman or a whiskey . . . but under the hood he was a genius.

A knot clogged in Nate's throat. The same knot that had clogged his throat for weeks now. There was a problem at Donneli Motors. A problem he hadn't shared with anyone, and hoped he'd never have to. But it was building into something bad, something big, something damn awful. And he was increasingly afraid that Daniel might be the source of it.

At that precise moment, though, give or take the telephone call with the Frenchman, Nate had a more pressing concern. The butts. Daniel's was expected. The plump fanny was just as familiar—Orwell was a mechanic who'd been working for them for seven years now—a lover of old cars, a temperamental cigar smoker, not creative in his thinking but thorough. But it was the third butt that made Nate suddenly say, "Look, we're on track here. Talk to you again at the end of the week, okay?"

He clicked the off button, shoved the phone onto his belt, and slapped the door to the garage open. That damn little butt—he recognized it.

"*Caitlin!*" he roared to his daughter. "Goddamnit. Why aren't you in school? And what the *hell* are you doing back here again?"

All three butts pivoted around. All three sets of eyes honed on him. They knew he was mad. Everyone in the place knew better than to make Nate Donneli mad. Except for the thirteen-year-old pipsqueak with the grease streak across her nose, and the lipstick she was too goddamn young to wear, and the sassy, sassy brown eyes.

"Come on, Dad. I told you at least twice that I had the afternoon off today. Some kind of teachers' in-service thing."

"You were supposed to be home!"

"Home's boring."

"How'd you get here—" He didn't finish the question because it simply wasn't worth asking. She had three Donneli uncles, all living in Ann Arbor, all who'd skin the world for her and never tell. And he'd just sworn this morning that he wasn't going to fight with Caitlin again, and here they were at it.

Caitlin was the one thing in his life that was right—or that he *thought* was right. Until seven months ago. He adored her. She might have been an unplanned, unexpected mistake to start with—but she was the best mistake he'd ever made and the light of his life. Further, the two of them had always been as thick as thieves. He could do no wrong in her eyes. He was better than God. He was her best pal, her hero, her idol. Then seven months ago she got her period.

That was it. The end of the glory days. Now he couldn't say anything right, didn't look right, didn't dress right, didn't think right. He embarrassed her by just breathing. He had permission to drive her places, but preferably if he didn't talk. He was unreasonable, dictatorial, mean, cruel, bossy, insensitive, didn't understand, would never understand, hateful, worse than anyone else's father, and—to the main point—wrong. Always wrong.

"Caitlin, I have asked you and asked you—"

She was already more bristled up than a porcupine. "There isn't one single reason why I shouldn't be here. The garage is mine, too. It has the Donneli name on it, doesn't it? It's not fair. All the guys say I'm not in the way, right, Uncle Dan? Right, Orwell?"

"Leave them out of it—"

"Well, if it doesn't bother them if I'm here, why should it bother you? They think I *help* around here. You're the only one who—"

Jesus, she had a voice like a shrew. That young, and already she could tear a strip off grown men and make them want to slink out of sight before she started sharing that temper of hers. Still, over his darling's shriek, he heard a door open and close, heard phones ring, heard a horn blast.

Since this was his business, he was tuned to hearing certain sounds—particularly when a noise intruded that didn't belong. Caitlin's shrieks really weren't all that unusual, and no matter how piercing her voice was, a completely different sound snapped his head around.

A woman had just walked in the front lobby. He knew, because he could hear her voice, talking to Martha, for those few seconds when the door was opened. The voice was actually quite a distance away—but his heart still heard it, the way a fireman sensed a fire, the way a farmer sensed a storm coming.

It was an alto, that woman's voice. Gentle. Cultured. Pretty. No nasals, no special accents. It was a voice that could sing, not well enough to make a living at it, but well enough to make a man's hormones perk up. It was a voice, in fact, that took him back to a spring in high school—the first time he'd walked next to a certain girl, holding hands as they ambled through the woods, and they'd just been talking when she suddenly laughed— laughed with him, laughed for him. And man, the intimacy of it, the high of it, had made his blood rush like a river.

"For God's sake, Dad, everybody but you—"

The door flashed open when a mechanic pushed through. Again he heard Martha's voice, talking, answering a question . . . but then he heard the other voice. The alto. That sexy, soft, unforgettable alto.

And suddenly his heart was thundering like a tornado wind.

The door was already closed again. Jason had come in—unusual for him to be anywhere near the bays, but Nate didn't notice or care enough to be curious. He'd twisted around faster than if someone had slapped him.

"What?" Caitlin demanded, when she suddenly realized that he'd stopped arguing with her.

"Nothing, honey. You can stay here," he said.

Her jaw dropped five feet. She hadn't even begun wiping the floor with him yet; she was just warming up. And he wasn't through arguing with her. He had to get through to his daughter. He had to. Soon. And far more effectively than he'd managed lately.

Only, damn. He must be losing his mind. Because that voice sounded like a woman's that he hadn't heard in fifteen years. It couldn't be Jeanne Claire Cassiday's. It just couldn't be.

chapter 3

Jeanne knew she'd been out of her mind to come there. Nobody sat on a train track and just blithely hoped everything would be okay. But she had assumed that she'd have the chance to talk to Nate's father before taking the risk of seeing Nate himself.

Instead there was a woman named Martha—who seemed to be a clone of the Martha at Oz Enterprises. A prison guard in personality. A gate-keeper. A martinet with hairsprayed hair and squinty eyes and pearls—and nobody, but nobody, was getting past that door without Martha's approval.

"Look, Mar—ma'am." The name tag just said Martha, so it wasn't as if Jeanne could call her

Mrs. Something. "I just want to see Mr. Donneli for a minute. If he's busy, I can come back another time. Or make an appointment. I'm not trying to create a problem—"

"You're not creating a problem, Ms. Cassiday." Those squinty eyes looked down on her from a scrawny-boned six-foot height. "We have no problem. I'm just trying to clearly communicate that if you want to see the senior Mr. Donneli, you'll have to tell me your reason. Of course, you can contact him privately. But if you want to see him in reference to business issues—"

"This isn't about business. It's personal. But not *that* personal." Jeanne was becoming inclined to tear out her hair. "I mean, I just wanted to ask him about his son—"

"Mr. Donneli doesn't have a son."

Okay. Maybe she was even more tempted to tear out Martha's hair first—but she was willing to give basic reason one more try. "Mr. Donneli has six kids. Four boys. Two girls—"

"There now. Everything's starting to make sense. You've got the wrong Donneli, that's what's going on here—"

"I don't have the wrong Donneli. This is Donneli Motors. That used to be Donneli Garage." Sheesh, the woman looked bright enough, but getting through to her was like a Democrat getting through to a Republican. "Look, I'm not trying to bother anyone. The reason I'm here is about a fifteenth high school class reunion. I'd lost track of Mr. Donneli's son, who I'm trying to contact to speak at the reunion. I don't know where he is. All I want to do is ask Mr. Donneli—"

"Mr. Donneli's *daughter* is thirteen years old. She's not even in high school yet, so she's hardly old enough to be worrying about a reunion. Ms. Cassiday, I'm sorry I can't help you, but . . ." Martha made a vague scooping motion with her hands, as if she'd had enough and was now determined to herd Jeanne toward the door.

Jeanne was becoming so confused she was almost willing to be herded. Almost. Unfortunately, it had taken so much blasted courage to come here that she couldn't just give up.

In these days of the Internet, anyone could find anyone. Only she'd tried cyberspace. And there was no problem finding zillions of Donnelis—or Nate Donnelis. But she had no way to identify *the* Nate Donneli she was trying to locate except through the connection of Donneli's Garage—his dad's business. And no, she'd never been there before. It was both geographically and emotionally miles from the kind of neighborhood where she grew up, but she'd still met his dad a couple of times when they were kids, always at school games or functions, and he'd seemed a nice guy. Gregarious, effusive, the kind of emotional man who waved his arms as he talked. Maybe he wouldn't remember her, but he'd surely give her

Nate's address if she explained that she was trying to contact his son because of the high school reunion.

She just couldn't imagine a reason he'd be unwilling to talk to her. And if she could just get to him—past this iron-haired guard with the pearls—maybe Mr. Donneli might reveal something about Nate. Like that he was married and had produced a houseful of choirboys and future nuns. Like that he'd graduated from Princeton and gone on to run the world. Something. Anything. Even the smallest iota of information could help her decide if she could really face him again . . . and if she could handle finding out why he'd thrown her out of his life so coldly all those years ago.

"I really don't know why you aren't willing to contact Mr. Donneli at home, if you consider yourself a friend—" The pearl-choking Martha was still herding her toward the door.

"I'm not exactly a friend. And I understand why you're so wary of letting strangers past. I'm sure he gets bugged with telemarketers and salesmen and all. I do, too. I hate it. Only, I swear, I'm not some interloper or salesperson who's going to bug him."

"Uh huh."

"He knows me. He met me years ago."

"Uh huh."

"He *did*. Why on earth would you think I would

45

make this up? I'm telling you I went out with his son—"

"And as I keep trying to tell you, Mr. Donneli doesn't have a son—"

"Peanut."

The sudden masculine voice shocked her like a gunshot . . . but that voice wrapped around her old nickname—the nickname only one man had ever called her—punched her right in the heart and squeezed tight.

It took only a second for her to turn around, but in that second, she saw the round clock with the white face on the far wall. The photographs of old cars—so many they filled one wall like wallpaper. The red leather couch, the red stone counter—furnishings that seemed crazy for a garage, but then, what the sam hill did she know about mechanics and garages? She also saw the pearl-choking Martha drop her aggressive stance in a blink, when it finally became obvious that Nate Donneli really did know her.

"Mr. Donneli," Martha said swiftly, sincerely, "I'm terribly sorry if I misunderstood this situation. I was trying to protect you from—"

"I know you were, Martha, and you're a wonderful protector. But the lady thinks she's looking for my father instead of me. That's what the source of the confusion is."

"I see." Martha obviously didn't.

Jeanne didn't, either. She was pretty sure she'd

grasp what was going on eventually. But just then she needed a minute to breathe, to gulp in some poise, to lock onto some sense somehow.

Only, damn. Temporarily her heart still felt sucker-punched. Her pulse started galloping and refused to calm down.

He looked just as he once had. More mature, of course. But those dark, sexy eyes were just as wicked, could still make a girl think, *Oh, yes, please take my virginity, please do anything you want, I don't care.* He still had the cocky, defensive, bad-boy chin. The dark hair, with the one shock on his temple that wouldn't stay brushed. The thin mouth and strong jaw and shoulders so square you'd think they were huge, when he wasn't that huge. He just had so damn much personality that he seemed big.

He was. So. Handsome. So in-your-face male. So take-on-all-comers wolf.

And double damn, but he'd called her Peanut.

She hadn't heard the nickname in all these years. Hadn't and didn't want to. But the fact that he even remembered it completely threw her. For God's sake, she'd been over her head, over her heart, over her life in love with him. And believed he'd felt the same way about her. And then suddenly he'd sent that cold note from Princeton, "Life's changed for me. Everything's different. I'm moving on. I don't want to hurt you, but this relationship isn't going any further. You go on with your life, find someone else. I'm never coming back."

Those weren't the exact words. She didn't remember the exact words, because it wasn't the words themselves that had devastated her. It was going from one day when she'd believed herself loved, believed she knew him, believed he was The One. Her Prince. The Only Man for Her. To being hurled out of his life after a semester in college because he'd "moved on"—as if that were some kind of explanation. As if real love could die as easily as a mood change.

She'd been stunned. So stunned, she realized now, that it wasn't as simple as being hurt. It rocked her world. And it was from that instant, that time when she'd been knocked flat and crushed, that she'd started down a different road. She'd started letting other people affect what she did, what she said, who she was.

It was that letter. His rejection. His dropping her the way he had. That was the catalyst for her losing Jeanne Claire Cassiday. And she'd never found herself since then.

And whatever she'd meant to say, on seeing him again, what came out was . . . "Damn it, Shadow!"

Shadow.

Hell, he hadn't heard that nickname in fifteen years. It came from basketball. At five-foot-eleven, he never had the height to compete well as a shooter, so he'd had to do something else to excel. He found his place in defense, shadowing the enemy's star player, never letting up, never giving up, until his teammates had started up with the Shadow tag. That was around the time he first took out Jeanne Claire. She called him that for different reasons, of course. She'd teased him about never letting up, never giving up around her.

Hearing her call him Shadow had made his blood pump back then. And damn near made the blood rush like a river now.

Only guilt colored the river darker than mud—because, damn, he knew what he'd done to her fifteen years ago. It's wasn't as if hurting her had been a choice. He'd never wanted to. And it was all so long ago—a thousand emotional lifetimes, at the very least. In fact, it should have been water so far over the dam that until he heard her name the other day, Nate would have sworn—to himself, to anyone, even to his mother—that Jeanne Claire never crossed his mind.

Only she had. One look at her, and Nate knew exactly how much she had.

Seconds kept ticking by, yet he stood there, as frozen as an ice cube. The shop and office were hustling, the way they should—business was booming, more work than they knew what to do with. Nothing was different. He heard all the usual phones and commotion, smelled the smells, saw Martha's head whipping back and forth between the two of them—and damn, but Martha could sniff out gossip faster than a mosquito could find fresh blood.

Still he looked at her. Still he couldn't look away. In a single blink of his mind, the past came rushing back to him.

The first time he saw her, she'd been walking down the hall at St. Sebastian's, coming back from the girl's bathroom, seventh grade. He'd just transferred from public school, and he was trying to find his way around. He remembered it all, the yellow and black tile floor, the crucifix at the end of the hall, the taped-up pictures in the hall that kids did for one project or another. And the smell—why did Catholic schools always smelled different from other schools? Was it the holy water? And why did parochial school buildings always seem to be one hundred and ten years older than other schools? Anyway, there was barbecued beef in the air that day, too, wafting out of the cafeteria.

It was crazy—silly to remember all those details, when none of them mattered and how could anyone care? But Nate's theory was that somehow a guy always remembered the first time he fell in love—at least if it was bad. And for him, that moment had been capital-B bad. She'd been the most forbidden female he'd ever seen. She wasn't just the epitome of a boy's wet dream. She was the holy, pure, impossible dream as well—the girl that made a boy want to be a hero and climb mountains and fight dragons, even if he never got to kiss her.

Well, maybe Nate never had a dream *that* pure—but it was close.

Right from that first day, he figured out that he was the poorest kid at St. Sebastian's. Other kids got church scholarships, but they were in better shape than his family. His dad was barely supporting six kids and a wife on a ne'er-do-well garage.

Nate had long seen the real truth of the family situation before then. His dad would rather stop and have a beer than work. No one fixed the hole in the screen door while his dad watched a football game. His mom was too tired to care about faucets that dripped or porch steps that sagged. Nate was the oldest, which meant that he came home from school to change diapers and start dinner and lug around a baby—or two. At least until someone told his mother that he needed to get out of public school. He was smart. Seriously smart. So smart that he had a shot at being an architect or a doctor or a lawyer—or president—or anything he wanted to be, if he could just get a decent education.

So he ended up at St. Sebastian's. Most of the kids came from gated neighborhoods, but even by a big-money standard, he knew right off that Jeanne Claire was a cut above. Even in seventh grade, he recognized aristocracy.

The forbidden attracted him from the first, but in the beginning he didn't expect to like her. He just assumed she was what she looked like—a prom queen. A princess. The darling of the class. A girl so beautiful that she was all wrapped up in herself, shallow the way a lot of ultra good-looking people could be.

But hell, back then, he didn't care if she was shallow as a brook. He'd been happy to drool after her for years. He had it so bad by ninth grade that he'd leave flowers by her locker sometimes—not that she ever knew they were from him. It was later he'd gotten to know her, but from the start, her looks alone could bring any red-blooded boy to his knees . . . and that went double for him.

And it seemed, it still did.

Damn woman was just as breathtaking as she used to be. In fact, way more so. He remembered her in a blackwatch plaid skirt rolled up at the waist and knee socks. Now she was wearing a suit. Navy blue, expensive and tasteful, but nothing flashy. White striped shirt. Red shoes. Gold bits in her ears, a skinny gold string at her throat. The style didn't cling, didn't show off. Didn't have to. She was as flat as a board as a teenager, didn't look much more built now, but damn, everything about her was sexily elegant, from her shoulder blades to her throat, from her so-feminine hands to the perfect curve of her calf.

In heels, she came to his nose. Maybe her hair

was a little darker, but she was still blond. Not California blond, not Barbie blond, but that rare natural blond that had a dozen colors—some gold, some flax, some honey, some just a sunlit-shimmer color. She was wearing it shoulder-length, simple, tipped under a little—she used to complain that her hair was so fine that it never held a style, but it always held *that* style, and that pale, crushably soft hair framed an exquisitely carved face. Her nose was small and straight. Her skin was porcelain with just a promise of rose under the surface. That bit of a mouth could look washed out when she didn't feel good—or when she had PMS—but she usually wore gloss or something, as now, and the least color added ten degrees of sexiness. Personally he'd rather see her mouth naked. He remembered her mouth naked. Too well.

The really killing part of her looks, though, were her eyes. They were light blue, almond-shaped, but not that special because of color or shape. Her eyes showed her heart. The vulnerability, the loneliness. She was beautiful, no question about it, but man, underneath, she didn't know herself. Then.

And possibly not now, either, since she didn't seem to have a clue to how he was reacting to her.

"Shadow?" she said again. "Nate?" Her voice echoed unsureness, as if she didn't know whether to step forward or leave, as if she wasn't even certain if he recognized her. And there was confusion in her expression, questions—some of which he could easily guess. Why was he in his father's garage? For that matter, where was his father? And why on earth was he wearing coveralls?

Then the metal door pushed open, coming from the shop, and eighty-five pounds of his favorite whirlwind bounded in. "Hey, Dad!" Caitlin took one look at Jeanne Claire and stopped on a dime. She tended to get anxious when he was talking to a woman—at least if the woman was attractive. She took one gander at Jeanne Claire and came up with an extraordinarily impressive scowl.

"Hey, Dad," Caitlin repeated more forcefully. Nate quickly tore his eyes from Peanut before the situation could deteriorate into anything worse—and with a thirteen-year-old more volatile than his mama's chili, most situations could get unbelievably worse. He lifted a hand and did the introduction thing.

"Jeanne, this is my daughter. And Caitlin, I want you to meet Jeanne Claire . . ." He hesitated just for a second, unsure what her last name was.

"Cassiday," she filled in, which was her maiden name—not that that necessarily verified whether she was married or not these days.

"I went to school with Jeanne at St. Sebastian's," he added for his daughter's sake.

"Hi, Caitlin." Jeanne had subtly stiffened when he identified his daughter, but her voice couldn't have been more poised, more careful. Maybe nobody but him could hear that tiny catch, the same catch that would slip into her tone when she was wary years ago.

"Yeah. Well, hi back." Caitlin stuck out her chin rather than a hand. "Nice to meet you." Then quickly, "Dad, since you don't want me around the shop, I'm all about going home. In fact, I could go right now, this minute."

Normally he had to drag his angel from the shop, kicking and screaming and giving him lip the whole way. Amazing how her tune changed when she was trying to separate him from a woman she didn't know.

"Can't do," Nate said easily. "I'll take you home, but I need a good fifteen minutes."

"I've got tons of homework—"

"And you'll have tons of time to do it." Nate waited, not sure whether to be amused or exasperated. Martha and Caitlin were both frowning, both standing as if rooted to the floor. Neither looked as if she intended to budge. "I'm taking Ms. Cassiday into my office for a few minutes. Don't go far, Cait."

"I won't. Trust me."

Jeanne piped in, "Look, I'm obviously in the way. You're in the middle of a business day—" Unlike the other two, she looked prepared to bolt for the door at the speed of light—at any excuse.

But if his worst nightmare had come back to

haunt him, Nate couldn't see ignoring it. He'd tried ignoring problems before. They came back to bite him in the butt, every single time. He had no idea why Jeanne Claire had come to see him—but for damn sure, she must have a reason.

The faster he found out what it was, the sooner he could go home and get a drink. Maybe two.

He was thinking, hard and yearningly, about how great a nice shot of whiskey would taste, as he ushered Jeanne down the carpeted hall. The shop and lobby bustled with constant noisy distractions. He motioned her into his office—which suddenly seemed too darn private.

Three buttons on his phone flashed messages and a fax was spewing out of his machine, but unfortunately, there was nothing he had to immediately jump for. His office wasn't fancy. One wall had a hundred pictures of cars. Another wall had a hundred pictures of his daughter. His desk was a long sweep of malachite, but God knew why he'd bothered buying something so handsome when the whole thing was covered in electronics. Of course, sometimes, he forgot that he tended to work 24/7.

Jeanne stepped in and took a studying look around, but she didn't seem inclined to take the leather chair across from his desk. "So Caitlin's your daughter?" she said brightly.

Nate mentally winced. If the first thing she managed to say was about his daughter, it seemed pretty obvious that she'd noticed Caitlin's age. Which meant that she could easily leap to the conclusion that he'd dropped her all those years ago because he'd gotten involved with someone else. "Cait's thirteen. Going on thirty."

He motioned her to sit, and then backed around the desk so he could sink into his swivel desk chair. Maybe with the door-sized desk between them, she could try to relax. Or he could. It was so ironic that fifteen years ago, he'd wanted her to think the worst of him—because that would have guaranteed she wouldn't try to find him. Now, though, hell. He didn't know what to say. Maybe it'd still be easier if she thought something bad about him—like he'd cheated with someone else.

But he hadn't. And he didn't like her thinking that.

She took the chair, crossed a leg, opened her mouth—and then closed it again with a wry smile. "Darn it, I'm so confused that I'm having trouble saying anything, Nate. The reason I came here in person was because I tried to telephone several times and couldn't reach your dad."

"You wanted my dad?"

"No, I wanted *you* ..." A petal-soft flush zoomed up her cheeks. She swiftly changed her choice of words. "I mean—I was trying to locate you, but after all these years, I had no idea where you were living. So I thought I'd track down your dad to ask him. Only I never got past your Martha, who just seemed convinced I was up to no good."

Nate had to grin. "Yup. You've pegged her. Martha is convinced that everyone is up to no good."

"Well, she's probably right, but—"

Time to put her out of her misery. He said gently, "My father died, Jeanne. I took over the business."

"Oh. God. I guess I should have realized that. Every time I asked about Nate Donneli, I meant your dad, and she thought I meant you. No wonder we were confusing each other. But he was so young that it never occurred to me—I'm so sorry, Nate."

"It's all right. I can't imagine any reason you would have known."

Still, she looked confused. "I guess I just never expected to find you here—"

She had that right. He remembered, clearly, telling her about a million times how much he hated his dad's mechanics business. "The place is a little different than in my father's time."

She nodded. "In fact, you always described your dad's place as a hole in the wall, where this is huge. And so extensive and interesting. And so busy—"

That direction was nothing but quicksand. Come to think of it, any conversational direction she could take was likely quicksand—at least for him. "There was a reason you wanted to contact me?"

She swallowed quickly, her eyes suddenly more careful than a cornered doe. But she said easily enough, "Yes. About the reunion."

"What reunion?"

"Our fifteenth high school reunion for St. Sebastian's. I'm on the three-person reunion committee—me, Tamara, and Arnold. We're just starting to organize, but I knew they were going to ask me to contact you. Even back then, you were the only one we all wanted to be the keynote speaker, because of being voted the Guy Most Likely to Succeed. I'm sure it's absolutely the last thing on your mind, but—"

Man. Talk about an unexpected stab in the gut. "I can't do it."

She blinked at his instant reaction. "Nate, you don't even know when the date for the reunion is. There's lots of time. Arnold threw out next fall, homecoming weekend for St. Sebastian, as a possible date. So we could combine events, and because that'd be a way for the alumni to support the game and the school, and then just have our class get together afterward. So if that idea flies, we're talking all the way to October—"

"I can't, Jeanne."

"Why?"

Why? Because he'd *been* voted the man Most

Likely to Succeed. Because, all those years ago, he'd been the man who was going to marry Jeanne Claire and love her forever. But that was before disaster had struck, and all his dreams had been lopped off at the knees. "Because I didn't live up to anything I said I'd do," he said bluntly.

She swallowed again. Hell. He'd only meant a reference to his career potential, but obviously he hadn't lived up to any promises he'd made to her, either. It seemed there was nothing he could say that wouldn't risk jamming his feet deeper into his mouth—and then the phone rang—the private button, not the outside line.

It was Martha, and she was all business. "Nate, it's the bank again. I've told them and told them that this is ridiculous, but they claim there's an overdraft, and this time they insist on speaking with you."

"No problem. Didn't I tell you, if this came up again, to turn it over to me right away?"

"Yes, you did. But I knew they were wrong, and I hated to have them bother you when you're busy."

The day seemed to be going from ghastly-bad to even worse. Jeanne Claire's showing up was an emotional bomb that compared with nothing else. He sure as hell didn't want to have to come out and tell her that he'd turned into the man Most Likely to Completely Fail all his dreams, all people's hopes for him. And on top of all that, he just didn't need this ugly, ugly nightmare creeping closer to the surface.

Someone seemed to be stealing from him. Nate didn't know who. But because there was a limited number of people who could pull this off, he couldn't tell the police. And he had to find some way to stop it.

Fast.

chapter 4

Jeanne sat frozen in the leather chair across from Nate's desk. She'd come directly from work, which meant that she was wearing the red shoes that were the trademark of Oz Enterprises, but just then, they struck her as totally ironic. She'd have done anything to be able to click her heels three times and land in Kansas—although she wasn't feeling picky. She'd have been happy if she could have disappeared anywhere, as long as it was out of Nate's sight.

Temporarily, Nate's back was turned as he continued with his phone conversation—a conversation that was totally none of her business. It was about money. It implied some kind of financial problem, something seriously wrong.

She couldn't feel more uncomfortable if she'd been caught naked in public. Nate couldn't possibly want her to hear this. Either that, or he was so troubled by the problem that he'd forgotten she was there.

Nervously she tugged on an earring, studying his office—but the look of the place didn't offer her answers, only confused her more.

For instance, the far wall was almost completely covered with photographs of old, gorgeous cars—the darlings in history, the Austin 7s and the Cords, the Duesenbergs and the oldest Rolls Royces.

Even for a woman who couldn't tell a carburetor from a fan belt—and who didn't give two hoots for cars—Jeanne could have fallen in love with those irresistible darlings. And in any other man's office, the photographs wouldn't have been odd. But the thing was . . . Nate violently, noisily, vociferously hated cars.

Years ago, his dad had a plain old fix-up-a-jalopy-type garage. Nate had hated everything to do with it. All through high school, he'd sworn a zillion times that he'd willingly do anything for a living that didn't involve grease under the fingernails. He'd done it, because he'd always helped his dad after school and summers. But by their senior year, he'd gotten a full scholarship to Princeton—his ticket out.

Again Jeanne tugged on an earring, remembering how passionately he'd wanted to be an architect. He'd wanted to leave his stamp, to make the world a better place his own way. He'd wanted to create better working environments for everyone—build dentists' offices with skylights, clinics as comfortable as living rooms, office spaces that had swirls and angles and beauty. But Nate was so full of dreams and goals. If the architect thing hadn't worked out, there were a half-dozen other fields of study he wanted to try. He always seemed open to absolutely anything— except for what his dad did.

Of course, the business had obviously expanded from the hole-in-the-wall garage it had once been, but the work was still cars. And although Nate was wearing an obviously nice striped shirt, he'd pulled on a working pair of coveralls over it—and there was another pair of coveralls hanging from a hook behind the door. That one had grease stains, so Nate wasn't just running around this place in a starched shirt, staying pristine all day.

He was still talking on the phone, his head still averted from her. "Mrs. Macpherson, I wish I could give you that answer immediately. I don't know. What I *do* know is that I'll have the overdraft corrected within the hour. And I'll talk to you again before the day's out . . ."

Again as she tried her best not to listen, Jeanne's gaze zoomed to the opposite wall, with all those pictures of his daughter. Caitlin. The photos showed all kinds of growing-up landmarks—a diaper picture, a sandbox picture, one of her in a Girl Scout uniform and another wearing a first communion dress. One showed Caitlin crying her eyes out—heaven knew why—another was obviously her first haircut, and a bunch of them were holiday photos, Halloween with all the different costumes she'd worn, and Christmas pictures, in which she was so surrounded by presents you could hardly see her.

Just looking at the pictures put a lump in Jeanne's throat. Caitlin could have been the child she'd dreamed of having with Nate. She looked so like him, with the same thick, dark hair. The same unforgettable eyes. The same cocky posture. Oh, she was a handful, that was obvious. It was also obvious that the girl was protective of her father— because she'd looked at Jeanne in the lobby as if she were as wanted around there as a snake.

But what did that *mean*? That she didn't trust women around her dad except for her mother? Could it mean that Nate had been hurt? Or just that Caitlin was the kind of daughter who was selfish and didn't want to share him?

For that matter, where was Caitlin's mother? On the whole wall, there wasn't a single photo of Caitlin with her mother—or *any* sign of a woman that could be her mother.

The more Jeanne looked around, the more confused and rattled she felt. They'd been so much in love . . . or so she'd thought. They'd sworn to marry after they both got out of college, to call each other every week, to be faithful, to never stop loving each other.

He hadn't lasted a college semester before writing her that ghastly letter. Down deep, in her heart, maybe she'd always expected him to drop her. She'd always known that she wasn't as smart as Nate. She'd been the prom queen type, not the mover and shaker type that he was.

Only that was precisely what unsettled her right now. All this time, she'd secretly believed that she simply wasn't strong enough, good enough, bright enough to hold him—but then why on earth was he back *here*? Back home? Back in the one business he'd always sworn he'd never do? Why had he torn up her heart and her life, if he'd been willing to come back home?

"Peanut . . ."

She hadn't realized that he'd hung up the phone until she heard him calling her that old nickname. Talk about twisting the knife. It hurt, hearing that low, sexy voice wrap around that old endearment he used to call her. Worse yet, there was something in his eyes—something she'd never expected to see again. Warmth. Yearning. An intimate sense of connection.

She swallowed, and then had to swallow again. She should never have come; that was for sure.

She thought she'd needed closure, and instead all she felt were old wounds razored open—and this overwhelming confusion. For Pete's sake, a man didn't throw over a woman . . . and then remember his pet name for her. He didn't look at a woman who meant nothing to him—as if she did. As if she really, really did.

"Damn it, Nate," she blurted out. "If it was about another woman, why didn't you just tell me that!"

She'd never meant to let that slip out, but Nate flinched as if she'd struck him.

"It wasn't about another woman," he said quietly.

"Come on. You said Caitlin was thirteen. Did you think I couldn't add? You must have been involved with someone awfully close to the time we were—"

"I'm sure the timing looks suspicious, Jeannie, but it isn't. I swear. When we were together, I never saw anyone else, and wasn't thinking about anyone else—even remotely."

He sounded so sincere that she wanted to believe him—even did believe him—but it wasn't as if there was only one huge question swimming in her head. "You were *never* coming back to your dad's garage. You hated this work. You wanted nothing to do with your dad's business. You hated the grease and the smells. You used to say over and over and over—"

"I know."

"I don't understand. You left me with such a . . . hole. Couples break up, for God's sake. We were children. We knew nothing about life. But I thought . . ." Once she'd started the flood, she couldn't seem to cut it off. She knew she was inviting him to hurt her again, but she still couldn't stop. "You were always bigger than life," she said fiercely. "Bigger than me. I knew that. I knew you could go miles farther than I ever could in life—"

He flinched again. "Jeannie—that was never, never true."

"It *is* true. My family had some money, and I had looks. Everyone always made so much of my looks. I was never afraid I couldn't survive, make some kind of life, but you were wearing such different shoes. You had real brains. Brains, the charisma, the drive, the everything. To do absolutely anything you wanted with your life. But damn it, if you wanted to be *here*, why did you drop me?"

She'd never known she was going to do it. Ask. Maybe she'd told Tamara she needed closure, needed to see him, but the reality was, it was too damn hard to volunteer for a sock in the heart. Only now . . . it was as if the cry rose from her heart and just couldn't be silenced. All these years, the ache and loss had always been there. For what?

Nate pushed out of his chair. "Peanut . . . I only

cut the ties with you because I had to. Because when my father died, everything changed."

"*Why?* I could have been there for you—"

"No, you couldn't. You were in college. Where you needed to be. Getting a degree, starting the life you were meant for."

"But so were you, just starting Princeton—"

"When my dad died, I dropped out of Princeton. College was over for me. You know I had three younger brothers and two younger sisters—and suddenly I had all of them to support. My dad hadn't prepared for spit; he left us with debts, and my mother—she couldn't possibly cope, financially or emotionally. She'd never even had a job outside the home. I was the only one old enough to step in. I had no choice."

They both fell silent. One minute stretched to two, then three. He'd painted a picture of his life that she'd never expected, couldn't quite grasp, couldn't suddenly make it fit against all her preconceptions of what his life was supposed to be. The way he'd blurted out his circumstances, she suddenly ached for him the way she'd ached all these years for herself, and she wondered if he felt as she did—as if the old hurts and pain had been bottled up too tight. For too long. And seeing each other . . . she didn't know what it meant. Except that she couldn't seem to stop looking at him.

And he couldn't seem to stop looking at her.

Restlessly he stood up, but then just leaned

back against the credenza, as if reminding himself to keep a careful distance from her. Well, she'd had it with distances. "You should have told me, Shadow," she said, low.

"I couldn't."

Old fury came out in a raw voice. "Horse hockey, you couldn't! You didn't even give me a chance to help you, to be there for you—"

"I was trying to give you a chance—at a life. Anything I'd hope to give you or have with you was gone."

"Maybe that's true. Maybe it's not. But either way—you decided what was right for me without ever asking me. I wasn't included in something that very much affected me, not just you!"

"Aw, Jeanne." His eyes reflected pain, and his voice seemed to have the same timber of loss that hers did. "At the time I thought I was protecting you. The best way I knew how. The only way I knew how."

Damn it. He kept clipping the wind from her sails, when she desperately wanted to lash some of that old fury onto him. "Even if you felt you couldn't tell me right then, you could have later. I understand that right after your dad died, everything had changed for you. But after a while—"

He was already shaking his head. "That's just it. There was no 'after a while.' From that day until now, my life has been getting my brothers and sisters raised. And they finally are, for the most part.

Tony isn't actually off the dole yet—he's in his first year of community college, working here part-time. But getting them all educated and grown up and then jobs—that's what I've been doing. There hasn't been a single gate in my fence."

"And you have Caitlin." She couldn't forget his daughter.

And he didn't duck from that subject, either. "Yes. Caitlin is part of that, too. And probably I'm making this sound wrong. I'm not complaining. My family needed me. I did what I had to do. And there's nothing I value more—that I could possibly love or value more—than my daughter." He scraped a hand through his hair. "I'm just trying to say—taking care of family became my life. Whatever you thought I was going to be or do—I knew I couldn't be that anymore. All those plans, they just had to be . . . erased."

She heard him. Unfortunately, she couldn't seem to absorb everything he'd told her all at once. Her heart was tumbling and stumbling around all the new information so fast she couldn't think. He'd dropped her because his life had changed. Not because he hadn't loved her.

She'd desperately wanted to believe that for so long. That he *had* loved her. That she hadn't totally misread her feelings and his. Only it seemed that it should change everything, realizing that he'd been hurt so badly himself.

Instead, certain critical things didn't seem changed at all. Her heart had still been broken. She'd still *felt* rejected, diminished, all these years. And whether the truth was different from what she'd believed, her reality was still that her life had become all screwed up—in ways she hadn't managed to fix, didn't know how to fix.

Suddenly Nate shook his head and let out a short, gruff laugh. "Nothing like diving into deep waters before we've barely said hello, is there?"

She shook her head, too, feeling just as bemused. "I don't know what got into me—asking such private questions out of the blue."

"Same thing—I can't imagine what I was thinking of, telling you all the family history out of the blue, either."

Again, a silence fell, uncertain, laden with nerves. Again, she found herself staring into his eyes. Found him staring back into hers. She said, "Shadow . . . you look so wonderful."

He said low, gruffly, "And you're a thousand times more beautiful than you were even then. You're obviously doing well. I'm proud for you."

His telephone rang. And before he could make the choice to either answer or ignore it, someone drummed knuckles on his door, and then a skinny guy in coveralls with a bushy red beard popped his head in. "Hey, Nate. The Stutz Chantilla Sedan's just pulled in—but the driver says he isn't even opening the truck door without you being there. Not for cargo that expensive. You know how they are about insurance—"

Jeanne jerked to her feet and grabbed her purse. "Nate, this is crazy. I'll go. Immediately. I'm in the middle of a workday, too, and for darn sure, I never meant to interrupt you—"

"You're not interrupting me, but I do have to go," he agreed. "Believe me, though—I'm sorry."

"That's all right, I—" By the time she reached the door, the red-bearded mechanic had charged off down the hall and Nate was suddenly in front of her. He wasn't blocking the door, not stopping her from leaving, but definitely making a point of face-to-face contact.

"No, we're not leaving this here." Maybe he was busy. Even pressure-cooker busy. But whatever a Stutz Chantilla Sedan was, it didn't seem to bother him right then, because for another long moment, his eyes met hers. Those dark, emotive eyes looked her over with infinite slowness, as if taking in her face, her hair, her mouth. Remembering her. Memorizing her.

Something kindled in the air, the way an invisible moodiness built up right before a summer electric storm.

"We'll find a way to talk again," he said.

To Jeanne, it sounded as if he were making a promise. And she wanted to talk to him again, wanted to see him . . . but she was also fifteen years older than she'd been at the time in her life when she'd believed anyone's promises. She would never trust anyone again the way she'd so blithely and completely trusted Nate.

Least of all herself.

The green banker's lamp illuminated ledgers and tax records and financial data from the last three years. For weeks now, Nate had been hiding in the study after dinner, scouring the pages up one side and down the other.

He'd discovered the first serious discrepancies a couple months ago. About a week after that, he'd confirmed something grave was going on. Money was missing. Not big money—but not horse feed, either. At this point, he was guessing somewhere between ten thousand dollars and twelve thousand dollars was missing. It had been siphoned off in small amounts over quite some time, which was why the problem had escaped notice for so long.

At this point Nate had established conclusively that there was no accident or coincidence or mistake. He had a thief. Cut and dried.

Only he couldn't find the culprit. The receipts reported all the moneys coming in. The bills totaled how much had gone out. It all added up. God knew, the records had passed the IRS—not that that was significant; everyone knew the IRS was stupid. But the records had passed his accountant's legal eye. And his own.

So how the hell could the bank accounts keep coming up short? How had the thief covered his tracks so well for so long? And dammit it, who *was* the thief?

Nate drummed a pencil on the desk, a familiar burn of acid churning in his stomach. He'd always fiercely guarded the family business because he had to. He'd had people to support, people dependent on him, which meant that only a very few had access to the financial records. Which meant . . . the thief had to be someone he trusted.

That hurt.

It hurt more, because he had an ugly, sick feeling who the thief had to be.

Abruptly he heard Caitlin yelling from the bottom of the stairs. "*Dad!* Come on down! Grandma made tiramisu!"

Nate opened his mouth to reply that he was busy, then closed it again. The whole family was mad at him, ranting that he was working too hard, being mean and dictatorial and ornery. Hell, he had to be mean to keep the family ship afloat over the years, but just then . . . well, he hadn't spent a minute with Caitlin since he got home.

Truth to tell, he hadn't done anything in two days but worry about his thief—and replay the meeting with Jeanne Claire over and over in his mind.

Both were getting him nowhere—and shredding his nerves in the process.

He scooped up the files, locked them in the top file cabinet drawer, and switched off the banker's lamp. The entire upstairs of this two-story white elephant was his and Caitlin's. He'd bought the house after Donneli Motors had finally started bringing in serious money. The whole family had been born in a house on the wrong side of Ypsilanti, a scooch away from Ann Arbor. That old place had been big, but rickety from the get-go, with stairways that creaked, windows that leaked, no insulation. Parked cars squished on the street because there were no driveways. Theirs had been the poorest house on the block, even there and even back then.

This house was better, but never what he would have chosen. His mother hadn't wanted to move at all, had insisted she'd only budge if he picked a neighborhood from which she could walk to her chosen parish. At the time, his brothers and sisters were still growing up, so they'd needed a place the size of an elephant, and at least this place had big, airy rooms, huge windows, lots of space. Of course, that was when he bought it.

He aimed for the stairs, already hearing raised voices below. Halfway down, the gloom descended. No matter how many conveniences and luxuries he brought to his mother's life, she still managed to make any place look the same.

The front hall was cluttered with doodads and fringed throw rugs. Smells of Italian cooking wafted through the entire downstairs. Crosses showed up wherever there was spare wall space. Heavy drapes darkened the rooms. He'd bought light-colored couches, but somehow they'd disappeared, been replaced by dark wood with dark colors.

Upstairs, he and Caitlin had chosen their own decor, but his mother—it was just easier on his sanity to let his mother be.

He poked his head in the kitchen. The sink was piled high with dishes, and every counter space crowded with cooking debris. An orange tabby cat was drinking from the faucet, where Caitlin was running the water to a thread, and typically, his mom was yelling.

"Caitlin, how many times do I have to tell you? I don't want the cat on the counters in my kitchen!"

"But she only likes kitchen water."

"Oh, you. I—" The instant his mother spotted him, she beamed. "There you are, Nate. Finally got around to joining the family. Tony's not here, and Jason's late. I thought everyone was coming for dinner and dessert today, but what do they care if they see their mother? And your daughter—"

"Dad, Grandma says I can't wear these jeans!"

"Next year, you go to the high school, wear a decent uniform, we won't have to be talking about these things. Those pants aren't decent!"

"That is so not true. Everybody shows their navel. It's the style."

"I don't care if it's the style. You're going to catch your death of cold. And it's immodest—"

"Didn't we just have this fight last week?" Nate asked mildly. "I thought we agreed Caitlin could wear whatever she wanted on weekends. But for school, no belly button showing."

"I never agreed to that," his mother said immediately. "What's right is right—"

"Grandma, that is so unfair. I get all A's. I'm not doing drugs and having sex like everybody else—"

"Mary, Mother of God—" Maria Donneli crossed herself. Twice. "I should hope you're not. But the point is, what the boys will think if they see you expose skin like that. You're a beautiful girl—"

"Grandma, it's just a stomach! Everybody has one, for Pete's sake! For that matter, I want a navel ring."

"Jesus, Mary, and Joseph, I can feel my heart pounding. It may be a heart attack. And when I'm dead, you'll be sorry you caused my heart failure. That you could even talk about putting a hole in your navel—"

"I think they're cute."

By then, voice levels had risen to shrieks and the tiramisu had been sliced and slid on plates, milk poured, napkins and forks put out, and Nate had shuffled through the day's mail. It was the same mail he got at work. Bills. Only these were home bills. Tony's college tuition bill for the next term. The usual electric and heating oil bills. A phone bill that could support a small country. A small charge from Old Navy—that was Caitlin. A massive lump to some godforsaken Catholic charity—that was his mother. Then . . .

Out of nowhere, just as he was staring at an envelope, Jeanne's face suddenly flashed in his mind. Not how she'd looked in his office. Not how she'd looked the day he met her. But the day—the night—they'd made love for the first time.

She'd been a virgin—which was one of the reasons he'd easily motivated himself to stay away from her. Sex was the only vice he'd allowed himself in high school. The girls went for him. He didn't know exactly what the deal was—maybe they forgave him for being a brain because he was a jock? Or there was some appeal in taking on the forbidden boy from the other side of the tracks? Whatever the reason, it had always been easy to score. And he'd always driven himself so hard that nailing every girl who'd been willing had seemed a worthwhile goal. In the guys' locker room, they'd started calling him the Stud of St. Sebastian—a tag he'd totally liked.

He'd been three-quarters of the way through the cheerleading team, in fact, when he came up against Ms. Forbidden. He'd known Jeanne all that time. Secretly suffered a nonstop crush on her for all those years. But as popular as she was, she'd never driven in the fast lane. She just wasn't like that. But she *was* a cheerleader, and somebody had dared him to see if he could get to any base because Jeanne Claire had the ice princess label. So he'd been dared into asking her out.

Only he'd never intended to score.

He never intended to make love to her at all . . . and for damn sure, he'd never guessed he'd fall in a real way for her. You didn't fall for an icon, for God's sake. You didn't screw an angel. She was an idol for him in every way. Hell, he'd have walked on nails before he risked hurting her.

But that night . . . it wasn't that simple.

That night . . . everything in his life got complicated.

That night . . .

"*Dad!* You're not listening!"

His head shot up. He couldn't believe he'd lost track of the conversation. He knew how dangerous these grandmother/granddaughter situations were. Caitlin always wanted him to take her side. His mother expected him to back up her authority. If he said one wrong word—or even tried refereeing between the two of them—they'd both turn on him. Big blood would get spilled. His blood. This was an absolute for-sure.

"Are we still on the jeans question?" he asked carefully.

Caitlin heaved a sigh, conveying the massive exhaustion with a parent that only another teenager could understand. "We were talking about that woman who came to see you the other day."

Both female faces suddenly peered up at him, studying his face with laserlike intensity. That was the thing with his mom and daughter—and the other fourteen thousand close female relatives he had on the Donneli side. They considered prying an innate female right. And they could smell when another female was anywhere near the borders of their territory.

"This was someone you went to school with, Caitlin said," his mother probed.

"Yup, it was. An old friend."

"She looked at you like you were way, way more than an old friend, Dad."

"So what was her name?" His mother was now standing next to Caitlin like they were joined at the hip, and never mind how often the two fought like cats and dogs.

On the other hand, Nate hadn't survived this long without knowing how this game was played.

"Her name is Jeanne Claire Cassiday. She was my first love in high school. And she stopped by with some silly excuse about the fifteen-year high school reunion for St. Sebastian's. But the truth is, she took one look and fell in love with me all over again. She suggested having a wild, promiscuous affair, and even tried to seduce me in the office, but—"

Both his girls had already looked at each other, rolled their eyes, and were turning away—back to the tiramisu.

"What, you don't believe me?"

"Sure, Dad. In your dreams."

"I'm going to take one piece up to the study and go back to work, okay?"

They waved him off. That was the trick to handling them, of course. Tell half the truth, and then invent something so outrageous that it stopped them from worrying for the other half.

But seeing Peanut had raised questions, in his mind, in his heart. All those years ago, he'd done the right thing, made the only choices he could make. He'd accepted that. Fifteen years ago, he hadn't only lost Jeanne Claire, but all the dreams he'd once believed in and wanted so much. He'd accepted that, too.

Or he thought he had.

Now, suddenly, he almost resented seeing her again. Maybe he was resentful of his life sometimes, but he'd toed the line, stayed the course. Now, sneaky as spring, he could feel this stupid, winsome hunger inside him. An impatience. A wondering.

He didn't want to *risk* anything. He just wanted to see her. One more time. Maybe one more time would do it. He just wanted to know if he could recapture even a cusp of that idealistic, hopeful man he'd been once. He'd liked himself back then.

He'd given a damn about everything and everyone back then.

Seeing Jeanne had made him remember the man he'd once wanted to be.

chapter 5

Arnold opened the front door to St. Sebastian's Senior High School and felt his confident smile immediately droop. He could have sworn he was happy to head the reunion committee, happy to be part of the whole reunion thing. He wanted to show his old classmates what he'd become and who he was now.

Only it seemed there was an eensy-teensy factor that he'd forgotten. Somehow, even after all these years, one look at the yellow and black tiled floors, the tall polished doors, the dark hallways, and phantom echoes trailed him like shadows. *Nerd. Dork. Arnee the Brainee.*

Eventually he was going to find this laugh-out-loud funny. How could all his adult, mature confidence dissolve so quickly? Still, he wasn't ready to laugh quite yet. The janitor who'd let him in started to offer his help, but Arnold said abruptly, "I know the way. I'm going to the library. Two others should be coming, Tamara Whitley and Jeanne Claire Cassiday. It's for a reunion committee."

"Yes, sir," the janitor said—with that tone of respect that Arnold was used to hearing from strangers these days.

"Keep an eye out for the women, would you? I know it's still light outside, but they're still walking alone from their cars." As soon as those extra words spilled from his mouth, Arnold wanted to kick himself. Was that a macho, authoritarian, cool-guy thing to say? No. It was his historically prissy, take-care-of-everybody type of thinking.

He could feel hiccups forming—he'd always had a sensitive esophagus. Weeks ago, when he'd established a place for the reunion committee to meet, he thought the high school library would be ideal. They'd be on the site. They all knew the place.

Only now he remembered how these long, echo-chamber corridors instinctively made him feel like tiptoeing and hugging tight to the walls. Anyone could jump out to confront him. The nuns and teachers used to love him—but the cool kids and the bullies could pop out of nowhere, and immediately have something to say about his shuffle, or his glasses, or the presumed small size of his wanger.

His wanger was a decent size. He had no problem being well hung. It was his ego that always seemed to limp.

He clipped down the main hall, trekked right, then tracked to the last room. He'd arranged for the library to be left unlocked, with at least one light on. Typically he never forgot to arrange such details—but now that made his wanger feel wilted, too. Taking care of details just wasn't a macho, studly thing to do.

He cleared his throat, and then aggressively flipped on the rest of the light switches. It seemed no one had updated the library decor since they'd been here. Just as before, the place smelled like old books and pencil dust. The librarians' oak work counter overlooked a cluster of varnished oak tables.

He chose a central table, opened his briefcase, immediately set out two color-coded files for Tamara and Jeanne Claire, then remembered to take off his jacket. And breathe. He had to remember to breathe.

He'd deliberately arrived fifteen minutes early to give himself ample time to settle. Unfortunately, that meant there was also ample time for memories of Tamara dissing and dismissing him to replay through his mind. He loosened his Italian silk tie—so he wouldn't look quite so buttoned down—checked to make sure his fly was zipped, patted down his hair. That morning he'd paid for a fifty-five-dollar stylist, yet as far as he could tell, his usual twenty-buck barber made him look exactly the same.

Money, though, wasn't the point. Tonight he'd have paid thousands if he could have bought a few ounces of confidence before seeing Tamara again.

He checked his trusty Rolex. A minute had passed since the last time he'd looked. It was now ten minutes until eight o'clock.

Then nine minutes until eight.

Then eight.

A hiccup interrupted the hallowed library silence—but it was only one; he was going to be all right. His parched throat gave him an excuse to hike over to the drinking fountain, though. The exercise made him feel like a kid again, remembering how the water gushed straight up from the library fountain, how he'd gulped it down, how he instinctively moved to wipe his mouth on his sleeve—and that was exactly when he heard the door swing open and the sound of chattering women's voices.

"Best Brain! You in here?" one called out. Tamara. Fifteen years later, and the sound of her voice still immediately made his hands sweat. He considered hiding behind European History—

who'd look for him back there?—but instead he charged out as if he had all the normal confidence.

Oh, God. Her hair was still red, still wild. Her voice and smile just as sassy. Her coat looked like patches of bright-colored velvet, unconventional and original, just like her. That was exactly the problem. There was no one else like her.

"Hey, Best Musician!" he greeted her in return, as if they'd had an old, comfortable habit of teasing each other this way.

She grinned at him—as if she was actually glad to see him. "Sheesh. Does it feel weird to be back in the high school after all this time or what? Didn't the halls feel haunted to you?"

"By the ghosts of kids past?"

"By the ghosts of all our sins past . . . Hi, Arnold." Jeanne Claire walked toward him with a warm smile and her hand extended. He shook it, then just watched the women get comfortable—peeling off their coats and gloves, stashing their purses, pushing at their hair.

"You look great," Jeanne said.

"Thanks. So do you." She did. He'd never known a woman more beautiful than Jeanne Claire, and it seemed the class princess had even more poise and elegance than she used to. If threatened at knife point, though, he couldn't have said what she was wearing.

He was too busy looking—or trying not to

look—at Tamara. "I think we can probably wrap this up in a few meetings, do the rest by phone or fax. I brought up a couple things in that first letter—like the keynote speaker. But there are some other things we need to immediately hash out—like a theme for the reunion. And a specific date. And we need to identify the jobs that have to be done, see who can volunteer."

He went into straight managerial mode, which actually he was pretty good at. He was just hoping Tamara—and Jeanne—noticed. No matter how much money he made now, she—they—had known him *then*. He just wanted her—them—to see that he was no longer the wallpaper dweeb who spit when he talked and knew every math answer.

A half hour later, he sat back, almost feeling relaxed. "So we're all agreed the homecoming weekend is a great date for this, the last weekend in October? We'll start the reunion day with the high school football game, making it easy for everyone to be in casual clothes—and the school colors—and then we'll do our reunion bash in the evening. Starting early, so people don't have to leave the game and go back home."

Both women nodded at every one of his suggestions. Nobody had any argument about anything.

"Tamara, you've got the address list, so you're going to take care of getting the invitations sent out. At least once we have the school hall lined up so we know for sure where we're putting on this gig—"

"Check."

And that's when everything suddenly went downhill. Arnold had no idea why. They were down to divvying up jobs, bringing up details, identifying needs. Obviously that was what they were there to do. So he gave himself and Tamara the hardest tasks, and then said, really nicely, to Jeanne, "You can do the decorations, okay?"

And both women were suddenly looking at him oddly. Who could figure? Everything had been going *fine.*

"What?" he said. "Is that too much to ask you to do, Jeanne?"

"No, of course not. You wouldn't be killing me to give me a little more, though," she said with a touch of humor.

"I'm sure you could handle more. I never doubted it for a minute. I just didn't want to give you anything too hard—"

"Hey!" Tamara said curtly, when he hadn't done or said anything but be completely nice.

He didn't understand, but he quickly veered to a safer subject—or what he assumed would be a safer subject. The speakers. "Jeanne, I don't know if you had the time to contact Nate Donneli about being our keynote speaker?"

Her smile seemed to freeze. "I contacted him. But I'm not sure he'll be willing to do it."

"You're kidding. He was valedictorian. And voted Most Likely to Succeed. No one was as well-known or well-liked as Nate. He has to do it—"

"Arnold, I'll ask him another time. One more time, anyway. But I have to say, he didn't want to do this at all. So I can't promise."

"Jeanne, if any person in the universe could get that man to do something, it has to be you," he began, but suddenly both women were giving him that arch look again. Like what, what? He didn't know what he was saying to offend them.

"Okay. Well, Tamara, I can't think of any possible better way to start the reunion than with a song and some comments from you. I mean, you weren't just voted Best Musician, but you went on to have hit records, become one of the famous ones in the class—"

"I don't think that's a good idea."

"What?"

"I think it's a bad idea," she repeated.

"But you're perfect. Everyone always loved you. You were lots of fun, and you knew everybody, and you could always get everybody going—"

"No," she said again. Not in a mean way, but she didn't add any explanation or reason or anything.

She wasn't making any sense, but he was afraid

of offending her by questioning her any further. "You know," he said finally, "we've really gotten a lot done for one night. How about if we call it quits for now, and meet in another couple weeks. We still have to decide on a theme, but that'll give everybody time to think up ideas."

Both women immediately popped out of their chairs, so he knew cutting it short was a good idea. Jeanne Claire checked her watch and said her goodbyes immediately, but Tamara didn't take off that quickly. She wandered off in the direction of the girls' bathroom.

Arnold fidgeted, putting stuff back in his briefcase, then pushing in the chairs. He could have left—he wanted to leave, was wary of being alone with Tamara altogether. Still, he couldn't just desert a woman alone in the building after dark.

Tamara ambled back in the room, but instead of pulling on her coat, she perched on one of the tables and just looked at him. "Arnold . . . don't do that to Jeanne Claire again, okay?"

"Don't do what?"

"She's a bright woman. Smart, responsible, resourceful. Capable. And fun. You really hurt her when you treat her as if she's stupid."

Arnold's jaw must have dropped fifty feet. "What? I never meant to do anything like that!"

"I know. No one means to, but everyone does. They take one look at that fabulous face and assume she's a witless blond. The reality is that she's kept her father's business afloat almost single-handed over the last couple years. Oz Enterprises."

"Are you serious? That whole hotel and conference complex?"

Tamara nodded. "Yeah. And that's the point. She could arrange the reunion in her sleep, if she had the spare time. It's what she does. Organize huge events. And I'm not trying to criticize you. It's practically everyone who misjudges her. I know you didn't mean to put her down."

"I didn't," he assured her.

That was all it took for her to smile at him—but she also pushed off the table as if that was that, she was now ready to leave. And suddenly—as if the Spirit of Idiots Past took over his vocal cords—words babbled out of his mouth in some insane effort to just keep her a little longer. In a room. With him. Any room.

"I was thinking about the reunion," he bumbled on. "That we should start it with music. I was always counting on starting it with your hit song—'Bucking the Tide.'"

She stilled, even as her hands had started to reach for her velvet-patch coat. He thought she might give him a reason why she was unwilling to play, so he could talk to her about it. But no, she said nothing, leaving him to trip on.

"But then I was thinking . . . we should also try to compile a list of songs the class'd remember.

Songs we could just play in the background, you know? Like remember the movie *Dirty Dancing*? 'The Time of My Life' song was from that. And Paula Abdul; her first album came out that year—"

"I remember."

"And then I just happened to remember some other songs." Actually, he'd racked his brain to recall the music she'd like. The songs he could remember her dancing to—with other guys. Or songs that he'd heard her practicing at lunch sometimes for fun. "Like . . . 'Tainted Love.' And 'Slow Hand.' 'Take Me Home Tonight.' 'Lay It Down.' 'Slippery When Wet'—"

She did pull on her coat then, slowly, her eyes meeting his from the other side of the table. "It's funny, how many rock and roll songs have a sexual theme, isn't it?"

"Yeah," he said, trying to sound suave and urbane.

"I think it's a great idea to play the hit songs from our senior year. Or the songs we all seemed hooked on."

"Good," he said, feeling gratified again, that she'd liked one of his ideas.

"But if you're trying to ask me again if I'd be willing to play 'Bucking the Tide' . . . or whether I changed my mind about starting the reunion with a little kickoff speech . . ."

He was. Because he couldn't imagine why she'd said no to begin with; both should have been something she'd love to do.

"Arnold," she said gently, "I know I said no initially. But if you really want me to give the kickoff speech, I will. You just need to understand—it's not going to be what you think. And I'm just afraid you'll regret asking me."

"There's no chance of that!"

Slowly she walked around the table toward him, still talking in the same conversational tone. " 'Bucking the Tide' was my first song that made gold. That was my dream, to have a band—a band that made it. To be able to do the music I loved. To be a hotshot. To be famous. But right now I'm selling shoes, did you know that?"

He said quickly, uncertainly, "No."

She stopped, a couple feet in front of him. "I live in a one-room efficiency. Sell shoes. Have an occasional drink. Pick up a guitar for friends sometimes. But that's it. I keep my life as simple as I possibly can. I got my dream—but the lifestyle sucked me into drugs. Maybe somebody else could have handled the fame and fortune. I sure couldn't. So I can't get up and say, 'I'm one of the real successes in the class.' Because my truth is—I *did* get my dream—but I flunked Success 101. Big time."

She didn't announce all that as if it was a confession, more as if she was simply informing him, sharing with him. There was no shame in her voice, no request for sympathy.

Only he didn't know what he was supposed to say, what he was supposed to do. He had no idea she'd had a drug problem. He hadn't known anything except that she'd hit it big, hard, and fast in music, and then dropped out of sight, as if she'd chosen to retire from the limelight. As far as he knew, she was the same idol she'd always been. The wild free spirit. The girl who dared anything. The girl who had the courage to defy any and all convention, to stand up for being different.

She was the sexiest girl he'd ever known, before or since. Sexy on the inside. Uninhibited, the way he'd always been the most inhibited, repressed human being in all of Ann Arbor, and possibly the entire state of Michigan.

That she'd gotten into drugs was hardly startling in this day and age. But that still didn't offer him answers. He had no idea what she wanted him to say. What the right thing to say could possibly be.

That she didn't have to do the opening reunion speech if she didn't want to?

She stood there for a long moment, watching him, meeting his eyes, but maybe she drew her own conclusions about why he couldn't manage to answer her. Or maybe not. When she took another step toward him, he had no idea what was on her mind—but suddenly she was as close as a breath, as close as a heartbeat. She lifted her hands. Toward him. She framed his face between those soft, white hands and looked right at him with those all-woman eyes.

"Let's just get it out in the open," she whispered. "I know you wanted me all those years ago, Arnold. I know I made you nervous. But now you know that I turned into a loser. So you can relax. I'm nobody you ever really wanted to be involved with, so you never have to worry about that stuff again, okay?"

She surged up and kissed him. He was pretty sure she meant it to be a light, friendly peck. A now-we've-cleared-the-air smack between old friends—or old classmates.

But Arnold . . . he didn't do light smooches. He didn't do we've-cleared-the-air kisses. He didn't do much kissing, period, but for damn sure, the chance to get his hands on his dream woman after all these years was hardly something he could take lightly.

For God's sake, the feel of her mouth alone became his entire universe for that instant. All blood flow stopped, then gushed straight to his groin. Rational thought went the way of the goony bird. Sight blurred. Hearing shut down.

He might have feared that he was going into a

coma except that his heart was galloping in his chest like a runaway gorilla, and in two seconds flat, he was harder than marble.

Her mouth . . . she was so sassy that who could guess her mouth would be that soft? That tentative and vulnerable? She was always so full of hell and attitude that who could guess she'd smell like some light, elusive flower?

It was over in seconds. Tamara suddenly bounced back down, opened her eyes, dropped her hands. Stared at him in bewilderment. "What on earth just happened there?" she demanded.

He could have told her . . . the world exploded. April turned into October. It snowed dandelions. The known universe—at least his known universe—was turned on its head. But somehow he couldn't believe that Tamara had quite the response to that kiss that he had.

"Are you coming to the next meeting?" he asked, because that was all he could manage to get out.

"Arnold. Get a grip. Something just happened here. Something crazy. And I'm not talking about *meetings*."

Well, he was. Because he wanted to see her again, and if that kiss had blown it, made her not want to attend the next reunion meeting, then he was gonna have to commit suicide. And he opened his mouth to say something intelligent and effective and careful, only—thank God—she grabbed her purse and file and one driving glove—she dropped the other one on the floor—and tore out of there.

He stared after her forever. At least a couple of minutes. Before pushing a hand through his hair and letting himself breathe. His heart was thumping as if he'd just endured a major trauma.

It was probably best that she'd charged out, since there was no question in his mind he'd have handled anything else badly. Said the wrong thing. Done the wrong thing. That was easy to assume because he was still completely confused by what had just happened. She'd rocked his world, yeah. But what had happened with her? Why had she kissed him? What had she felt?

All these years, he'd daydreamed about seeing her again. Daydreamed about talking to her. And now that he'd finally had his chance, it seemed as if the actual event had been both less than he'd hoped . . . and a thousand times more.

chapter 6

When Nate needed to track down his brother Daniel, he always looked first in the obvious place. This morning, typically, Daniel was in the shop, his head buried under the hood of a car. Their mother always said it was one of those mysteries of life, how the car engine could be spotless and his brother coated with grease from his chin to his knees.

"How's she coming?" Nate elbowed next to Daniel, studying the '37 Hudson. She was a Custom 8, Series 77—one of the first automatic shifts and a prize by any collector's standards.

Daniel's voice came from the depths of the engine's shadows, colored by the smells of grease and oil—and moody as mud. "You know how it

100

is. The original owner respected her fine, but once a girl gets into the collector's market . . . well, there's a lot of ignorance out there. She wasn't abused. Just not treated right. I can easily get her running again, but I can't get her up to prize value."

"We knew that when we took her on."

"Yeah, but I'd hoped."

"She only cost $965 new, Daniel," Nate said wryly. "And we bought her for a song. No matter what, we'll get an easy ten thousand for her."

"I *know* that," Daniel said testily. "But I'd still like to horsewhip her last owner. It should be a crime to treat a girl like this rough or careless."

Normally Nate would have chuckled. Daniel was the notorious Donneli, by far the best sinner in the family, had trouble with women, credit cards, gambling, and any other vice he could think up. He resisted responsibility in any form, always had—but get him near a classic car, and he was more protective than a mama lion with her cub.

Recently, though, Nate was too damn worried to tease Daniel. And his brother looked just as crabby.

"What'd you come by for?" Daniel stopped working long enough to wipe his hands on a rag.

"A trip I thought you'd want to take. The usual annual car show's in Hershey, Pennsylvania, this fall—I just caught the dates, first days in October. I was tempted to say skip it; we've got too much on our plate now through the summer and fall. But I saw some of the goodies they were listing, including original parts for a 1926 Pierce Arrow Runabout. You know the one, the seventy-horse, where the hood lifts up from the side—"

For an instant Daniel's eyes lost their defensiveness. "Like that's a car I'd ever forget. Man. Just thinking about her is enough to give a guy a hard-on."

"She's a beauty, all right. But I don't trust the dealer listing the parts—I think he's a junker. I can't see buying something we haven't seen firsthand. I want you to go."

Daniel stopped wiping his hands, glanced around for his coffee mug. The coffee had to be stone cold by this time in the morning, but he still took a long pull. "Last year you told me I was never going again," he said warily.

Last year his brother had run up several thousand bucks in motel and entertainment bills. They'd had a three-day shouting match over Daniel's partying habits. But their constant wrangling made Nate worry that if the family had a thief, the most likely candidate had to be Daniel. Until there was proof, Nate didn't know what he could do . . . except to keep a dialogue going between them, no matter how difficult that could be sometimes. "If you don't want to go, I could ask Jason," he said.

"Jason would rather get the clap than go to a car show."

That was true. Jason was a whiz with numbers, but he dressed like an urban stud for the office and never stepped foot in the shop if he could help it. "Whether he'd go or not isn't the point. I thought you'd want to—"

"I do." Daniel tossed down the rag. "Can I take Caitlin?"

Then it was Nate's turn to stiffen. "No."

"She's asked to go with me. Over and over. And she wouldn't be any trouble."

Sometimes Nate felt as if he were the only one in the entire family with any common sense. "Of course she asked you. You're her favorite uncle, partly because you always say yes to her. But she's bugged me about it, too, and the answer's no."

Daniel was already bristling, always quick to bite. "Hell, why do you always have to be such a tight ass! You think I wouldn't watch out for her, you know better. I love that kid, and she asked me so many times that I finally said the next time I went to one of the car shows—"

"Damn it. You promised her, didn't you?"

"Yeah, I did," Daniel admitted.

Nate swallowed back his temper. Daniel had a long history of making promises he was in no position to keep. But this morning Nate was doing his damnedest to avoid another fight. Instead, he tried to win his brother's understanding. "Look, Dan. She's already too attached to this place. She thinks she wants to be a mechanic—"

"And would that be so bad?"

"With her brains, she could be a brain surgeon, for God's sake. Or a rocket scientist. You think I'm going to let her aim for a job where she gets constant grease under her fingernails?"

"Sometime you should hear yourself. You shoved the business down all of our throats. I happen to love it—but Jason and Tony sure don't. What kills me, though, is how you'd figure it's good enough for all of us—but not for your daughter."

Nate's jaw dropped. "Hey. I never said or thought any such thing. The business was a way of giving everybody in the family jobs, for God's sake. Good-paying jobs. But that isn't at all the same thing with Caitlin."

"I sure don't see why it's different," Daniel snapped.

Nate sucked in some patience and tried one more time. "Look. Cat's hanging out here all the time now. And that was okay when she was just a tyke. But now she's growing up. Talking navel rings and makeup. Getting little breasts. Boys are calling. It's scaring the holy hell out of me."

"I don't see what that has to do with—"

"I'm trying to explain why I don't want her any

more attached to the cars and the business than she already is. Except for Martha, it's almost all men here. Family's fine. Obviously. But you know the rich jerks that walk in here. Sometimes those guys are real creeps, arrogant, think they can take anything they want. And Caitlin's on her way to being beautiful."

Daniel rolled his eyes to the ceiling. "Jesus, Nate. She's just a kid. You think things out so far ahead. Can't you just let her be? Let her do what she loves? Why do you have to manage everybody's life?"

The accusation stung. "I don't."

"Yeah, you do. Hell, when I was a little kid, you used to be my idol. But ever since Dad died, you turned yourself into the boss of the world. It always has to be your way. You think you know what's right for everyone." The last was said as Daniel huffed toward the door—which he slammed when he stormed out.

The other two mechanics in the shop magically bent their heads over cars as if the action could make them disappear—not that everyone in the place hadn't heard the brothers argue before. No Donneli had ever managed to be passive about anything. They laughed at the top of their lungs, but they sure fought that way, too.

Nate strode back to his office. Daniel's temper tantrums weren't new, and normally he'd slough off a few moody words, but today it wasn't that easy. He couldn't talk to any of his brothers without feeling suspicious, and he hated it.

Nate sank into his desk chair. He loved his family. Hell, he'd given up his whole damn life for his family—which was exactly why it was so painful to believe that one of his brothers could have betrayed him. Maybe he fought with Daniel more than anyone else—maybe they even regularly came close to strangling each other. But he'd honestly never doubted that the brother bond was fiercer than fire until recently.

Man, he was so sick of worrying about this.

He had a dozen things to do, was about to push out of the chair and charge back to work . . . yet impulsively he suddenly grabbed a phone book, thumbed through, then dialed a number. He asked for Jeanne Claire before he could change his mind, but then the doubts set in. This was crazy. He had no excuse for calling her, nothing planned to say—and he never did anything impulsive because he was so bad at it. He was a pinch away from hanging up when he suddenly heard her velvet voice.

"Nate?"

"Yeah, it's me . . ." And then he stumbled over what to say next, just as if he were a gum-chewing teenage boy again. Finally a short bark of a chuckle escaped him. There was just no choice but to laugh at himself. "Calling you is totally nuts.

Don't worry about saying no. It just happened to be one of those few days when I could grab a couple hours for lunch. And I just had a wild hair, thought maybe if you were free—"

"I can't break loose at noon. But I can get free around one, if that would work for you."

"Yeah, that's fine. Is there any easy place convenient for you?"

It was her turn to hesitate. "Mariner's. Off State Street."

He knew it. The name hadn't been Mariner's when they were in high school, but the cafe had long been a hangout for University of Michigan students and faculty—which was exactly why they'd snuck off there as often as they could. It had been a long walk from St. Sebastian's, but being around the college kids had made them feel cool. More important, they could talk there for hours without anyone paying any attention to them.

He arrived at twelve-forty—giving him ample time to fidget. The ambiance hadn't changed a whit. The place had the same scarred booths, same menu scribbled on a blackboard, same fancy teas and coffees, same deli sandwiches with fancy breads. He kept mulling why she'd picked the place . . . Did she remember how many hours they'd spent there? Did she think of the place as theirs, the way he once had? Maybe her choice was simply accidental, convenient? Maybe he was losing his mind?

And then he watched her push through the door, and quit giving a damn whether he'd lost his mind or not. His throat parched. His palms slicked. Suddenly he was a damn fool seventeen-year-old all over again.

She was wearing red shoes again, but today her blond hair was brushed back in a sleek coil. Outside, the blinding April sun could have fooled anyone into believing it was a nice spring day outside, but the wind still had winter's sharp teeth. Her cheeks were as rosy as her blouse. She was wearing black business slacks and a long black coat that looked expensive but completely concealed her figure. Nothing concealed the expression in her eyes. She stood at the door, searching for him over the crowd of heads, oblivious to how many guys—all ages—swiveled around to get a better look at her. Finally she spotted him in the booth at the back and immediately offered a vulnerable, luminous smile. She reached the table before his heart remembered that trick about the need to beat regularly.

"I wasn't sure if you'd come," he admitted.

She peeled off her coat, slid in across from him. "Well . . . I'd worked up an excuse to call you, because I met with the reunion committee. But the truth is . . ." She suddenly shook her head with a cheeky grin. "Shoot, I'm not sure I have a clue what the truth is. Except that I was happy you called. I just wanted to see you."

"I didn't have a good reason, either, Peanut. Beyond thinking . . . I'd never expected to see you again. But now I have. And now I can't get you off my mind." A waitress intruded, seeming to think they wanted food. He ordered something. She ordered something. And then he had her alone again.

She folded her arms on the table. "I'm supposed to ask you again if you'll consider being the keynote speaker at the reunion." Before giving him a chance to respond, she added, "But I'm not going to. Instead I'm going to ask why you look so tired."

"It's been one of those long mornings."

"You used to be a morning lover. A really annoying crack-of-dawn kind of person."

"Still am."

"So there was something unusual about this morning—?"

"Not unusual. I regularly seem to annoy everyone I come in contact with, but today I scored extra high. My daughter was ticked at me first, then my brothers at work. Lately the whole family's been calling me The Crank. In fact, Caitlin's told me several times that I'm the bully of the universe."

"And are you?"

"Yes. To both the crank and bully labels. I think that's partly why I wanted to see you. You knew me back when I was a relatively nice guy. I was trying to see if I could remember back—a thousand years ago—when I felt like I was a nice guy, too."

Another smile, this one full of amusement. "So you've turned into a complete dictator and tyrant now?"

"Yup." The waitress interrupted, serving corned beef sandwiches slathered with mustard, kosher dills, and hot spiced chai for both of them. Jeanne sat back while the meal was served, but her eyes met his, and once the waitress turned around, her voice turned quiet and serious.

"Okay, all joking aside . . . something's actually wrong, isn't it, Nate? Are you having some kind of trouble with your business? The day I was there, it sure looked as if you were going great guns."

He remembered how perceptive she was. But he'd forgotten how naturally he talked to her, how easily things came out that never seemed to with anyone else. He started on the wolf-sized corned beef sandwich, hungry for the first time in days. "The business is doing great. When my dad ran the place, it barely kept the family in peanut butter—I know you heard me whine on that when I was a kid, how lazy my dad was, how it used to drive me nuts. Anyway, when I got stuck taking it on, I was damn young . . . but it was still obvious that it had to be completely overhauled if there was going to be any chance of making it. So I moved to classic cars, and then to fancy antique cars. And it's done fine."

"It looked as if you were doing way more than fine." She took one look at her sandwich and immediately divided it. There was no way that small mouth could get around three inches—but she dove in, obviously as hungry as he was. "I don't know anything about cars, but every single one I saw looked like a treasure."

"They are. In fact, the truly unique models are priceless to collectors. People who love them *really* love them—which is why the business has grown so well. Except that we've been so busy, especially this last year, that apparently I wasn't watching the till close enough." He took on her chips, when it was obvious she wasn't going to touch them. "I've got a thief."

He'd told no one about his private nightmare, yet it came out to her easier than melted butter. The déjà vu sensation kept wrapping around him. For so long he'd had no one he could tell, no one he could unload to, and here he was, sitting in a scarred oak booth with corned beef hanging from a sandwich and she was listening to him. She was his again. She was listening again. They were two against the world again.

"I know there's more than ten thousand dollars missing. Probably close to fifteen. It's been siphoned off, bits at a time. I haven't figured out how. For weeks now, I've been pulling up the records of bills and receipts. Everything was recorded the way it should be. Everything adds up. It's only when one bank account showed up overdrawn that I had a clue something was going on. And there have to be answers in the computer accounting program, but damn it, I can't find them."

"Good grief, Nate. No wonder you're upset."

Hell. Once the faucet was turned on, he couldn't stop leaking. "What kills me is that there are only a handful of people who have access to the accounting records. Myself. Martha. And my three brothers. And the thief isn't Martha, because there are figures even she doesn't see."

"Martha?"

"You met her. She's the woman who runs the whole place and me with it. I think we hired her a decade ago to be a receptionist, but she didn't limit herself to that, even the first day. She's kind of the traffic control, general majordomo, the only person who knows everybody's schedule."

"We have a Martha at our place, too. Same name. Same job. Same bossy temperament." She added in a conspirator's whisper, "I'm afraid of her."

"It must be in the name. Maybe if you name your daughter Martha, you're inbreeding some kind of terrorizing personality." He said it dead serious, so he'd win another of those cheeky grins—and he did. But then she reached over to steal his pickle.

"So you think you've got a thief, but you haven't been to the police or a lawyer?" At his expression, she answered her own question. "Of course you wouldn't. Not if you thought it was one of your brothers. But why, Nate? What kind of problem would motivate someone in the family to steal like this?"

It was such a relief to get it out. And she voiced the exact same questions that his mind had been circling around for weeks—if one of his brothers was the thief, then which one and why, and how could it possibly have happened? Only he couldn't seem to come up with the answers alone.

"I know I told you about the family years ago, even if you didn't meet them all. You know I'm oldest of six kids. My two sisters—Mary and Anne—they're both doing fine. Married. Mary lives in Arlington, and Anne just got married and moved to Atlanta last year. Neither of them gave a moment's trouble. But the boys . . ." He sighed.

"I thought you always got along great with your brothers."

"I did. We did. Until my dad died and I took over. And they all still get along fine—with one another. I'm the only ogre in the clan."

"Come on, Nate. You're no ogre."

"Yeah. I am. The thing is, Peanut, I had to be. When Dad died, I was a bare, spare nineteen. Mary was the next oldest, at fifteen. Then came Daniel. He was just thirteen. He was crazy about our dad, so the loss hit him extra hard, and suddenly there was me, giving him orders, telling him what to do, right when he was reaching adolescence."

"That went over like a ton of bricks."

"To put it mildly. We butted heads like mountain rams. Still do. Daniel . . ." He shook his head. "Just getting him through high school took a full-time war. He's smart. In fact, he's damn near a genius under a car hood, and I'm not kidding. But he could never settle down. Skipped school, partied, raised hell with alcohol and women. Even now, he gambles, runs up his credit cards. He's a charmer. Everybody loves him. But he just couldn't spell responsibility if his life depended on it."

"Okay. So, age wise, after Daniel comes—?"

"Anne. She was eleven when dad died. A total sweetheart, then and now. I had to watch the guys around her, chase a few off—she had a tendency to bring home the lame ducks. She bucked me if I forbade her from seeing some guy, but what the hell was I supposed to do?" He couldn't help the aggrieved tone in his voice. "I was a kid, too, remember. Suddenly trying to father all of them, trying to keep us financially afloat. Anyway, that's all water under the dam. Anne found herself a good man, and she and I are totally fine together. Talk at least once a week."

"Okay. So after Anne, comes—"

"My two youngest brothers. Jason is twenty-four now. Two years younger than Anne. He's our accountant—well, actually, he hasn't passed his CPA test yet, but that's only because it took him extra time to finish his degree at the University of Michigan and work at the same time. The CPA thing's moot anyway. He could have done the books in his sleep from the time he was a kid."

"And you get along with Jason?"

"No. Hell. I don't get along with any of my brothers. With Jason, the problem is that he's a natural with numbers, but he claims he never wanted to be an accountant. He wanted to run off to California and be a photographer. Like who wouldn't?" Since she still wasn't eating her chips, he copped a few more. "But I had all five kids to put through school, make sure they were set up in jobs, in life. I didn't have the luxury of saying, Sure, go lie on the beach and don't worry about preparing to make a real living."

"Hey. I'm not attacking you, Shadow. You don't have to sound defensive with me."

"I didn't mean to. I'm just trying to explain—they all think I'm dictatorial. A tyrant. The boys resented me for any rules I laid down, anything I said. Maybe I could have been nicer. I don't know. All I know is that I suddenly had five kids to raise when I was still a kid myself. I swear I did the best I could—"

"Of course you did. But you have one more brother; fill me in there."

"Tony. Sometimes we forget and still call him Sonny, which he hates. Anyway, he's nineteen, so he was only five when Dad died. Everybody babied him, but he's a good kid. He still doesn't know what he wants to do—except that he wants nothing to do with cars. So temporarily he's in community college, living in an apartment with kids—and that was one of our wars, the cost of him living there when he could live free at home. And he's working for Donneli Motors, which I know perfectly well he doesn't want to. But I can give him any hours he wants, working around his classes, and he's smarter than anyone I could hire off the street . . . so I can give him parts runs, cars to deliver, whatever comes up."

"That sounds like a good deal for him."

"It is. I swear it is. But Tony's on me all the time. He didn't want to go to school locally. He didn't want to live at home. He doesn't want to do anything—ever—that I think he should do. I don't listen. I always have to have things my own way . . . What? What?" She was suddenly giving him a look.

"I'm just rolling my eyes. You sound exactly like the ogre the guys claim you are. So. Are they telling the truth? You don't listen to them? You always have to have things your own way?"

He considered, as he chewed the last of her

chips. "Yeah. I guess I am an ogre, come to think of it. But why would I listen to them when I know what's best for everyone?"

That really made her laugh. Until that moment, Nate hadn't realized that he still remembered that certain laugh of hers. It wasn't a big belly buster of a laugh; it was just uniquely *her* laugh . . . a laugh that was just for him, a laugh that cut out the rest of the world.

He was suddenly reminded of all he'd lost—all he'd given up. Lately everything in his life seemed to open up that old sore, but seeing Jeanne felt like an extra bruise on an old, deep wound. It was too late for them, obviously. Fifteen years too late. He wasn't so foolish to believe otherwise. But it still sliced hard, that it was this easy to be with her, to get those feelings back, even after all this time.

Swiftly he glanced at the wall clock. "Hell. I've kept you here more than two hours. I've got to get going, and I know you do, too."

"I do. But it's been a month of Sundays since I took any free time, so it's not like I'm feeling guilty."

Maybe she wasn't feeling guilty, but she quickly gathered up her coat—making Nate sure she was more than ready to leave. He motioned the waitress for the check. As soon she brought it, Jeanne said suddenly, "Nate? Could I help you?"

"Help me? Help me how?"

"You're worried that one of your brothers is a thief. I don't know what I can do, but I'm offering. I'm pretty good with computer programs, and I know my way around accounting and tax statements. Maybe a fresh set of eyes might notice something you missed?"

She suddenly held her breath, although he wasn't sure why. There just seemed something in her expression—a wariness, a defensiveness—as if she expected him to doubt that she had the brains to analyze an accounting problem.

"I don't want to ask you."

"I volunteered. You didn't ask. But if you don't want me—"

"I do." Hell, her wording made heat shoot up his neck. But that wasn't what he meant. "I could use another pair of eyes. I'd appreciate it—especially because this isn't something I want to take to an outsider. I don't want lawyers or outsiders in our personal business, don't want my brothers thinking I don't trust them, either. But that means that so far it's just been me, staring at the same data hour after hour. If you can spare the time, maybe I could just show you the files and records. For darn sure, I'm missing something."

"I'd be glad to."

"Jeanne. . . ." He cleared his throat. They walked toward the cash register, with his hand at the small of her back, steering past students and professors. No one paid them any attention.

Someone was arguing about green space, someone else about Middle East politics. ". . . . I took up all our time talking about me, my life. Is there someone in yours?"

"Pardon?"

"Are you with someone? In a relationship?" So maybe he wasn't Mr. Tactful. So maybe he had no business asking. But one way or another he needed that answer—now. Immediately. Yesterday. Before he said another word to her. Before he thought another thought about her.

She couldn't instantly answer. By then he'd reached the cash register, after which he got change and had to hike back to leave a tip, then hike ahead to push open the door. Outside, clouds had scuttled in front of the sun and the wind had kicked up a temper.

She snugged the collar of her trench coat to her throat. "Yes and no."

"Those dice won't spin. There's either a man in your life or there isn't, Peanut."

She scrunched up her nose the way she used to. "You want the nutshell summary, I was married for a short time after college. He wanted a corporate wife. I could have sworn that was me, but it didn't seem to work out that way. The divorce wasn't fun, so it just seemed wise to live solo for a while—besides which, my dad needed me. So it wasn't until last year that I really considered looking around again. And then I met someone . . . we seemed to click, until recently the relationship came to a place I was uncomfortable with. I broke it off . . . only he hasn't been taking it very well. He's still calling."

Whew. She'd summarized a lot of heavy stuff damn fast—but he still caught the weed in the garden. "Forget what he wants. I'm asking about you. Is that relationship totally over for you or not?"

"I don't want to be in it. I want it completely over. But it's complicated, Nate."

It wasn't to him. When a woman said "complicated," what she invariably meant was that she still had feelings for somebody else and a guy was smart to run—at a full gallop—in the opposite direction. Nate opened his mouth to change the subject, when she suddenly twisted in front of him.

"But this isn't complicated at all," she said softly. "I can't stop thinking about how much you've been through, how much you've done. Raising five brothers and sisters when you were just a kid yourself—"

He frowned. "I told you. I screwed it all up. Most of them are mad at me."

"Shut up, Shadow. You're so dumb, you don't even see how special you are." And then she kissed him.

Of course, he'd seen her twisting in front of him; of course, he'd seen her lift up on tiptoe. But they were on State Street. Noisy traffic was zooming past, red-cheeked kids jostling them. It was a weekday. A workday. A middle-of-the-day day. How could he possibly have anticipated that she'd kiss him?

So he had good excuses for being confused. Outstanding excuses, in fact. Brilliant, outstanding excuses that would hold up in any court of law—especially if the jury were all guys.

But that still didn't quite explain how he did an instant time travel back fifteen years.

The thing about Jeanne was that she put on such a good show. She was so gorgeous. She was always dressed right, always had a look of poise and competence. She never said the wrong thing, never spit when she talked, never had lettuce hanging between her teeth. She was so damn perfect that strangers never realized the truth. The truth was that Peanut had no confidence.

She sure could kiss, though.

Back then, Nate well remembered that he'd been overendowed with ego—especially ego about his prowess. The cheerleaders used to chase after him nonstop. He never denied enjoying the attention. The point, though, was that by the time he'd had his shot at Jeanne Claire, he'd studied and practiced intensively, and his kissing skills were right up there.

Back then, she didn't have skill worth a dime. She didn't seem all that skillful now, either—

considering that she jolted off balance toward him and their noses initially collided and her hat tried to slide off when she pushed up on tiptoe.

But she still shook him clear to the bone. Even at his age. Even on a crowded, public street. Even when he couldn't possibly be trigger hard and aroused as if he were a teenage boy in two seconds flat. Even . . . aw hell. He couldn't think.

He had enough sense to back her into a doorway, which was at least more shadowed and private than kissing her in front of a street full of gawking strangers. She didn't seem to care. The damn woman simply wound her arms around his neck, sighed, closed her eyes, and let go. Her lips touched his, sank against his, as if she'd been waiting fifteen years for the touch of him and nobody in hell better try getting between them.

A candle sputtered to flame, where Nate could have sworn there was no flame inside him, not anymore. He didn't feel sweetness, not anymore. He wasn't a man for sentiment or softness. He didn't have time. Those were a boy's feelings, a boy's joys—great memories and all, but for God's sake, a man had real-life pressures and responsibilities.

Yet suddenly his heart was full of her again.

That sassy scent on her neck had nothing to do with perfume. And that soft, vulnerable skin was such an impossible contrast to that wild, wicked tongue of hers. Most women were too smart to reveal too much vulnerability. They didn't just lay themselves up against a guy, let him feel those warm, firm breasts, the tummy, the tenseness in her thighs from being on tiptoe. Her trench coat was too thick, intrusive. The fabric made hissy sounds when he ironed harder against her, hands sliding down her shoulders, down her spine to her fanny to push her tighter against him.

Minutes before, there had been anger inside him. The anger had been seeping into him for years, resentments and frustrations festering in corners and his mind's shadows—he knew about the anger, just didn't know what to do with it or about it.

Years ago, he'd given up everything because that's what he had to do. He'd even felt pride for doing the right thing . . . but sometime since, he'd lost that pride and become a lesser man. These days he seemed to feel angry all the time because of everything he'd had to give up. Pissed all the time because he'd never had his turn. Resentful all the time for all the dreams he'd once had— dreams so close that he was a pinch away from actually owning them, having them, making them real in his life—and now they were all completely gone.

Peanut brought them all back. Not just those dreams, but the time before the anger. The time when he really believed he owned the whole damn world. She kissed him as if he were the hottest, most dangerous guy she'd ever come across. As if she were a little bit afraid but couldn't help herself. As if she shivered from the sensation of danger but kept coming back for more, because she liked feeling dangerous, with him.

Hell. He wasn't especially hot and never had been. He was just Nate Donneli. But with her, for her—man. It wasn't as if he suddenly believed he was a red-hot lover . . . but that he wanted to be. That was the whole problem with Jeanne. He wanted everything for her. He wanted to be everything, do everything, bring her everything. . . .

The thought slipped away from him, the way every other coherent thought couldn't seem to hold for more than milliseconds. Her lips were softer than a warm rose petal. Her fingers whispered through his hair. Her face tilted to his in that posture of take me, tempting him to do just that, right there, right then, and to hell with anyone and anything else.

He pulled back, a frown pleating his forehead, his eyes snapping open to look at her, look at her, look at her. His breathing was coming in hitches. Her lips were still parted, still wet . . . her eyes still smoky, honed on his face, on his mouth.

"Hey," he said.

"Hey back, Donneli." For a moment she stared back at him with those dazed eyes, that lethally soft smile. Whole seconds passed before that smile faded, and then she swallowed. "Whew."

"That's what I thinking. Whew. In fact . . . double whew."

"I vaguely remember offering a kiss. But I had no idea it was going to turn into a tornado."

She was tensing on him. Not jerking away, not backing away, but not his again—at least not his the way she'd been a moment before. People charged past them; the wind nipped at their cheeks; traffic sounds blared. It hadn't taken long for the world to catch up with them again, yet he felt the oddest sense of loss. "If either of us wanted to know if there was still a strong spark, I do believe we just found out."

Those soft eyes of hers didn't deny it, but the worried pleat between her brows was becoming deeper. "A spark is one thing. Jumping headfirst into a fire is another. I didn't come here looking for this, Nate."

He could see the power of that embrace had scared her. And told himself that he should be scared, too.

She'd turned into everything he'd dreamed she would. She looked exactly like the million-dollar success she was—while he'd never left home base. She'd gotten her degree—where he'd never stepped inside another college door. And there was a guy in her picture. He'd have to be crazy to forget that guy.

Which all added up to trouble. To know there was still a powder keg of emotion between them made absolutely nothing easier. What was that old saying—"The things we fear the most have already happened to us." Well, he'd let Jeanne Claire Cassiday free once, and almost hadn't survived it.

He couldn't afford to lose her a second time.

chapter 7

At zoom speed, Jeanne hustled through the lobby doors of Oz and bolted toward her office. It was one of those salt-and-pepper-sky days—brilliant sun one minute, blustery and cloudy the next. Just like her mood lately.

Her work schedule had been a pressure cooker for the last few days, but she knew perfectly well that wasn't what had her on edge. It was Nate. She intended to see him. She wanted to see him. And soon.

But not until she managed to untangle her confused emotions much better than she had so far.

A dozen times she'd told herself that a few kisses on a public street couldn't possibly have rattled her cage. She'd been married, for Pete's sake. She'd gone out with lots of men; she worked with tons of them. Further, the memory of her debacle with her almost-fiance Donald was still fresh enough to sting. Her precarious history with men should have guaranteed that she'd learned how to be cautious.

Only she hadn't been remotely cautious with Nate, and for days now, she'd wanted to kick herself upside the head. It was one thing to give in to an impulsive kiss—for God's sake, she'd loved him once. Naturally she'd been thrown to hear about his dad dying, his being stuck with the whole family to care for and all the other responsibilities that had been heaped on his head. Her heart had ached for him.

And there was no denying that that shock had made her heart ache for herself, too. All these years, she'd assumed *he'd* dumped *her*. All these years, she'd assumed that she'd never been worth keeping, that she was the kind of fish a guy threw back. All these years, she'd *felt* like that thrown-back fish.

But that was still no excuse or reason for coming apart in his arms. Granted, she'd been unprepared to feel that fierce well of yearning after all these years. She'd never expected all that hunger and hope—not to count the lust—and normally she didn't like to underplay lust.

But my God. This wasn't just a guy. It was *Nate*. Past the lobby was a long windowed hall, leading to the corridor of private offices. Just in the last few days, daffodils and hyacinths had started blooming. The grass had turned that brighter, silkier shade of green. College couples were underfoot everywhere, smooching and snuggling in public. The trees were blurry with buds, and the breeze had that winsome kiss of spring fever.

She badly wanted to call him. And she had an honest excuse, because she'd offered to help him with his thief. Only she still felt . . . discombobulated. No matter how much passion those kisses invoked, the fifteen years since high school was a lifetime. He had a completely different life now— including a daughter. And maybe it salved her ego to realize he hadn't dropped her by choice— but she'd still suffered a soul-deep hurt. That hurt didn't erase in the blink of a second. She wasn't remotely the same person she'd been years ago.

She knew all that. She just wished she could figure out exactly what those kisses *meant*. Or could mean.

"Jeanne Claire!" She'd just reached her office when Martha caught up with her. She should have known better than to try dodging the general. Typically, Martha had swept up her gray-blond hair in an impeccable twist; her makeup was flawless and her lips pursed in disapproval. "You were gone a half hour longer than you said."

"I couldn't help it. The meeting just went on and on."

"Well, important things piled up." Slicker than a Las Vegas card dealer, Martha started dealing out pink phone messages. "The Vargas and Connelly wedding people called. Your father wanted to know if you could make that dinner on Tuesday. Then the insurance people left a message about the animals for that Rigby party. Then those lingerie people that your father set up"—she sniffed to express her opinion of that particular group—"called to set up a time for their so-called executive retreat. Then a personal call, that Mr. Donald—"

"Got it, got it, got it." Once Martha left, Jeanne settled in, dumping her purse, shivering out of her suit jacket, and sorting the notes into priorities. The one call from Donald went straight to her nerves; how many times did she have to say no before he heard her? But otherwise, the messages represented nothing more than a pile of work. Work, she wasn't afraid of.

In keeping with the theme of Oz Enterprises, her office was done in yellow. The color scheme had been one of her dad's creative ideas. The yellow brick road in the Oz story ended up at the wizard. Here the road ended up in her office, where the events manager was supposed to plan any fabulous dream you wanted and make it happen.

This afternoon, the yellow desk, fake yellow brick floor, and yellow walls struck her as just too much blooming yellow. She'd tried to be the wizard her dad wanted her to be, but sometimes the magic sure proved elusive. Her gaze snagged on the clipped black file she'd just brought in with her. Profit and loss projections. She'd gone into today's lunch meeting with the accountant, believing Oz was headed for a stronger financial period. She'd known what March's profit figures should have been . . . unfortunately, she'd forgotten how blithely her father could orchestrate sweeping changes without telling anyone. They simply couldn't afford going in the red fifty grand. Not another fifty grand. Not again.

Swiftly she reminded herself that April marked the beginning of summer events. She'd already ensured that there was some good, solid money coming in. June weddings already crowded the calendar. She'd gone after businesses for their spring retreats and seminars, then searched out new companies who wanted a place to set up their company picnics and golf outings.

When it came down to it, she wasn't avoiding Nate. She'd honestly been too busy to breathe. In fact, she'd just kicked off her red heels and knuckled down when the telephone rang.

"Jeanne Claire? It's Arnold Grafton. Did you get Nate to be our speaker for the reunion?"

"Um, not yet . . ." The déjà vu struck her sense of humor. Fifteen years ago, talking with Arnold had been just this challenging. He never did say hello or goodbye, just bumbled straight into conversations. "Like I told you, I'm almost sure Nate won't agree to do it."

"Aw, come on. He *has* to. He was the leader of the class in every way. What reason did he give you for saying no, for Pete's sake?"

She closed her eyes, recalling that conversation, thinking that Nate had never really given a reason. He'd just implied that he wasn't the "success" implied by the Most Likely to Succeed label. His attitude had startled her then and still did—my God, look at all he'd done in spite of the grief and trouble he'd had. But none of that was Arnold's business. "He didn't give me a precise reason, but lots of people have a phobia about public speaking. If we have to—"

"Jeanne." She wasn't sure why Arnold interrupted her, but she could hear him nervously clearing his throat. "Tamara said I hurt your feelings." More throat clearing. "If I did, I'm sorry."

"Huh? You didn't hurt my feelings."

"I didn't mean to. I swear."

"You didn't. Stop worrying."

"I was trying to be nice."

"You were nice."

"I was—"

"Arnold, good grief, it's all right, let it go." She was close to laughing out loud. How ironic. Two seconds talking to Arnold and they both regressed to their mutually insecure high school behaviors.

"Well, that was really the main reason I was

calling. To apologize. But I also wanted to run some other names by you if Nate really won't agree to be the speaker. Do you have a minute to hear the list?"

She didn't, but that was neither here nor there. "Shoot. Go for it." Johann, one of the clerks in payroll, paused in her doorway with his mouth open. She shook her head, mouthing the word, "Later."

"Okay, first I tracked down Baker Somerfeld. Remember him? Best Athlete. You know, the maestro jock, won the full scholarship to Notre Dame, went on to play professional ball." Arnold sighed. "He just had a sex change operation."

"Oops. Maybe he may not be our best choice for the reunion keynote speaker, huh?"

"I'll say not. Worse yet, he'd love to. He told me he'd want to talk about 'evolving gender roles.'" Arnold coughed. "So I told him that naturally Nate was our speaker, that I was just checking in case Nate got sick or something. And in the meantime, I tracked down everybody else I could think of. You remember Lara Reed? Best Dancer?"

"Sure."

"Well, her name's Lara Bartley now. Third marriage. This time she married a podiatrist. Had her boobs and nose done. She's telling me all this—I never even knew her—in the first three minutes of the call."

Poor Arnold sounded so freaked, she had to

smile. "Okay, possibly she isn't the best substitute for Nate, either, but sheesh. We had a great class of comers. There have to be other people who could do that speech—"

"Yeah, there were. Like Butterball Dingle—you remember him? The Science Whiz? He shed the pounds, buffed up, got a big grant, working on some fancy medical cure for some terrible disease. But darn it, he's in Africa."

"Not exactly a help."

"And then there was Rachel Baker—"

"I remember her." Since Jeanne wasn't getting any work done anyway, she pulled open a drawer and propped her stockinged feet on it. "She was the artist. Really cute."

"I never thought of her as cute. At least not like Tamara. But whatever. The point is that she's gone on, even did a sculpture for the White House, really made a name for herself." Another one of those Arnold sighs. "Only she's due her second baby in October, and they're saying it could be twins. Pretty risky to count on her." Arnold said abruptly, "Look, we need Nate."

"All right. I'll ask him again. I promise."

"There were some people I couldn't reach. Like Buzz Sawyer—"

"Ugh. Mr. Obnoxious."

"He's a judge now—"

"I know he is. But he's still a dog. Let's not ask him unless we absolutely have to, okay?"

"Okay. Now . . . I scheduled the next reunion meeting for a week from Thursday, seven, at the school again. But Jeanne—?"

"What?" She was listening, yet suddenly there was complete silence on the other end. "What, Arnold?" Finally, she heard him clearing his throat again.

"Look, would you mind if I asked you something about Tamara? Was she really into drugs?"

Jeanne tugged on an earring. Was this awkward or was this awkward? She tried deflecting from a direct answer. "Where did you hear that?"

"From her."

"Well, then. I can't imagine Tam telling you something so personal if it weren't true, can you? Really, though, if you want to know more, I think you should ask Tamara yourself."

"I just can't . . . seem to believe it. I mean, she was everything. She had everything. Talent. Looks. Pizzazz."

Jeanne's expression softened. Most people didn't think of Tamara as remotely pretty—but she wasn't surprised that Arnold did. She'd known he had a crush on her. Everyone in the class did. Until that moment, though, she hadn't realized that he still cared.

So she wasn't the only one who'd carried a very long, very bright torch.

"I'm not asking to pry," Arnold bungled on. "I guess I'm trying to ask . . . if she needs anything. I mean, not that she'd ever want anything from me. But—"

Hearing how much he cared made Jeanne willing to fill him in a bit more. "Tam's been on a long, rough road. But she's also been substance-free for two years now—except for an occasional glass of wine. But wine, alcohol, was never a problem for her. I think a lot of people try to stay away from all substances, but for her—"

"Does she date anyone?"

"Um, Arnold. I don't think anyone's used the word date in more than a decade."

"I mean, is she *seeing* anyone?"

"I don't think so."

"How do you think she feels about kids?"

Jeanne lifted the phone to stare at it. "Arnold," she said patiently. "If you want to ask her out, ask her out. We're grown-ups now, remember? We don't need the go-betweens anymore, where Mary asks John who asks Mike who asks Sally if someone would say yes before asking her out."

"Yeah, well, I was never part of that chain, Jeannie. If you'll remember I was the class retard. Still am."

"Hey. You were the class multi-brain," she corrected him.

"But a social retard."

Since they weren't in the same room, she could hardly wring his neck for being so exasperating. "Arnold, you're too old to ask for reassurance as if you were still a kid. Get off your tush. Pick up the phone. Ask her. If she says no, you'll feel rejected. That'll suck. But you're an adult, you'll survive it."

Well, she got him chuckling, but once she hung up, she found herself sitting there, feeling bemused. Arnold had never been a friend in high school. He'd just been one of those kids who was there, part of the fabric of their high school life. Everyone knew he was a nerd. Everyone knew he couldn't make a personal comment without putting his foot in his mouth. Everyone knew he could answer any question any teacher could ask.

She'd never made fun of him. But he'd never made an effort to talk to her any more than she had to him. She also knew why—because Arnold thought of her as untouchable, too pretty, too cool, to have anything to do with him.

That's not how it was. But people had distanced themselves her whole life because of presumptions and assumptions they made about her looks. So it struck her as funny, in a bittersweet way, to have a friendly, adolescent conversation with Arnold now.

In high school, she'd been so alone. Apparently, so had he.

In fact, the only man with whom she hadn't felt that loneliness was Nate. And suddenly she was rubbing her forehead, eyes closed, remembering those kisses outside the cafe again. That was precisely what had pulled her in. That was precisely what she couldn't let go of—didn't want to let go of. She'd never had that feeling with anyone else, and by damn—right or wrong, smart or not smart—she wanted it back.

Realizing that she was thinking about Nate—again—she swore, then determinedly pushed in her chair and grabbed a handful of papers from her inbox. This was nuts. If she didn't finish some work, she'd be stuck in her office all night. She grabbed a pen and dove in—just as someone knocked on her open office door. She glanced up.

Her stomach instantly twisted tighter than a sailor's knot.

"Hi, Jeannie."

"Donald." He didn't look much different than the first time she'd seen him. He was wearing a blue sweater, Zegna jacket, casual pants, and Italian boots in leather softer than a baby's butt. There was nothing wrong with him—absolutely nothing. He looked what he was—a wealthy, forty-one-year-old man who'd earned the confidence and poise to do whatever he wanted with his life. Money had bought him the kind of freedom everyone dreamed of. He never dressed pretentiously or lorded it over anyone . . . but he could wear his blond hair a little long, do a workday in a sweater when others felt obligated to wear suits, and yeah, he could probably get in anyone's office, anywhere, without having to worry about a receptionist stopping him.

"I could have called first—" he said smoothly as he stepped in.

"I wish you had."

"—but then, every time I've called, you've found an excuse to either say no or hang up before I could finish a conversation with you." His eyes met hers, unmoving. When her telephone rang again, he said, "Leave it. Let your voice mail pick up. You know you have no reason to be afraid of me, Jeannie. And I won't stay long. But I'm determined we're going to talk before any more time has passed."

Her palms felt so squishy damp from nerves that she wanted to kick herself. "Donald . . . I never wanted to hurt you. But when I called it off, I meant it. I wish things could have worked out. You were nothing but good to me, but the fact is—"

"The fact is, Jeanne, that everything was going fine between us until the one night when we finally had sex."

Hoboy. Was she glad he'd brought *that* up. It was precisely that sexual debacle with Donald that motivated her to call off the relationship— and to take a good hard look at the emotional abyss she'd let her life become. It wasn't his fault, though, that she'd turned out to be the coldest fish in the Great Lakes. "It may have looked as if sex were the reason—"

"It looked that way because it was that way." He didn't close her office door, as if he sensing she'd bolt if he cornered her too tight. But he stood in the doorway, where she'd have to pass him to leave. "It may not have been great, but nothing terrible or frightening happened, now did it?"

"Of course not. And that wasn't why I called it off, Donald—"

Again he gently interrupted her. "We were getting along fine."

It was true. Possibly they'd only met because her father was hoping to find a new funding source in Donald, but he'd never pushed business on her. She'd liked him. He had a cottage in the U.P., a boat on Lake St. Clair. When they had dinner at his house, he'd hire a chef. He'd shown up with orchids and tulips, lobster from Maine and beignets from New Orleans.

He'd spoiled her.

She admitted liking it. She didn't like him because of his money, but for darn sure, no one had ever courted her with such style. He'd never tried giving her a too-expensive gift, but who could turn down a box of See's chocolates? A basket of fresh lavender?

Behind the scenes, her dad pushed for the relationship to develop. He was crazy about Donald, but then, her dad was crazy about anyone with money. And Donald was good to her dad.

Nothing specifically wrong ever happened. There was no sudden moment or event when she realized the relationship wasn't working for her. But it was like watching someone walk on a train track with the sound of the train's warning hoot in the distance. She didn't love Donald, but she kept telling herself that maybe she would in time. That she should. That only a stupid, foolish woman wouldn't love a guy who cared, who showed her such constant attentiveness, who spoiled and romanced her. What was not to love?

The night he'd seduced her, she knew it was coming. For weeks, he'd been bringing up long-term plans. He'd talked about house styles. He'd mentioned marriages. He'd pretended to idly window shop jewelry windows, steering her toward rings. Besides which, she was a grown woman, and she knew perfectly well he'd been patient as Job. No guy was going to be held off with good night kisses forever. It was amazing he'd waited as patiently as he had. And it was just sex, right?

"We were getting along fine," she agreed quietly. "And I enjoyed our friendship, our time together, so much I can't tell you. But I couldn't give you the feeling you wanted, Donald. I'm sorry. It just wasn't there."

He shook his head. "Come on. You're not a teenager. Neither am I. Good sex isn't about rockets going off and magic. It's about two people working at it. Sometimes you get the rockets right at the start. That's nice. That's great. But there's no reason to think a couple can't have a good sex life—a great sex life—with some time and effort. If you were scared—"

Could this conversation possibly get any more fun? "I wasn't afraid of you."

"Good. I'd sure hope not. I didn't see how you could be. Maybe I was too patient, too slow, because I knew you were wary. But one occasion is hardly a judge of anything in bed, Jeannie. Especially when we were so compatible in other ways. If there was something else going wrong—you never told me."

"Donald, there was nothing wrong with anything you did in any way. It was me. My fault. My feelings. My problem. Not yours."

He repeated the same refrain. "Everything was going fine until we went to bed. You're judging the whole relationship based on one time under the sheets that wasn't stellar. I don't get it."

Stellar? She'd frozen up like a Popsicle. He'd hurt her, not because he'd done anything wrong, but because she had as much lubrication as the Sahara at high noon. She'd gone into the encounter determined to have sex. Determined to fake it. Determined to make Donald believe he was a great lover.

It kept seeping through her consciousness that she'd been doing this for fifteen years. Not having bad sex. But being a fake. A fake with men. A fake with herself.

That was when it hit her. She really had changed in the last fifteen years. Everybody tried to protect themselves once they'd been hurt—but she wasn't the freely loving girl Nate had once known. She wasn't as free, and no matter how much she'd accomplished, she wasn't as strong.

When she didn't immediately answer him, Donald said bluntly, "I want to know—is there someone else?"

"I wasn't seeing anyone else when we were going out, if that's what you're asking." She added, "I understand that you want a more specific answer. But I don't have it. I just don't feel . . . loving toward you . . . the way a woman should feel for a lover, the way you have every reason to have a woman feel. You're a super man. It's only me that's wrong. Not you."

"You're not giving me a reason not to call you."

How many times had she tried to tell him no since that awful night? What was she failing to say? "Donald, I don't want to be enemies with you. I don't want to say anything mean. I don't *feel* anything mean. But I'm serious—completely—

about having no further interest in pursuing any kind of personal relationship with you."

He looked at her for a long time. Her phone rang again. Voice mail picked up. Outside the window, the sky darkened, clouding up in thick gray fists. People walked past her door, talking, laughing.

Finally he shifted, as if staring at her for a length of time had enabled him to come to certain clear conclusions. "There's someone else," he said flatly. "Another man."

"There was never—"

"We'll talk again. Don't worry about it, Jeanne. I didn't come here to be unpleasant. I just wanted both of us to have a clearer understanding what had happened, where we stood."

He was gone before she could say anything else. She didn't know she'd been holding her breath until her lungs exhaled an exasperated sigh.

Typically Donald had been kind. Typically Donald treated her like an incomparably treasured possession, a princess, a fragile sweet thing that deserved constant cherishing.

Only she wasn't a princess. She wasn't fragile. She wasn't a sweet thing. And his attitude made her want to smash something. Why did she let it happen, for Pete's sake? Donald. Her first husband. Even her father. She didn't knowingly cave for the men in her life—but somehow she'd stopped standing up for what she wanted and needed in her life.

It hadn't always been that way. Nate had always made her feel reckless and strong. He'd always invoked the explosive thrill of passion—but he'd also wanted her to be everything she could be.

What on earth did it take to get over that man?

Or to win him.

The thought surfaced in her mind, as sneaky as a promise, as stubborn as resolve. Maybe, for some women, there really was only one man. Maybe, for her, that man was Nate.

And maybe not. Jeanne took a long, slow breath. She might love being taken over in passion—but nowhere else. She didn't want to risk being hurt the way she had the first time. She didn't want a relationship where she disappeared under a strong-willed man. But there certainly was no better test in the entire universe than Nate.

Only a strong woman could stand up to Nate's kind of powerful personality. Whether she still had that potential was unknown. But it was time, she thought, to take a risk, to take control of her life—with no holds barred.

chapter 8

Tamara knew something was bugging Jeanne, but getting it out of her was like pulling teeth. "I can get you a deal on shoes."

"That's okay," Jeanne said. "I don't need shoes. In fact, I don't really need anything."

Tamara shook her head. "Next thing, you'll be saying you don't need to shop."

"Actually, I don't—"

Tamara was almost too shocked to interrupt. Almost. "Don't say it! The feeling'll pass, I promise! Let's just put you in sight of a sale sign and see if that doesn't perk you up. Come on. Think greed. Materialism. Vanity. It's the American way. And if that doesn't motivate you, think how righteous you'll feel to help the economy . . ."

There now. She finally got a chuckle out of Jeanne but it was a distracted one. She pushed through the entrance doors to the Briarwood Mall and hustled Jeanne in before she could balk. Tamara often needlessly took a bossy role in their friendship, but this afternoon it was actually necessary. When she'd dragged Jeanne out of that ghastly yellow office, her friend had been neck-deep in paper. Two o'clock on a Saturday afternoon and she hadn't even stopped working to grab some lunch! Obviously Tamara had had to get tough.

"I never see you in the dumps. You're always so damn cheerful that you usually annoy the hell out of me. So what is this? Oh. You haven't mentioned Donald the-wannabe-Trump in weeks now. It's him, isn't it. Damn it. Is he still chasing you?"

"I know you don't like him, but that's because you're allergic to anyone with money, Tam. He's never been unkind to me."

"It's not his money I don't like. It's that he looks at you like a diamond he wants to own. And he's manipulative. Like you call off the relationship and does he listen? No. He only hears what he wants to hear."

Jeanne paused to unzip her jacket. "Donald did come to see me. He did upset me. But if he were the worst problem I had, he'd be a piece of cake, okay? Honest, there's nothing there worth talking about."

Tamara thought, *Okay, so we can rule out Donald.* No matter what Mr. Money had or hadn't done, Jeanne simply didn't sound remotely shook up about him . . . only there had to be some other problem then, because she sure wasn't behaving like herself. She was antsy, vague, distracted. Jeanne was always the rock in their friendship. The unshakably calm voice. The one who never failed to be rational. For her to behave this way was totally unnerving.

But maybe it was partly the weather, Tam considered, as they ducked and dodged around shoppers. The mall was unusually busy, probably because the stores had just stocked up on all the new summer clothes. Why they sold bikinis in April made no sense, but all the bright colors and new fashions were disarming on such a stormy spring afternoon. Tons of flowers might come out of this, but it was sure hell on hair.

While her hair was turning into a punk rocker's frizz fest, though, Jeanne's was just hanging limp and damp. Jeanne even looked beautiful when she had the flu. That her hair could look bedraggled— that *she* could look bedraggled—was enough to put steel in Tamara's spine. Before this afternoon was over, she was going to help Jeanne or die trying . . . but in the meantime, she figured she might as well take advantage of the bonding time. As they neared Banana Republic, she said, "He kissed me."

"Who?"

"Arnold. He kissed me . . . or I kissed him. After that first reunion meeting, in the school, right after you left. And now we've got another meeting coming up and I'm nervous."

"Because of a kiss? Somehow I wouldn't think just kissing a guy would put you in a tizzy—"

"Neither would I. But I'm telling you, this was different. It was like . . . a whiff of Vera Wang. A trip off planet. A something I never expected. It was unbelievable. Underneath that thinning hair, those button-down shirts, those boring eyes, I'm telling you, there's a red-hot wolf."

"Say what? Are you sure we're talking about Arnold Grafton?"

"Yeah. And I *mean* it. I wasn't trying to start anything serious, just kind of impulsively gave him a little smack. Then—whammo. My nerves melted into a puddle at my feet. I saw stars. I saw magic. I see a blouse that would just be perfect for you." She squinted, then sprinted straight for the Ann Taylor window.

"It's cute," Jeanne agreed.

Tamara leaned closer. Cute didn't begin to cut it. On the surface it was just a blouse, but it was navy and white striped, silk, fitted. It was the kind of hint-of-sexy but tasteful blouse that Tamara only wished were her style. It was a lady's blouse—the kind of lady who let it all hang out with her guy when the lights finally went off at night. "You've got to have it, Jeanne. It's absolutely perfect for y—" She turned around, but Jeanne was gone.

And then her jaw dropped, aghast, when she saw Jeanne had ambled over to the Victoria's Secret window, and was staring speculatively at a red satin bra and thong. It was skimpy. It was flashy. It was in-your-face sexy. It was something *she'd* pick. "Jeanne!"

"Don't you think it's fun?"

"Well, yeah, but have you forgotten? I'm the slut in this friendship. You're the good girl. And we're here to shop for you today, so let's get you back in Ann Taylor's where you belong—"

"You know what? I've never tried on anything like that in my entire life," Jeanne said.

"Well, of course you haven't. You have class and taste," Tamara explained patiently. "See, there are two kinds of women in this world. Your kind and my kind. Didn't I explain this to you in ninth grade?"

"I think I should try on that bra," Jeanne repeated. "And also that top over there—" She motioned.

Tamara noted the top in question. It was a black T-shirt with slits—zig-zaggy slits—that allowed bare skin to show through. In places Jeanne would never let skin show through. Not in public. Not in this life. "All right, you're starting to scare me. I thought you needed shopping. Now I think I should have taken you straight to the emergency room."

Jeanne looked at her firmly. "You loved that blouse in Ann Taylor's. Go try it on."

"It's not me, don't be silly."

"You loved it."

"It's not me," Tamara repeated.

"Today," Jeanne said, "I think we should try thinking outside the envelope. Let's both buy something we'd never normally buy. Starting with you." Relentless as a steamroller, she grabbed Tamara's arm and steered her toward Ann Taylor's.

"Jeanne, I can't afford anything in there—"

"You don't have to. I'm going to buy it for you, an early birthday present."

"It won't look right on me."

"Then you won't buy it. But . . . it might."

"I don't have anything to go with a blouse that . . . tailored."

"Then we'll buy pants or a skirt."

"I don't wear skirts. At least nice-girl skirts." Cripes. When Jeanne got a rare bug up her butt, she was harder to stop than a runaway bulldozer. That quickly, she'd taken off through the store, gathering shirts and pants and skirts at wind-generator speed, and now was pushing Tamara into a dressing room with the whole stack. When Tamara turned around, Jeanne settled on the upholstered bench outside like a sentinel—or a rabid watch goose. "And I don't think you were very nice to Arnold," she said.

"What wasn't nice?"

"Your kissing him. You know perfectly well he had a terrible crush on you back in high school."

"But that was fifteen years ago. And that's exactly why I kissed him—because I could see he was nervous around me. And I thought if I told him about the drugs, if I kissed him, then he'd know for sure that I wasn't the kind of women to put on a pedestal. And it was just a little smack. There's no way two adults could possibly think that meant anything!"

"But it obviously did mean something, at least to you, because it's still bothering you after almost two weeks, right? And you hurt him once, Tam."

Well, hell, if Jeanne was gonna poke at old, painful sticky stuff like the truth, then two could play that game. "Nate Donneli hurt you once, too. But that hasn't stopped you from stumbling around with stars in your eyes even since you ran into him again."

"He kissed me."

Tamara was positive she'd misheard the soft-spoken words, but just to make sure, she yanked open the dressing-room door to look in her friend's eyes. Never mind if she was mostly naked. It was just a body. So some strangers saw. Who cared? She bent down to make sure she got a full view of Jeanne's face. "Did you say Nate kissed you? Really? So how was it?"

Jeanne hadn't moved; she was still sitting on the upholstered bench outside the dressing room. But for just that moment, her eyes looked almost as big as her heart—and for darn sure, almost as haunted. "You remember after Nate dropped me? How Quent just seemed to . . . find me when I was at my lowest point in college? He took one look and said he knew I'd be the perfect wife for him. He was so sure. And after Nate, he was someone who seemed to . . . value me."

"I remember him," Tamara said warily. Those were the years when her life had started getting hazy; the music was still coming, but the drugs had started taking their toll. Still, she'd seen Jeanne regularly until the couple had moved to Philadelphia. She'd seemed happy enough with Quent. Not as animated or full of hell as when she'd been with Nate, but much more contented than in that dark period after the breakup.

Slowly she pulled on the silky blouse, but her eyes never left Jeanne. There was honesty and then there was Honesty. It wasn't easy for either of them to get down to this level, but it'd always been harder for Jeanne.

"The whole time we were together in college . . . I felt safe with Quent. I always knew what he wanted to do, what he wanted me to say. And afterward, I knew how to be a corporate wife, how to entertain and play the political games, what to wear, what groups to join, how to look. I even knew how to give a great blow job. I know, I know, that sounds terrible . . . but I mean, it was part of feeling safe, that I knew exactly what and how he wanted me to do anything."

Tamara frowned worriedly. Blow job was a term she used, but hearing Jeanne say it aloud was on a par with a nun stripping in public. Cripes, she made the sexual act sound like a job, nothing personal about it. Maybe Tamara had never known her friend's ex-husband very well, but now she realized he was an ass and she'd have hated him. "I'm glad you divorced him."

"Yeah, well, maybe he should have divorced me. It's not that I didn't care. I did. But I closed off. I didn't see it that way at the time. But now I realize that I closed all the doors where he could have gotten in to hurt me." Jeanne suddenly shook off the serious mood, tried to say lightly, "Either you're buying that blouse or I am, because it looks fabulous on you."

"Shut up, Jeanne." Tamara hunkered down and said fiercely. "You're one of the warmest, most loving people I know. If some son of a jerk made you think you were frigid, then he was a complete dodo bird."

That won her a pastel smile. "I swear, you'd stand up for me no matter what I did. But I'm trying to be honest, Tam. I wasn't frigid. Sex wasn't terrible. It was just . . . I thought of pleasing him as part of the job. Not as something that needed to come from my heart."

Tamara had an easy response to that impossible news. "If Quent didn't manage to stir you up—and you have the easiest, softest heart this side of Poughkeepsie—then he was less than a dodo bird. I'd put him in the witless ignorant idiot class."

"Would you quit being loyal and listen?"

"I'm not loyal. I'm just smarter about men than you are. But yeah, I'm listening."

Jeanne took a breath. "The point I'm trying to make is that I realize I've been sabotaging myself. All this time, I blamed Nate for hurting me. It always felt good to blame him. I *liked* blaming him. It was comfortable. It kept me safe. But I forgot what it was like to feel totally *Un*safe . . . until Nate kissed me the other day. I swear I was a pinch away from having an orgasm right then, outside, standing up, wearing my coat, all our clothes on. Just like that. Just from that kiss."

"Well, that's good," Tamara said firmly.

"How is it good? I had more control over myself when I was a teenager." She said darkly, "Maybe I should buy a vibrator."

"Vibrators are overrated. And you know the answer to this. You never got over being in love with him. So do the obvious. Skip the vibrator, sleep with Nate."

"That's what I've been thinking. Maybe. Try

again. Risk again. But at this point, I've got more experience sinking into wrong relationships than in developing good ones. Then I start thinking I'm completely crazy. Don't you think it's bananas to skydive with a guy who threw me over before?"

"But you told me he had reasons. You told me about his dad dying—"

"I know. He had a terrible time." Jeanne pushed at her hair. "But he also should have known—and felt—that he could turn to me, if he'd really loved me."

"You were a kid. He was a kid. Then is then, and now is now. Don't you think it's time you took a risk?"

Jeanne rolled her eyes. "Yeah, I do. But that's so easy to say, and so hard to really do. I mean, are you so ready to take a risk with Arnold?"

"Arnold! Arnold has nothing to do with this. I'm an addict, for Pete's sake."

"A recovering addict. An addict who hasn't used in more than two years now. Almost three."

"It wouldn't matter if I hadn't used in a decade. He's got a *kid*. Nobody's gonna consider a drug user to be a mother for their kid. That's just reality. Besides. As nerdy as he is, Arnold's not just an inkhorn. He's a nice guy. And we both know I don't sleep with nice guys."

"Exactly. We've both been sleeping with the wrong guys for fifteen years. Don't you think it's time we changed that around?" Jeanne pushed to her feet and pointed her finger. "You're buying that blouse."

"I can't."

"And after we find you some pants or a skirt to go with it, I'm going to try on that stuff at VS. You know why?"

"Because you've become psychotic?"

"No. Because we were happier when we were seventeen, for Pete's sake. We had more guts. We *believed* in ourselves. Tamara . . ." Jeanne stood up. "We need to take back our lives."

"Couldn't you do it and send me a postcard about how it went?"

"No. We're both doing it. We're both going to chart a different course. We're going to be happier. We're going to go after what we actually need and want in our lives."

Tamara had never seen Jeanne like this. Determined. Strong. Assertive. Not particularly polite. Even bossy.

On the other hand, as she'd discovered in her own life the hard way, if you were going to make a damn fool of yourself, it was no fun to do it alone.

"All right, all right. If you're looking for someone to kick ass with, Jeanne Claire, I guess I'm volunteering to be your wing woman." Having stated that, Tam got back to more immediate crises. "You did bring a credit card, didn't you?"

* * *

Arnold knew he wasn't the most flexible guy in town, but he really did much, much better on days when life didn't throw him curve balls. He knew he was well prepared for the second reunion meeting. And he'd pep-talked himself into believing he could cope with a few rolling readjustments. Yet he'd just hung his jacket on the back of the library chair when Tamara breezed in. Instantly, his pulse kicked in with the buck of a colt, and he had to work to make his voice sound natural and hearty.

"I'm so glad you got here early. I was hoping Jeanne Claire might get here a little early, too, because I came up with an unexpected glitch, and can only spare an hour for our reunion meeting tonight."

"That's okay. We'll cope. Jeanne called me an hour ago to say she'd be late, that we should just get started. I'll fill her in on whatever she misses." Tamara plunked down a Starbucks, then peeled off her spring jacket. "The only critical thing tonight is agreeing on a theme for the reunion, right?"

"Right."

She smiled at him. He smiled back, but inside, his heart was going thunk-thunk-thunk. Memories of that torrid kiss slammed in his mind with the power of poison ivy—and not for the first time. For the last two weeks, he'd been replaying that kiss several times a day, but seeing her in person accelerated the oomph of those memories tenfold.

Unfortunately, that meant he was hammer-hard in ten seconds flat. He sat down, opened a folder, smiled at her again, and wondered if it was possible for a man to swallow his tongue. And then he got a good look at her. "Have you been okay?"

"Just fine."

"You're sure? You haven't been sick or anything?" He didn't want to pull one of his classic inconsiderate moves, but something was definitely odd about her tonight, even if he couldn't pin down what it was.

Her smile faded abruptly. "Why, do I look sick?"

"No, no, you look wonderful. Like always. I just had the impression . . ." Pearls of sweat prickled the back of his neck. The more he catalogued her appearance, the more he was certain that something was seriously wrong. Nothing about her looked quite . . . normal. Her hair was pulled back, fenced in with some clips, tidy. What was that about, for Pete's sake? And she was wearing a white blouse with blue stripes, navy pants. The pants and shirt fit her skinny frame okay, but they looked like borrowed clothes. And then there was her face . . . something was way, way strange about her face—then it came to him. No makeup.

There was nothing on her face but clean soft freckles and a little lip gloss. "You *don't* feel well," he said more worriedly.

"Arnold, damnit, I'm trying out a new look, some new styles."

"Oh. I see." He yanked at his tie, then remembered he wasn't wearing one.

"Every time you've ever seen me, I've worn prints and bright colors. I thought I'd try more conservative styles for a change. I like them. I *am* capable of being conservative, you know. Did you think I always wore cheap, flamboyant stuff?"

"No. God, no." Hell, how had he managed to hurt her feelings so fast? "I never thought you looked cheap." He tried to regroup. "And I think that's a really beautiful blouse. I like your flamboyant stuff, but I like this, too. It looks very businesslike. Very, um, very tasteful. Very, um . . ."

"Very unlike me?"

That's it. As soon as this meeting was over, he was going to buy a gun and shoot himself. Well, actually, he had to wait until Howie grew up, but the very minute that happened and his son didn't need him anymore . . . "Tamara, I really think it's a nice blouse. Look, I'm not very good with things like clothes. You're the one who always had the style and class and all. I didn't mean—"

She plopped down in the library chair, made an Italian gesture to indicate that enough was enough of this conversation, then swiftly spread her stuff out. "Let's just get on with it, okay?" she asked wearily. "We need to settle on a theme—"

"Jeanne *will* be here, won't she?"

"Yeah, she said she wou—wait a minute? Did you know there was a kid in here?" Tamara suddenly spotted movement by the far book stacks.

Arnold didn't have to look behind him to know. "Yeah, that's Howie. My son. I have a live-in housekeeper during the week, Mrs. Hernandez, but she needed a night off to help her sister, so I brought Howie with me. He loves libraries. But he's only eight, so I don't want to keep him out too late. That's why I said I wanted to cut this meeting to an hour. He has school tomorrow."

"No problem at all."

Sticky beads of sweat had started to accumulate behind his knees now. "So. Do you have any ideas for the reunion theme?"

"I didn't. But Jeanne Claire did. She thinks the theme should revolve around dreams."

"Dreams?"

"Yeah." Tamara gestured. "We all had dreams in high school. We all had hopes and ideas about who we were going to be, what we were going to do. But now it's fifteen years later, and reality has come home to roost. Some of us got our dreams. Some of us realized our original dreams were goofy and impossible. And some of us . . ."

Her voice trailed off. Because her attention kept

jumping to the far bookshelves, Arnold figured Howie must be doing something to draw her attention—which meant it was time to introduce the two.

Usually, his offspring was miserably shy around new grown-ups, but this time all Arnold had to do was call his son's name.

Howie immediately bounded closer with an exuberant "Hi!" But then he hesitated. Arnold wanted to sigh when he saw his son's expression. Apparently the problem was inherited, because Howie had clearly stolen one look at Tamara and fallen in love. Moony eyes looked at Tam through thick lenses. His forty-seven cowlicks had been slicked down before coming, but they were dry now and springing free again. A green T-shirt hung haphazardly over pants that drooped over his shoes.

"Hi," Tamara said back, this time with a genuine smile for him.

After that momentous meeting, Arnold figured enough was enough. "Howie, we really have to work for a few minutes. I told you—"

"Oh, that's okay, Arnold." Tamara offered his son another smile. A wowza dazzling grin. "Bored back there?" she asked him sympathetically.

"A little." He edged forward. "I like libraries and all. And I like physics, but these physics books . . ." He screwed up his face, illustrating what he thought of the high school library's offerings. "You're going to a party with my dad, huh?"

"We're trying to plan one," she agreed. "You like parties?"

"Nope. You have to talk to people. And you can't read or go on the computer or anything fun. And you have to be nice." He edged closer yet.

"You're so right. I hadn't thought about all that. And this party your dad and I are stuck planning . . . it may be even more boring than that."

"It sounds awful."

"Yeah. That's what we're afraid of. That's why we're trying to plan some fun into it."

"Okay." Typical of his son, that was about all the adult conversation he could handle in one dose, and he ducked behind some bookshelves again.

"So this dream concept," Arnold prodded Tamara. "I don't quite understand how Jeanne wanted to apply it to a reunion theme."

"I didn't, either, but Jeanne said, just think. Graduating from high school was a landmark, but fifteen years later, we're all at another pivot point in our lives. We know more about the world, more about ourselves. Some of us lost the dreams we once had, some of us found our dreams. But right now, we've got a shot at *new dreams*, you know? So that would make a good theme for the reunion— because we can look back at what we all thought our lives would be . . . and now we can look ahead to what we really want and we're really capable of doing."

"I get you. Like—"

As if she could see he didn't understand, she went into more detail. "Like me. I wanted to be a musician. That was my big dream. And I was one of the people in the class who totally got the dream I asked for . . . only it was the wrong dream for me, and my life went completely in the tank. But now . . . now I may have been through fire, but I'd like to believe I won't make the same mistakes again. That's why a theme like New Dreams could work for everyone. Because we've all been through *something* and are facing different life choices now. You have to know what I mean—"

"Yeah, I do." He was finally getting it. "In high school, I can't say I ever had a dream. I thought I was always going to be the nerd of the universe. It never occurred to me that I could own my own business, be successful. I have totally different dreams now than I did then—"

"Arnold, you can't be serious. You had to know how brilliant you were."

"But I was a complete misfit."

Her eyes widened. "No, you weren't. You weren't with the jocks or the social crowd, but that didn't mean people didn't like you. All kinds of people looked up to you all the time."

Discovering that she could be stupid about some things made her far less intimidating. Besides which, he couldn't see wasting time arguing with her. "Anyway, the point is that I see what Jeanne means about making 'New Dreams' a theme for the reunion. No matter what anyone thought in high school, probably no one got what they expected. So a reunion's a good excuse to relook at hopes and goals. Or even lost dreams and disappointments. To relook at who we are, anyway."

"Yeah . . ."

They kept talking about the themes and dream thing, but he watched her flash a wave, then a wink, then a funny face to Howie. Howie wasn't afraid of grown-ups or strangers, but he was generally too shy and too serious to engage in mindless play . . . much less to flirt, eight-year-old fashion, with a woman he didn't know from Adam. When the squirt finally peeled off to the bathroom for a few minutes, Arnold had to shake his head. "Man, are you ever good with kids."

"What? Oh, no. Not me. In fact, I've never had any chance to be around kids. If you don't mind my asking, though . . . where's his mom in this picture?"

"I'm afraid she's not. I thought I told you. She died of cancer a few years ago."

Tamara's eyes filled faster than a well. "Sheesh,

I'm sorry. I guess I just assumed there was a divorce, because everybody divorces these days. I didn't mean to callously ask you something that was painful or none of my business—"

"It wasn't callous. It was a natural question." And it was always easier for him to have it out in the open.

"I'm sure she was wonderful."

"She was," he said honestly. "One of the best people I've ever known. And a great mom to Howie." That was part of his problem lately, he'd believed. He'd had his wife for only a short time. But she'd opened his world, his life . . . and when she was gone, he'd seemed to shrivel back to all his old insecure ways. No matter how much money he made, he couldn't seem to buy himself confidence for any price in the last few years.

Abruptly, though, he realized that he'd faded out of the conversation . . . and that for some reason, Tamara was looking stricken. "I'm glad for your Howie, that he had such a great mom." She added awkwardly, "I can probably appreciate that even more, because I've never seemed to have a maternal instinct myself. So I've always been in awe of the women who do the mom thing really well."

It just didn't seem to be his night. Somehow he seemed to invoke the most confounding responses in her. Like her implying that she wasn't maternal when she so obviously and totally was. She'd won over Howie the way strangers never did. And she hadn't looked at Howie as if he were a nerdy kid, either. She smiled at him as if she meant it—as if she thought he was adorable and full of personality and life.

In fact, she smiled at his son the way Arnold only wished she'd smile at him. And with his son gone from the room, suddenly she stood up and started shuffling papers together. "We might as well fold up, don't you think? I mean, we've got the reunion ball rolling. And we settled on the New Dreams theme—"

"We sure have."

"Then we can call this meeting short, right? I don't know what made Jeanne this late, but I'll catch up with her and fill her in." Tamara whisked him a blinding smile, then yanked on her jacket at top-gun speed.

So he bellowed for Howie, then yanked on his jacket faster than a bullet, too.

"Planning this reunion thing isn't that tough. We're doing great, don't you think?" she asked cheerfully.

"We sure are," he said heartily.

"I mean, there's a lot of work to do, but agreeing on all the key issues has been easy. And we're sharing it all."

"We sure are," he said heartily.

His heart crashed like a lead zombie when she zoomed out the door. Within a few minutes, he'd scooped up his files and jacket and Howie and hiked outside. Howie peppered after him, asking a dozen questions about the school, life, God, and frogs. Dusk had fallen, a purple sheen softening the crisp night. Someone had mowed grass. Between the smell of buds and daffodils and lilacs and fresh-mown grass, a guy could come close to throwing up on spring fever.

"Hey, Dad." Howie had barely climbed into their SUV before he was buckling himself in. Howie was the kind of kid who never forgot to buckle his seat belt. "She was okay. I'll come to more meetings if you want. I liked her."

So did Arnold, but that didn't stop him from feeling sickly-sad.

Tam had obviously forgotten that kiss—or else it hadn't meant anything to her—or else she took kisses that wild and red-hot for granted.

He didn't blame her. He seemed to be just as sick in love with her as he used to be. Just as in high school, he stumbled over his own tongue, said everything wrong.

In the last fifteen years, he'd gone from pauper to prince financially, had a good life, and for damn sure had the best son in the universe. But the one and only dream he'd really wanted was a woman to love . . . a woman who took his whole heart, a woman he could give his whole heart to. For him, that woman had always been Tamara.

But it seemed she was just as unattainable and unreachable for him as she'd always been.

Chapter 9

Jeanne had every intention of making the reunion meeting, but work problems started intruding from early afternoon and never let up. First, she found out that her dad had signed on another two events without asking her—committing to both of them below cost. It wasn't the first time he'd made a crazy financial move—she knew he didn't get numbers—but she couldn't seem to get through his darling head that Oz was headed for a crisis.

"But these are friends, honey," her dad cajoled her. "And I promised. And these are the kinds of events that bring in great publicity, so it'll all work out in the long run."

To her father, everything would work out "in

the long run." "Dad, this is like the card game of war. When you run out of cards, you lose. It's over. Good publicity won't bail us out of anything. We've run out of places we can borrow money. So we're on the line—either we start bringing in big amounts in the profit column, or we're not going to be in business by next year."

"You worry too much, princess," her dad said affectionately, and then snapped his fingers as if a brilliant idea had suddenly occurred to him. "I know just what you need. Some relaxing time. Go out with Donald. Get dressed up, have a nice dinner, forget all about Oz Enterprises for the night. Life's too short to be thinking about work all the time."

By the time she strode back to her office, she was nursing a headache. It's not as if any of these problems were new. Oz had been flirting with Chapter Eleven when she climbed on board. Right from the start—whether she'd ever wanted the job or not—she'd knuckled down, brought in events, brought in publicity, brought in business to turn the red ink around. And she had. But nothing she could do was enough to bail out her dad if he was determined to make impulsive, financially unstable moves. It wasn't her fault.

Right?

Right.

Only somehow she always felt as if it were her

responsibility. There simply was no one else to save her dad if she couldn't. How could she just desert him? He was her *dad*, for Pete's sake.

Her headache had turned into a serious hammer-snapper by late afternoon, and then her stomach started whining about too much coffee and too much worry. She stood up, stretched. It was almost five; she had just enough time to grab a sandwich from the restaurant kitchen before going to the reunion meeting—or that was the plan, until a couple suddenly showed up in the office doorway.

"Hi there. You're Jeanne Cassiday, right?"

"You bet. What can I do for you?" She smiled when they introduced themselves. They were quite a pair. On a nippy April afternoon when everyone else was wearing jackets and pants, these two wore tank tops and shorts. Their Nikes matched. They both had short, curly blond hair that had apparently been styled by the same hairdresser. They were color coordinated. They were holding hands and unable to stop looking at each other adoringly.

". . . so we'd like to have our wedding here."

She nodded. "We do weddings all the time, although I have to say, we're completely booked for June and most of July. But if we can agree on a date, I'll—"

"We can be flexible on the date. Timing isn't the problem," Bobby interrupted delicately. "The problem is that we don't want a regular wedding. That is, we want the vows to be regular. And the wedding march and all that. And the champagne and cake and everything. But . . ."

She looked at her Robert. "But," Robert picked up her sentence, "We want to be married in the pool."

"We've had pool-side weddings before," Jeanne assured them. "We can do all kinds of—"

"No, not pool *side*," Bobby said. "*In* the pool. We're both divers. And we'd like to say our vows on the diving board, then dive in and put on our rings underwater."

"She had a dream about it last night," Robert clarified.

"I was thinking we could both wear white bathing suits. And have floats in the water with white candles."

"And we could have bridesmaids form a circle in the water for us to dive into together."

"And we could have those underwater lights. You know, a night wedding. Romantic. But the thing is, we'd want to rent your whole pool area and showers and all that—"

"Okay . . . okay." Jeanne started scribbling notes at the speed of sound. This was exactly how she'd tried to turn this place around—by taking on projects and events too unconventional for other conference centers to touch. But this one, like all the others, raised a unique set of problems. Insurance would raise hell if they had food and alcohol around swimmers. And there were other liability issues if nonswimmers were part of the wedding party. And how were they going to exclude the regular guests from using the pool?

"All right, now, how large a wedding are you talking about? What kind of number...?" Jeanne's cell phone beeped.

It was Tamara, reminding her of the reunion meeting. One glance at her watch and all Jeanne could say was that she was stuck being late for sure. She went on talking to the couple for another fifteen minutes—long past office hours by then— when her cell phone interrupted the lovebirds' brainstorming yet again.

"Jeanne Claire," she said crisply.

"It's just me. And you sound busy—"

"No problem," she said. But there was a terrible problem. He wasn't even in the room, yet just hearing Nate's tenor made her body melt thirty degrees. She forgot the couple in her office. Her mood was suddenly parasailing over a waterfall in the Amazon—or that equivalent of a lunatic high.

She'd determined that she was willing to take a risk with him—but dagnabbit, she was supposed to keep her head.

"I've been doing some more research on my thief," Nate said. "And I pinned down some more evidence of discrepancies and missing money. I just can't seem to tie all the clues together. I wondered if there was any chance you could pop over to the shop—unfortunately, all the numbers I've got are on the system here. I hate to ask you to go out of your way, but I can promise it shouldn't take more than a half hour—"

"Yes," she said.

"Hey. You don't have to say yes that fast. I wasn't through groveling. I was going to offer you dinner, diamonds, a foot rub, chocolate—"

She told herself she wasn't charmed, but damn it, she was. "That'll do for a down payment, Donneli. But give your imagination some exercise, for heaven's sake. You just keep thinking up more payment ideas and I'll see you shortly."

She heard him laugh before hanging up. The sound spun in her mind, an almost forgotten echo of how easily they'd once made each other laugh—but then she glanced at her watch and put a hustle on. It didn't take five minutes for her to get rid of the couple, chase upstairs to her apartment, peel off her clothes, and climb into the shower. Minutes after that, she realized she was humming over the sound of the hair dryer. Mere minutes after that, she watched herself don the red satin bra and matching thong she'd bought on that crazy shopping expedition with Tam.

She stopped momentarily to reassure herself that she hadn't become a complete immature lunatic. She hadn't forgotten how badly he'd hurt her. She didn't believe for a second that she and Nate were a couple again—or even that they should be. The sound of his laugh hadn't gone to her head.

She was just stronger than she used to be. Strong enough to admit that she was fascinated by the challenge of seeing him again. Of wanting to know what might happen with all that chemistry. Of being tantalized by the idea of a second chance.

Having recovered her common sense, she slowly pulled on a concealing black sweater and demure black pants—nothing seductive, nothing enticing. Slowly she scooped up her car keys—and then a Rice Krispies bar, because she really didn't know when she was going to find time for dinner. Slowly she took the elevator down, checked out at the front desk, walked out the door at a poised, sedate pace.

And then galloped for her car.

Twenty minutes later, she bounced into the parking lot of Donneli Motors. A night watchman motioned her past the gates and the closed sign, as if he'd been waiting for her. Her car had always seemed nice enough, but it looked like a derelict next to the old, ruby Ferrari and ivory Austin-Healey Sprite she parked next to.

The night watchman insisted on walking her to the building, which gave her no chance to reapply lipstick, or for that matter, to adjust her underwear. It wasn't a good time to discover that the red satin bra tugged and itched.

Inside the lobby, the watchman told her that Mr. Donneli was waiting for her and motioned for her to go straight back. She remembered the look of the front lobby, but not all the guy smells. Leather and oil and waxes mixed with a whiff of lemon hand soap. The smells were all pleasant—but nothing as comfortingly familiar as scents she used on her own turf.

She'd taken only a few steps when Nate came barreling out of his office. "I was listening for you," he said warmly. But as fast as he met up with her, both seemed trapped in a sudden, short silence. That wild embrace was suddenly between them, making them feel like robbers trying to look innocent . . . trying to *be* innocent. She couldn't seem to stand still or find anything intelligent to say.

"What's wrong?" he asked.

She took a breath. "Nothing. Just an itch." It was the bra straps, she told herself. God, what had convinced her to buy such an insane piece of lingerie?

Nate took the bull by the horns, quieting her nerves by simply talking. "I'm not sure what I found, so I'm really grateful you could come and were willing to take a look."

"No problem."

"I've gone back three full years now. I've been

through all the receipts. Everything's recorded on this computer spreadsheet. Then all the bank deposits are in this file, see? All the receipts match up, but the bank deposits don't equal the receipts. And this file here, this is where I first pinned down that there was a discrepancy, cash missing for sure . . ."

She listened, then took his desk chair and started studying. He brought her a mug of coffee and a bowl of Hershey Kisses, then pulled up a chair next to her. He'd done all the tough work— weeks of it, from the look of the meticulously arranged information. And he'd obviously grappled with the records over and over and over.

She wasn't sure if he really trusted her to evaluate any of the records. She'd barely copped a C in high school math classes. She was never supposed to be smart, and the truth was, she hadn't wasted much time studying in school. It was only because her father was a magician at muddling numbers that she'd gotten serious about learning accounting. And for the same reason, she could recognize a well-run, honest business when she saw one.

Nate had built that darn hole-in-the-wall garage into one heck of an enterprise. But that made his problem all the more distressing.

Finally, she lifted her head and just looked at him. Aching. "You have a thief, Nate."

"I know. I told you."

"But you were hoping that somehow it could just all be a mistake?" she said softly.

"I want it to be a mistake."

She shook her head. So fiercely, she wanted to kiss him again—to console him for having to deal with a painful problem, she told herself. But that wasn't it. It was just . . . him. The whisker shadows on his chin. His ruffled, rumpled hair and sexy eyes. His shirtsleeves cuffed up. Everything about him ignited her senses, her mind, her heart, and the errant thought dawdled through her mind . . . What would happen if she jumped him right there? Just . . . pounced.

Would all life end as she knew it? Would she suffer guilt for being a wicked tramp forever? Would he say no?

Would he say yes?

Or maybe, would he kiss her back as furiously, as tenderly, as completely, as she wanted to kiss him?

She set down the coffee mug he'd given her and behaved herself. "How many people make deposits for your business?"

"Family. Which means me and my brothers. And Martha. No one else."

"And can all of you get into the computer records? Do each of you have a special password or sign to identify which one of you is inputting figures?"

He shook his head. "No. There is a lock-out

code, so no stranger can just come in off the street and get into the system. But we're family . . . I thought we trusted each other. And we're all so busy, so if someone's headed out the door, they're usually given the bank chore. Jason has primary responsibility for the records, so he spends the most time here, of course. But he's also the one who first noticed the money missing and brought the problem to me."

"He couldn't explain it?"

"No. In fact, he said that it might be something he did. He was worried about it. Said that was the whole problem was his doing the books before he got to be a CPA, and that maybe he'd never make his CPA. Maybe there was something he didn't do right."

"This isn't like that," she said gently. "This has been a deliberate, systematic removal of small cash amounts. There's no way it was accidental."

"Yeah. Damn it." He scraped a hand through his hair, leaned back in the creaky office chair. "I just don't know what to do from here."

"You want to talk about your choices?"

"Yes. But not quite yet. Tonight, I just really wanted confirmation—I needed to hear from someone else that I was interpreting the figures correctly. Someone I trusted—and someone definitely not part of my family. But the next step, I think, is for me to determine what I have to do next."

"Okay." She hesitated, but he sounded as if he actually wanted to change the subject. So she asked quietly, "Tell me about Caitlin's mother, Nate."

He met her eyes. "From one tough subject to another, huh?" he asked wryly, but he didn't duck answering. "She's not in the picture. Not part of Caitlin's life. Or mine. In any way."

"And that's all you want to say? All you want me to know?"

He pushed out of the chair, slugged his hands in his pockets, and restlessly paced over to the window. "It's not easy to tell you something I'm ashamed of," he said roughly. "When my dad died, I came home, realized almost immediately that the family was sinking financially, and dropped out of college. I already told you that part. What I didn't tell you was that I went through a rough personal stretch. I just couldn't seem to accept that everything I'd wanted to do with my life had been erased. I wasn't going to be getting a degree, wasn't going to be an architect. I was stuck with grease under my fingernails—the one kind of work I never, never wanted to do. And I was angry." His gaze seared her. "Maybe more than anything, I was angry about losing you."

She listened.

"I did the family responsibility thing seven days a week. But on Friday nights, I went to the local bar, a neighborhood hangout. I was looking to get drunk and feel sorry for myself. And I did. Friday after Friday. One of those Fridays—early on—early after I broke it off with you, I picked up a woman."

Okay. She'd been waiting for it. The hurt. She'd known it was coming; she just hadn't known how bad it was going to be.

"I'm not proud of what I did. She didn't care about me. I didn't care about her. I was trying to force myself to believe that this was my life now; I was going to be blue-collar, just like my dad, and somehow she seemed part of making myself accept that. Anyway, one shot out of the barn, and she found me six weeks later, claiming I'd gotten her pregnant."

"And you believed her?"

"Hell, no. The thrill in her week was picking up a new guy on Friday nights. But once I had proof the baby was mine . . . that sobered me up damn fast. From her viewpoint, she didn't want to be a mother. If I'd give her money for a kid, she'd raise it. Otherwise she wanted money to have an abortion. And from my viewpoint, I didn't want her raising a child of mine, so there was only one answer."

"For you to take the baby," Jeanne said quietly.

"Yeah. It's what she wanted; it's what I wanted. I gave her money for health care during the pregnancy. In return, she agreed not to drink, to take care of herself. Right from the hospital, I took Caitlin home. If she changed her mind, she never contacted me again. And once I had Caitlin . . . hell. Once I held that squirt in my arms, she was mine. Nothing else mattered. There was no chance of my giving her up."

She found herself swallowing. And then swallowing again. "I want to say it's okay, it's okay, I understand. And I do understand how much you love your daughter, Shadow. But not about the woman. I'll never like it."

"I'm not asking you to."

"It stinks. How you used her. How you'd pick someone who'd use you. How you went so fast to someone else."

He lifted his head, faced her square. "That's exactly what I did. When I look back now, I realize . . . I was using her to make me forget you. To wipe you out of my mind, so I'd quit pining about you. Sleeping with her was a way of crossing a line where I couldn't go back, had to stop pretending that I could ever get that life back again."

Damn man. She wanted to slug him, chew on him some more, vent more to let some of those old, old hurts loose. But he made it impossibly tough, both by being honest and by being so hard on himself.

"Jeanne, I'm not excusing myself. What I did was dead wrong. To her. Wrong for me, too. But I don't want you afraid I won't tell you the complete truth. I didn't in the past because I felt I couldn't. But anything you ask me, I'll try to give the whole truth now."

She would have answered him, except that his telephone suddenly rang. The sound made her jump. Until that moment, she felt as if she and Nate were alone in the universe. It wasn't easy, talking this way, sharing this way, but his honesty seemed to reach right into her heart and squeeze.

Initially she thought he was going to ignore the call. He looked as if he wanted to keep on talking . . . but the phone jangled again, and then his fax started spewing out paper. Obviously life was determined to intrude on them. He grabbed the receiver. Almost immediately he started talking in Spanish or Italian. She could tell the subject was cars, but not much else.

It seemed the most polite thing to just get out of his way. She motioned that she was going to walk outside his office for a bit. He nodded, mouthed that he'd be off in five minutes, no longer.

Right then, she was just as glad to have a few minutes alone. He'd basically told her before about Caitlin's mother, but not in this much detail.

It bit—that he'd gone so fast from her arms to a stranger's. It bit more to think of Nate unhappy enough to reach out to a woman he cared nothing about. Yet he hadn't made excuses or prettied up his behavior. The uncomfortable level of honesty he'd offered struck Jeanne as a kind of quiet showdown. He had no reason to open those uncomfortable doors unless he thought the two of them might have a future.

And that was a two-way street, Jeanne sensed. What she did and said to him now could make or break whether they had another chance together.

Hugging her arms under her chest, she wandered around, not consciously exploring but too unsettled to sit still. She poked her head in the bathroom off the lobby—clearly Martha kept that one up, because it was spotless, decorated with a nice mirror, a rug. She glanced at his brother Jason's office again. After that came a coffee room.

The garage bays shouldn't have drawn her. She didn't know zip about the cars . . . but then this wasn't like any garage she'd ever seen either. The floor was clean enough to stage a picnic. Although only dim security lights lit the long room, she could still see enough. Paint gleamed; leather smelled fresh-rubbed; chrome shone mirror-bright.

She bent down, saw the label on one car. A 1930 Rolls-Royce Maharajas Victoria. She had no clue if the name had some special meaning, but the car was a gorgeous creamy yellow and green.

After that came another old Rolls. This one had wooden running boards and was made of polished aluminum. A sheet on the hood claimed the car had forty-three horsepower. Who knew cars ever had that kind of horsepower?

The next bay had some godawful thing— maybe it was originally a car, but it didn't look like much more than beat-up tin. But the bay after that had a glossy convertible, adorable beyond belief. A Pierce Arrow Roadster, L929, it said on the fender.

Then came something called a Stanhope . . . it looked more like a carriage than a car, with brass lanterns that gleamed in the light, gas contained in a copper tank, and a brass horn that looked like something that belonged in John Philip Sousa's time.

She was only trying to understand Nate's world, Jeanne told herself, yet instead found herself falling in love. These weren't just cars. Each was a treasure. Someone's dream. A mama couldn't take care of her first newborn better than these cars were pampered and protected.

And loved.

They weren't just taken care of. They'd been spoiled down to the last detail. There wasn't a speck of dust to be seen. There wasn't a tool lying loose anywhere. The garage was more like an operating room than a mechanics' workstation.

At the end of the long garage bay area was a connecting set of doors. Curious, she walked over and peered in the small window, saw the tip of a red fender, and froze. Technically the doors led to another service bay area like all the others, except that this one was private, isolated from the areas that customers were normally exposed to.

There was only one car inside. For all her ignorance about cars—old or new—Jeanne knew this one. It was a 1965 Ford Mustang. And her heart was suddenly slamming, slamming.

Impulsively, she turned the knob, found the door unlocked, and silently slipped inside. A wall security light provided enough illumination for her to tiptoe closer, even if most of the car was in shadow.

The Mustang wasn't as expensive as the other cars—not as fancy, not as sexy, not in the same elite class in any way. A collector might not even find the car particularly cool, so on the surface, it seemed even odder that the car was housed in its own private bay.

Jeanne remembered when it was called a pony car—and yes, she recognized it. The horse on the grill was faced the wrong way. She wouldn't have known which way the silly horse was supposed to face, but Nate had told her. The way the horse faced on the Mustang grille had become part of the car's mystique.

There was really no telling if this was the exact same Mustang she'd once known, but the car was red on the outside, red on the inside. It wasn't as souped-up as some of its brother '65s—just a stock six-cylinder engine, none of that V–8 stuff. It had a hard top, unlike the sportier convertible models. These days, deep-foam bucket seats were nothing special; neither was wall-to-wall carpeting or the padded instrument panel.

The first time she'd seen it, it had just been a used car. Nate had driven it to pick her up. It stalled three times on the way to a movie. Actually, as she recalled, the car stalled whenever it darn well felt like it. It had air-conditioning that almost never worked; a radio that played at will; windshield wipers that sounded like battering rams and barely kept off the rain . . . but in her favor, that baby had a heater that could cook you out of your clothes in summer and winter both.

She knew.

She knew the car.

Her fingertip grazed the roof, trailed the shape. She knew this damn car in a different way than she'd ever known any car, before or since.

Behind her, the door opened. She knew it was Nate without looking up.

"This is our car?" She tried to ask it in a normal voice, but there was a drumming in her blood, a thickness in her throat. Her fingertip trailed down the back window to the fender, as if the car were demanding all her attention.

"It's the same one," Nate affirmed.

"After all these years, she still runs?"

"No more predictably than she ever did." It seemed as if the whole world had gone quiet, because she could hear him moving one footfall closer, then another. "This was the only car on my dad's lot that he'd let me borrow for a date— and then only because he couldn't sell the damn thing for love or money. She wasn't classic then. Just old. And unreliable—as I'm sure you remember. My dad could never figure out what was wrong with her—but then he was a lousy mechanic. When I inherited her, I figured I'd make her right."

"And did you?" Still she hadn't looked at him. Still her fingertips tiptoed down the length of the car.

"Hell, no. This car has a mind of her own. She was a spoiled brat from the day she came off the assembly line. Never yet found a mechanic who could fix her, and I've got the best. I should have just junked her years ago."

"But you didn't." That seemed to be why she couldn't catch her breath. Because the car still existed. Because he'd kept it. It didn't even matter why . . . but Nate, of course, came up with a reasonable reason.

He said, "Caitlin's got her eye on it. She thinks the old Mustangs are in a class all their own. She wants it when she turns sixteen. At least, that's

how I've justified holding on to the damn thing."
He was on the other side of the trunk by then. He
leaned on his side; she leaned on hers, and their
eyes met for the first time since he'd walked in.

Her heart stalled. Maybe she was committed to
being careful. Maybe she knew—in her heart, in
her head, in every way—that being thrown away
all those years ago had affected her. It wasn't simple. It wasn't about blaming Nate anymore for the
messes she'd made in her life. It was about starting to understand that nothing was going to work
until she acted strong, was strong, believed herself strong. With him. With herself. Her resolve
was so clear.

Yet suddenly she found herself lifting her head,
meeting his eyes. And suddenly she couldn't
seem to give a royal damn whether she made the
safe, responsible choices or took all the impossible
risks.

It was so quiet that there was nothing in that
room, maybe nothing in the universe in that instant, but her, him, and the memories they had of
that car.

"So that's the only reason you kept her, huh?"
she asked lightly.

She saw the dark gleam in his eyes, but he
didn't answer the question. Just asked her lightly,
"Remember the song 'Tainted Love'?"

She remembered. In fact, she remembered it
blaring out of that hiccupping car radio.

"And do you remember 'Take Me Home To-night'?"

She remembered.

"There's another song we seemed to play all the time that year. I can't remember the title, who sang it, nothing. But it's the song about 'Never gonna give you up . . . never gonna let you down . . . or hurt you.'"

Her throat was suddenly so full she could hardly swallow. "That wasn't a new song when we were dating."

"Not new. But it seemed to play on the radio every time we were in the car. We saw a movie that first date."

"Dirty Dancing," she said softly.

"You were never Jewish and I was never a muscle-bound Patrick Swayze. But secretly, I always thought that movie was about us. *Top Gun* came out the next year. And *Die Hard.* Hell, in our house, *Die Hard*'s practically a tradition on the holidays no different than cranberry sauce and oyster dressing. So there were great movies our junior and senior years. But *Dirty Dancing . . .*"

He'd been leaned over that red car hood, but now he stood, pushed his hands in his jeans pockets, ambled around the fender. Around the back. Around. Toward her.

"They were us. You were that sheltered princess who'd never seen any life, but never doubted what was right. You weren't just beautiful, but good clear to the bone. And I was the no-good loner from the wrong side of the tracks who knew damn well he had no right to touch you."

"You and I weren't about a movie, buster. And the touching we did wasn't just up to you."

"Oh, yeah, it was. You didn't know what hit you. I did. I knew all about the power of hormones, because I'd been torpedoed by them before—and with you, I couldn't even be in this car and think of anything but having you. But you were still innocent as grass, so you were vulnerable."

"Hey. You're saying you weren't vulnerable because you were a guy?"

"No. I was a complete shambles. I'm not denying it—but I still could have stopped us. And I didn't. I wanted in your pants more than I wanted to live. But not because you were a princess, Peanut. And not because you were a sheltered virgin."

"Why then?" Funny, but she couldn't make her voice rise above a whisper. He'd never really said why he used to call her Peanut, but she thought it was because everyone else gave her fancy, elegant nicknames. He saw her differently. He saw the real her, or that's what she believed then, and hearing that nickname still made her pulse sing.

"Because you believed in me—more than I believed in myself. Because I wanted to see myself for the rest of my life—through your eyes. Because fifteen years ago I believed I could have anything, be anything, be anyone . . . as long as you were in my life."

If he didn't quit, her heart was going to sink in a fat, liquid puddle on the floor and never beat again. "Don't waste all that sweet talk on me, Donneli. You wanted to nail me. It wasn't all about love or romance or anything complicated. Not in the beginning."

"Oh, yeah, it was. I wanted to nail you. True. But I also remember—as red-hot as those hormones were running—I also couldn't seem to stop talking to you, either. You ruined me for every other woman. My whole family claims I don't talk at all, don't ever communicate. And I don't. Go figure. Because I could never seem to shut up around you."

"I never shut up around you, either. I always told you things that I never told anyone else."

"Remember skipping school? Senior English. Nowhere to go, middle of the winter, so we hightailed it to the U of M library and hid behind the stacks. Thinking people would believe we were college students, not catch us.

"I remember taking you home from the Christmas dance in this darn car. Snow up to our knees. We skidded and slipped and came to a dead stop under a traffic light. You started crying buckets—"

"Hey! You don't have to remember every little thing."

He said, "But I do remember. Every. Little. Thing." And then he snagged her in his arms and kissed her.

chapter 10

He'd claimed that she'd ruined him for any other woman, but Jeanne knew the truth. He'd ruined her. She'd slept with other guys. Cripes, she'd even married one, but no one ever came close to putting the shivers in her pulse the way Nate did.

It wasn't fair. Having to risk getting her heart broken by a man who'd dumped her once already was even less fair.

On the other hand, who would have thought revenge could be so heady and immensely, consumingly sizzling?

His mouth covered hers in a kiss too short. But then his lips hovered over hers, whisper close, until her pulse charged with impatience and anticipation. When he finally kissed her again, he let out all the stops. His mouth wooed, warmed, then deeply, darkly claimed hers.

She looped her arms around his neck for balance, tasting him, meeting the pressure of his mouth with pressure of her own. She felt the heat pour off his skin, heard his groan when her abdomen molded against his, tasted the delicious, dangerous recklessness that only Nate had ever invoked.

In a single kiss, she zoomed back fifteen years. She was a virgin again. Leaned back against the same wicked red car. Surrounded by dark, velvet night shadows that inspired both of them to share abandoned kisses and impossible dares. When his hand found its way to her breast, she whispered, "No, Nate," when inside, her heart was racing, *Yes, yes*. When she gulped out a "We shouldn't," inside her mind was singing, *Do it, Nate. Love me*.

She suddenly couldn't keep the past and present straight. This was *now*, and right now she was wearing a black pullover and slacks . . . yet her heart remembered his hand sliding down her side, pushing up her skirt, palming her through her tights. A thrill shot through her blood, fast and red-hot. She felt owned, possessed . . . but by her alpha guy, her mate, her chosen love. It was a scary sensation, to give up control, to give up herself—but it felt safe, too. Because this was Nate. Because whatever could have been—would have been—wrong with anyone else, was always, always right with him.

"Jesus. How do you do this to me?" He'd said that then, too. The same words. In the same whiskey-rough groan. "I'm half crazy and I've barely kissed you."

So was she. It was the restaurant all over again, when she'd felt a pinch away from coming and he'd barely done more than kiss her. But they were rubbed against each other now. Heat, delicious, cruel, clutched her belly and tightened. She remembered this part from their past, too. "Don't you dare open the back door to that car," she whispered.

But he did. Maybe he was reading her mind— she just couldn't stand up much longer, not with knees turning weaker than water. She heard the click of the back car door opening, but she couldn't stop kissing him—and he damn sure refused to stop kissing her. They slid into the backseat in an awkward tangle of knees and elbows and feet, making her want to laugh at their urgency, laugh at their crazy speed. The leather was colder than a slap and made crunch sounds when they climbed in. The backseat went down—oh, she remembered exactly how it went down. But there still wasn't enough space. Not when they were kids and not now. Especially not for a man as broad-shouldered as Nate had become.

Still, in that squashed space, on the cold leather, it was dark as a secret, and when she kissed him, he tasted as forbidden as ever. She'd never felt hunger like this. She pushed at his shirt. He pushed at hers. Teeth nipped her neck. Her tongue found the shell of his ear. Then, for a moment, suddenly his hands were framing her face, her hands framing his . . . and the kiss between them was as winsome and desperate and wonderful as the air they needed to breathe.

"I swear, I didn't ask you to come here tonight to start anything like this," he said fiercely.

"You always said that. You always believed it. But darn it, Nate, why did you have to keep this car all these years?"

"You know why."

"Well, it's not fair."

"That night wasn't fair, either. You remember—"

"Of course I remember. You hurt me."

"God. I didn't want to."

"Well, I wanted you to. I went into that backseat thinking that you'd slept with every cheerleader in school, every popular girl, that I was just another score for you. And I didn't care."

"I cared. You were never a score for me, Peanut. I never expected to touch you. Not make-love kind of touching. You were on a pedestal for me. I was positive I was gonna be a hero for you—"

"You were."

"I was gonna be a hero by *not* touching you."

"Well, as it happened, you were a hero because you did. For God's sake, get it off me, would you?"

"What? What the hell is this?"

"It's a fancy bra. But something about the wire doesn't seem to fit right. It's been digging into me every time I move. I—" Why waste all that breath explaining? Just like fifteen years ago, he had the hooks undone and the straps wrestled from her in three and a half seconds flat, maybe faster. A flash of red satin caught in the security light before it landed outside the car window.

"Did you wear that for me?"

"Of course I wore it for you. Even if I didn't think you'd ever see it."

"I didn't see it," he assured her. "I only see you."

Melt. He'd always been able to make her melt. When his mouth laved down her throat to her breasts, he soothed one, then the other, for the tortuous treatment the bra had put them through. His kisses were reverent, soothing. Then sassy and teasing.

But then, so were hers. He'd always been ticklish for a certain kind of kiss, a certain light touch. A trailed touch through his nest of chest hair. Her lips on his navel. Taking his zipper down slow, real slow, one silver tooth at a time.

"You been saving this up for fifteen years?" he asked her. They shuffled, gasping for air and sanity. Gymnasts couldn't have pulled off the contortions required to finesse lovemaking in the backseat, but both of them were laughing, his eyes gleaming with light and fire both. Hers were gleaming with the reflection of him. She couldn't seem to stop feeling breathless, high.

And then they sank lower, deeper into another kiss. This one tipped into a new, deeper realm of madness. "Okay," he said when they came up for air. "Okay." As if this established what they were doing was okay for posterity, when nothing was remotely okay for either one of them or posterity, but he fought again for a shred of sanity. "The thing is, Peanut, if we're only temporarily out of our minds, that's one thing. If we're only necking because we're damn fools trying to reclaim something long gone, that's one thing, too. But damn. If you're remotely willing—?"

"Are you?"

He sucked in another lungful of air. Or tried to. "The thing is, I think there's a good chance that trying to have sex in the backseat at our age could kill us both."

"So that's the question. If it's worth a life-or-death risk."

He said, "No question, it's worth it for me."

He made her laugh—good grief, he was as hot and randy as he'd always been. But the laughter didn't last, not then. She reached for him.

Tender, teasing kisses turned demanding and

urgent. Heat swelled in the car, colored touch and scent and taste. His sweatshirt followed her sweater, tossed to the land of somewhere. Wherever their clothes landed, she didn't know, didn't care. Only what she could touch, see, smell, taste of him mattered. They tugged off shoes, pants. She kissed him places that had never been erotic. He kissed her places she'd only dreamed of. She told herself this was a huge risk, an impossible risk, an insane risk.

But she wasn't trying to sell herself promises about the future. This was so much simpler. It was about the hurt all those years ago—she'd hurt so much, believing that she'd meant so little that he'd easily tossed aside her love. All these years, she'd never gotten that confidence back. All these years, somewhere deep in her heart, she'd just assumed she wasn't worth keeping.

And now, these kisses, this moment, brought it all back. The strong young woman she'd once been. The reckless willingness to risk all, give everything, invest all her emotional savings in what she hoped they were together.

Her elbows jabbed him in a rib. His one arm got trapped under her weight, lost feeling. Socks . . . neither of them had remembered to take off socks. She lost an earring. She lost her heart. They were too darn old to do this in the backseat of a car; she was almost positive it couldn't happen . . .

But it did. Her leg seemed to be over his shoulder, her other tucked somewhere around his waist, and there was an instant when they were both laughing, low and gruff, at what contortions they were going through . . . yet suddenly their playing was all done. She wanted him more than she wanted to breathe; he seemed to want her with the same fury and fire. She'd have done any amount of twisting or contorting to feel that cataclysmic sensation of being filled, by him, and then filled up, by him. He groaned from the inside out.

"Oh, Nate . . ." Her head fell back, eyes closed, just from the lush sensation of feeling him inside her, part of her. For an instant she again remembered another long-ago night, the car, the dark night, the pain of losing her virginity. The pain this time was entirely different. He completed as if he'd been made to satisfy specifically her, only her, emotionally, physically, and in every other way. The pain was only from not having known this or anything like this in fifteen years.

"Don't move," he whispered.

But she had to move. And so did he. He knew her body better than she did, then and now, seemed to know what drove the hunger, drove the need, drove her senses beyond sanity. And back then, she might not have felt up to his level, but something else mattered more. She knew Nate, not just the popular, cool, overachiever Nate Donneli, but the lonely boy . . . the boy who was as afraid of letting go as she was, who couldn't admit to weakness because he was so afraid of failing, afraid of turning out like his father, of being a loser, of letting anyone see his fears. With her, though, those walls crumbled. With her, those doors opened. And now, just as it had in the past, vulnerability was something they shared and exulted in rather than feared.

She could feel her body clenching, starting the climb, craving release. Speed and need galloped through her pulse. It wasn't just that she wanted to come, but that she wanted to be there for him, with him, right then, right *then*. His eyes sheened in the darkness, the intensity in his face matched by her own. Hunger clawed through her, a hunger that named all the flavors of loneliness she knew, that only he—

"Hey, Dad? Cripes, I've been looking all *over* for you! What on earth are you doing back here—oh. *Oh.* I . . . *oh.*"

Faster than a scald, Nate's whole body suddenly locked, still as stone. Jeanne heard the voice, too, but her mind couldn't seem to instantly accept that the most intimate of private moments had suddenly turned public. Her head whipped around—past Nate's shoulder, past the partially open car door. Even in that dim wedge of light, she identified his daughter standing in the far doorway. Caitlin's eyes looked wide with first confusion and then shock, her mouth gaping open like a fish.

The inside of the car was so shadowy that Jeanne was positive Cait couldn't see how nude they were—or exactly what they were doing—but for darn sure she could see the nest of clothes on the ground . . . especially the red spangled bra. Even at thirteen, the child could undoubtedly fill in the blanks from there.

Nate responded first. And fast. His voice came out as if he'd been swallowing rocks, but the tone was unmistakably clear. "Caitlin. Go wait for me in my office. Now, honey."

Caitlin started to say something else. Nate repeated, "*Now.*"

She whirled around and disappeared immediately then, but Jeanne still couldn't breathe. Maybe Caitlin had obeyed her dad and aimed straight for the office . . . but maybe she'd just gone behind the door out of sight and could still hear them.

Her pulse was still thrumming need, her skin still flushed with desire—and his body was still buried inside her, hot and hard. But her mood wilted a ton faster than he did.

His daughter was already a handful, and Caitlin had already made crystal-clear that she was against any woman in her dad's life. It was a double yikes to have his daughter catch them in a moment like this, before they even remotely had a chance to know each other.

For just an instant, Nate's eyes met hers. Exasperation and frustration were easy to read in his tight features . . . but there was more in his expression, a play of emotions and feelings on his face that she desperately wanted to understand, needed to understand. Was he angry with her? Angry with them? Being interrupted by his daughter, of course, immediately changed things . . . but the interruption also forced them to stop, might make him relieved of the excuse. For all she knew, he could believe that making love was a terrible mistake, an impulse he'd never wanted to give in to.

And then he said, "Peanut, I *have* to find her, talk to her."

"Of course you do." Whatever she needed to say to him, this obviously wasn't the time. Both of them fumbled and grabbed for clothes. "She's so young. Maybe it would help if I talked to her, too—"

"No." He must have seen her instinctive flinch of hurt, because he immediately added, "I want you to get to know her, Jeanne. But not like this. I don't even know what I'm going to say to her, so I'm sure as hell not going to pass the buck to you." He reached over and kissed her, hard, ardently, fast. Again, she saw the blaze of emotion in his eyes.

But she felt a sudden blaze of emotion, too. "You shut me out before, Nate. You never gave me the chance to be part of a problem with you, for you."

"I didn't shut you out—"

"Yes. You did."

"This isn't the same thing," he insisted.

She heard him. And there was no more time to argue. But there was a stab in her heart that warned her, this could well be exactly the same thing.

"Okay. Like this is impossible. I can't stand it." Caitlin had hunkered in the car seat next to him and said nothing for most of the ride home, just steadily popped gum bubbles that got increasingly bigger and noisier. "I was just gonna shut up and chill out, but it's not working. You're being too quiet, Dad. Especially when you can usually yell about everything. So maybe we better try talking about this."

Nate *wanted* to talk to his daughter. He planned to say something intelligent and wise and philosophical—the very minute he thought of it. Somehow he just couldn't shake the pictures replaying in his head. The moment when Jeanne's warm, willing, naked body had been joined with his. The moment when they'd almost climaxed together. The moment when they'd almost been together the way they'd always wanted to be.

And then—just as years ago—life had somehow found a way to separate them.

He had to find the correct things to say to his daughter. But he didn't know the correct things—

any more than he'd known how to magically make everything all right with Jeanne Claire. She'd made him feel guilty for not dragging her into this father-daughter confrontation, which was plain crazy. Obviously it was up to him to fix this. A man didn't drag a woman into taking on his problems for him.

Only right now, he couldn't seem to solve any problem he had. And although normally he loved taking charge, right now he'd just as soon take off for Tahiti—under an assumed name—where no one could find him for a while. Where he couldn't find himself even.

Caitlin blew another bubble. The inside of the car smelled distinctly like Double Cherry bubble gum. "You didn't even ask me why I came to the shop. So I'll tell you. It was because I'd left my science report in the backseat of the Duesenberg, because that's where I was working on it a few days ago. Only after dinner, I remembered the report was due tomorrow. And I knew you were at the shop for sure, because you said you had work and also because I knew you had that Pierre guy calling you from France tonight about the Triumph TR6."

Nate switched on the radio. Caitlin switched it off. Since she was obviously determined that he was going to say something, he tried, "Why in the universe would you have been working on your science report in the Duesenberg?"

"Come on, Dad. The J-dual Cowl Phaeton with the 265 horsepower? That French blue with the silver? If *you* had some icky science report that's so boring you could die, wouldn't you try to make it up to yourself by doing it in a cool place like the Duesenberg?"

"The question is why you were even in the shop to be in the Duesenberg to begin with, much less to do a school report."

"No, that's not the question." Caitlin blew a series of little pops, but they were starting to sound dejected. Her gum was losing bubble power. "The question that you should be yelling at me about is why I came to the shop at night. And that's what I've been trying to tell you. Because I remembered that report was due tomorrow, and when I remembered where I left it—well, Uncle Tony stopped over to see Grandma tonight, and he stayed for dinner. Uncle Jason was supposed to come, but he keeps not showing up lately. Anyway, Tony was driving back to his apartment. So, like, he said it was no sweat to give me a ride. And when he saw your car there, he just dropped me off, because we both knew for sure you were there. And if you were busy, like, I just had to study anyway. I could do it there probably better than home. So I had no reason to think you'd mind."

Again she waited, as if giving him ample opportunity to add something constructive to the conversation. She even quit blowing bubbles. The silence stabbed his nerves until he finally came through with "You should have called to let me know you were coming."

"But Grandma knew. And Uncle Tony knew. And I did call you once, but the office line was busy. I figured that was good, you know, that you were likely talking to that Pierre guy—and if you were on the phone, I was all the more positive that you were in the office for sure."

He switched on the radio, this time punching into one of the rap stations she loved and he couldn't stand. But she still switched it off. "We need to face this, Dad," she said sternly. "This is not the kind of thing you can hide under the rug."

"Hey. I'm not trying to hide anything under a rug. I've never hidden from a problem, Caitlin, and I've tried to teach you never to."

"I know, I know. But this is different, because it's about . . . you know." She twisted in the car seat, looking like eighty-five pounds of ragamuffin, her hair in one of those kid styles that stuck out all over, her shirt looking man-sized, her shoes looking bigger than her whole body. But something about her eyes had changed in the last year. Sometimes she could get one of those *knowing* expressions. Woman knowing. Female knowing. At some point his squirt of a daughter had become adult female enough to look at him as if she knew things he didn't and never could. She said baldly, "So. There's a woman in your life."

Oh, man. He thought he was strong and tough enough to face anything. Wrong. "Caitlin," he started to say heavily—without a clue where he was going from there.

"It's okay, Dad. I know it's embarrassing. But if it's embarrassing for you, think how bad it is for me. You're my *father*, for God's sake. Maybe you have sex, but I never wanted to know about it. I just always like to think that you didn't."

Hoboy. He opened his mouth, but then closed it again. He'd never, ever ducked talking to his daughter about anything. But this time, he desperately needed some space to think about what to say—and she wasn't giving him any.

"But the fact is," she continued relentlessly, "if there's a woman in your life, you should be telling me, because obviously she'll end up part of my life, too. Of course, maybe she isn't very important. Like maybe she was just a random for you?"

"A random?"

"Yeah, a random. You know, a one-shot deal. Accidental. Casual. Nothing you're planning on doing again."

That's it, from now on, he was supervising what Caitlin watched on TV and maybe eavesdropping on her phone as well. Hell, where did she get this information? And what did he owe his thirteen-year-old daughter in the way of truth, honesty, and parenting in this circumstance? He jammed on the brake when he meant to push on the gas for a green light. "There is no chance I'd be doing 'a random.'"

"You did with my birth mother."

If he ever had any more kids, he was going to lie to them. No more of this honesty stuff. This was impossible. "You're right. But that was fifteen years ago. I was stupid, and your birth mother was stupid, too. That's not an excuse, but I can promise you that there's no chance in the universe I would behave in an accidental or careless way with a woman now."

He thought that was a pretty good speech, but Caitlin went straight back for the bone she wanted undug. "Okay. So you obviously care about her. Her name is Cassiday, right? Jeanne Claire Cassiday. She came to see you a few weeks ago. That one. The woman who came to see you about the high school reunion."

"Yes." He switched on his turn signal, even though he had no intention of turning in either direction. "For the record, I knew her for years and years. It's not as if this were someone I just met—"

"She looks like money. It showed in her clothes and everything. She looked like Grosse Pointe or Birmingham or like that."

"She comes from a solid family—"

"You call it solid. I call it money. Whatever, she

doesn't look like our kind. Which is the point. Is she serious, or is she just playing with you?"

Where did she get these questions? Some teen magazine? "Caitlin, this just isn't a subject that I think we need to immediately talk ab—"

"Of course we need to talk about it. Look, Dad. You don't have anyone to protect you except me." She paused to blow another bubble. "That is, you've got a bunch of brothers and sisters, and Grandma, and Martha and all—but honestly, I don't think you want any of them to know what you were doing in the backseat of my Mustang—"

"It's not your Mustang."

Caitlin made a vague motion. She'd staked her claim to that car when she was four years old. She had no idea he'd saved it for other reasons, which wouldn't have mattered to her, anyway. Damn kid knew he'd never denied her anything over the long haul. "The point is that I think I should meet her. Talk to her. Because of my mother."

"Huh?" God, it wasn't just in the eyes. It was in the words, too. She was starting to think as confoundingly as a grown-up woman.

"My mother," she repeated. "I already knew she was a random, Dad, partly from stuff you told me, partly from stuff I got out of Grandma. It's not like I'm a kid anymore." She wadded up her gum in a wrapper, then dove into her school bag and pawed wildly around until she found her Pez. She flipped the lid and popped one. "After Gramps died, you had a short thing with my birth mother. Probably because you were, like, vulnerable. And that's what I'm saying, that you've got a little history of not having real great judgment with women. So I think I should meet her."

"Caitlin, in case you haven't noticed, I'm a grown man who's been protecting and supporting a family—and extended family—for years. With no help from anyone. I'm the last person on the planet who needs protecting, and just for the record, I'm an *excellent* judge of character."

Caitlin, deep into the Pez container now, either didn't hear him or simply chose to ignore him. "I'm thinking . . . your birthday's coming up. She could come over and have cake with us."

"I don't need help or advice with women. From you. From anyone. I love you more than my life, but I'll see who I want to see. If I think a relationship's going somewhere for sure, then of course I'll include you—"

"You're not ashamed of her, are you?"

Nate's jaw dropped. He was so disconcerted he turned north on their street. When they lived south. "Of course not—"

"And you're not ashamed of your relationship with her—"

"Of *course* not—"

"And I know you're not ashamed of me. So why wouldn't you want us to get together?"

"Because." Nate flipped up a hand.

"Because why?"

"Because this isn't your business at this point, for God's sake."

"You're, like, sleeping with her. And you said, like, that it wasn't casual. So she means something important to you. So unless you're ashamed of me, I can't think of any reason why you wouldn't like the idea of my getting to know her."

My God, if he kept making wrong turns, they were going to end up in Ypsilanti. At midnight. On a school night. Nate told himself to get it together, take control of the conversation—and his daughter—and get this all straightened out promptly.

There was no way he was subjecting Jeanne to a Donneli family gathering. It'd be like a Roman thinking it'd be charming to invite a Christian to a den of lions. He didn't bring strange women home. He didn't bring un-strange women home, either. He knew what they'd put her through.

It was out of the question.

chapter 11

Someone pounded on her apartment door so loudly and insistently that Jeanne pelted out of the shower and grabbed a towel. For Pete's sake, was it impossible to claim a few free hours?

Of course, by late April, Oz Enterprises was running full speed with nonstop events. Today alone, there were two weddings and an executive golf outing scheduled—but it *was* Saturday afternoon. Just once it wouldn't kill the staff to call her dad if there was a problem.

The pounding began again. She was just reaching for a robe when she recognized Tamara's screech from outside the door. Immediately, she relaxed.

"I'm coming, I'm coming!" Since it was just

Tam, she pushed on the terry cloth robe and grabbed a towel to dry her hair. Truthfully, she pretty desperately needed a few minutes of calm, quiet time, especially when she had to be dressed and out of here by four—but Tamara never visited without a reason. She opened the door, greeting her with "Sheesh, where's the fire?"

There definitely seemed to be one. The instant the door was opened, Tam lumbered inside, lugging a suitcase bigger than Nebraska. Her jacket was flapping open, her cheeks puffing-pink. "God, it took me forever to carry this thing up here."

"Um, did I know you were going to show up? The last I knew, about a half hour ago, we were talking on the phone and you suddenly hung up."

Tamara peeled off her neon orange jacket. "I didn't hang up to be rude. I hung up because you said you said you were going out later, so you only had a few minutes. I need that few minutes— desperately—so I came right over."

"Well, I *am* glad to help but I thought all you wanted was some clothing advice. What's with the suitcase? Are you moving in?"

"Stop looking so panicked." Tam hustled over to the kitchen area and opened the cupboard that stocked the Oreos. "I'm going to Howie's Little League tryouts this afternoon at four. Or something like Little League. Whatever you do when you're only eight years old. Howie is Arnold's son, of course. I told you about Howie before, didn't I?" Still talking with an Oreo in her mouth, she heaved the massive suitcase on the couch and started unzipping. "You know I'm not mother material. I know I'm not mother material. But I don't want Arnold ashamed he asked me to be part of this. So I have to wear the right thing."

Jeanne had started to towel-dry her hair, but now she dropped the towel and peered worriedly into her friend's face. "You have a fever? A violent allergy to something? Hit your head recently?"

Tamara swallowed the last of the Oreo so she could enunciate clearly. "I'm serious, Jeanne."

"So am I. We're talking about Arnold. For the first eighteen years of his life, he didn't know how to tuck his shirt in. Now he's totally tucked in, but probably only because he makes so much money that someone does it for him, because I doubt he cares any more about clothes than he ever did. In fact, I'm pretty sure he wouldn't know a style if it bit him in the tush."

"Maybe not. But he cares about his son."

"I'm sure he does." Jeanne was still confounded at the mess Tamara was making. Clothes were swiftly covering every surface in her living room. "But offhand, it wouldn't seem too traumatic to attend some Little League tryouts—"

"Well, it is. Arnold's so dumb that he thinks I'm good with kids. And God, I'm so nervous I want a drink. And you know I drink, but the one time I never touch alcohol is when I'm nervous, because I don't want to play that dependence game, you know? Not with my history. Do you have any more Oreos? I don't give a damn if I'm addicted to Oreos. Anyway, this is the thing. I have to sit in the stands for these tryouts. It's about fifty-eight degrees outside. Breezy. So what do you think?"

Jeanne surveyed the rainbow assortment of outfits. One top and pants looked as if it had been personally fingerpainted by a three-year-old. Another outfit was a blend of plaid and polka dots. Then came some frayed purple jeans with a jeweled belt paired with an army surplus top. A vintage lace blouse. On and on.

"Tam," Jeanne said tactfully, "I think you might be taking this just a little bit too seriously. I mean, you can just wear jeans. That's what most of the moms'll be wearing. Jeans, a sweatshirt. Lipstick and blush. Play shoes."

"No. Forget that. I tried the blue-striped-blouse routine—it was a bomb. A big, big bomb. He hated it. So I can't dress like you. And I'm not trying to dress *appropriately*. I have to dress like me. Only not the recovering-pill-guzzler, ex-musician, loser me. The clever, artsy me. The nonconformist me. The me that people tend to accept because they don't know what else to do with me anyway." Tam gulped. "Oh, God. You don't like any of these outfits, do you? Well, maybe you have something in your closet that I can steal."

Before Jeanne could stop her, Tamara peeled down the hall. Seconds later, she let out a shriek that would make a tomcat proud. *"Jeanne Claire! What is this? You have a fever? A nervous breakdown? A violent allergy to something?"* She skidded back out to the living room. "There are clothes all over your bed! Not on hangers! Getting wrinkled!" Deliberately mimicking Jeanne's earlier actions, she galloped closer to peer directly into Jeanne's face. "You *must* be sick," she announced.

"No, um, I'm just trying to decide what to wear for something this afternoon, too."

"Since when is that a problem? Just close your eyes, spin around, and pin your finger on anything in your closet. It'll be perfect. Everything you own is perfect."

"Perfect isn't good enough." The way Tamara looked suddenly gave Jeanne a ticklish déjà vu sensation. They might as well have been girls again, dressing for a Saturday night date together— telling all. Only it had been a long time since Jeanne Claire had told anything to anyone, much less "all." On the other hand, if she was going to regress to her panicked teenage years in maturity—or lack thereof—Tamara was certainly the ideal person to do it with. "It seems I'm going to Nate's house. It's his birthday, and apparently his family do it up the old-fashioned way—an early dinner, cake and ice cream, presents."

"A family birthday party," Tamara echoed, as if verbally testing out the feasibility of growing an extra head. "I'm obviously missing something. How exactly did you get conned into this?"

"I didn't get conned." But she knew she was nervous. They'd talked several times since that night in his shop, but each time something had interrupted them. With two people as busy as they both were, work interruptions were sometimes unavoidable. She understood. It was just that there'd been no real chance to discuss that crazy night, no matter how much they'd left hanging— and then came this invitation.

She'd told herself she was happy to go. He'd shut her out before. His asking her to this implied he understood that she needed—*they* needed—to trust each other. Not just with the easy stuff, but the mountains, too. Only . . . now she couldn't help but worry. What if she didn't handle this well? What if she didn't come through for him the way he needed?

"If he didn't con you, how come you're looking so stressed?" Tamara demanded.

"Because the situation is a little awkward."

Tamara immediately perked up. "What kind of awkward?"

"Well, let's just say that I'm only wearing plain

white underwear for the rest of my life. In fact, I'm never wearing sexy underwear again as long as I live."

"Oh, man. This sounds *good*." Tamara gestured with a wait-a-second finger, then fetched the rest of the Oreos. " 'Fess up."

Jeanne provided the abridged version. "His daughter caught me with Nate."

"Caught you doing what?"

Now it was Jeanne's turn to dive for the Oreos. "Well, let's just say, Caitlin got a look at the red satin bra."

"Damn. I am *so* proud of you. That's a real mess. I didn't think you ever got yourself into *real* messes."

Jeanne sank down on the edge of a chair. "The thing is . . . now his daughter thinks I've got my hooks into her father. So she wants to spend some time together. She specifically asked Nate to include me in the birthday thing."

Tam shook her head. Firmly. "So that's great. Go spend some time with her. Go to the mall, a movie, whatever. But for God's sake, get yourself out of this birthday thing. Think about it. You've got a young teenager on the family home turf. You have his mother. Are you out of your mind? Plead sick. Plead ptomaine poisoning. Hell, I'd volunteer to *get* a case of ptomaine poisoning before I'd agree to go to that. You're making my Little League game look like a piece of cake."

Tam's doubts fed straight into Jeanne's. "But I need to go."

"Why?"

"Because his daughter's so important to him. Because the more time passes before I have some face-to-face time with Caitlin, the tougher it's going to be. So we either have to get past this, or the ball game's over and the loser goes home. The loser being me."

"Don't give me baseball analogies. I don't do sports. That's partly why I'm having such a crisis over the Little League thing. But never mind that." Tamara curled up on top of her outfits in the lotus position. "Somehow I seem to have missed some major scenes in this movie. A month ago, you went to see Nate to find out once and for all if you could get him out of your system. Now, I know you've seen him. I know he explained what happened all those years ago. But you didn't tell me you'd fallen hard in love with him all over again."

"I didn't exactly say—"

"You didn't have to. If you're willing to face the tortures of the damned—meaning facing his mother and teenage daughter at the same time— just to be with him . . . you're in love."

"Okay. I am." It was like taking a great, big heaping gulp of air after being stuck under water forever. "Oh, God. I really am. But I'm not at all sure it can work out. Nate's the same dynamo he always was. But I never thought about it before—how he always called the shots, took charge, didn't count on me. Obviously, I can't be there for him unless he gives me a chance. But I don't want to be with anyone—even Nate—who doesn't want me to hold my own. Do you understand?"

"Of course. The whole damn world always treated you like a face. A looker with no brain. Men, especially, always thought you were too soft, the way they always seem to think that I'm really tough." Tam cocked her head. "But you *do* have a too-soft side, Jeanne."

"I know."

"In fact, you're worse than you used to be. If somebody says they need you, you jump."

"It's a disgusting quality," Jeanne agreed.

"If Nate tries to run over you, I'll have to kill him."

"That's so nice of you," Jeanne said dryly, "But—"

"I know. The clock's ticking. We don't have time for inconsequential chit-chat." So much for the lotus position. Tamara was already up and sprinting down the hall again. "Back to serious stuff. Clothes. I'm headed for your closet. I trust your judgment on telling me what to wear, but believe me, for your problem, nobody could give you better advice than *me*. Pendleton and pearls just won't cut this. You have to think Scarlett—like what Rhett made her wear after she was caught kissing Ashley."

"Say what?"

"*Gone With the Wind*. It was probably the only book I ever read. Anyway. What you need is an I'm-a-strong-cookie outfit. Something with color. Something with guts. Trust me, if there's one thing I know in life, it's how to fool people into thinking I'm someone I'm not."

Tamara got her to laugh—Tam's irreverence always lifted her spirits. But an hour later, as she drove to Nate's, worries were crowding her mind again.

Contrary to advice from Tam—who thought she should wear a red halter top and tight white slacks—she'd worn a turquoise silk shirt and tan slacks, plugged in some opal earrings, and brushed her hair loose. They simply defined "dress for success" just a wee bit differently. Traffic snarled in downtown Ann Arbor, making her later and frazzling another layer of nerves. It was almost four-thirty before she squeezed her car into a spot on the street two houses down from Nate's. Her heart started hiccuping in earnest then.

Maybe she was plumb crazy to come here.

They'd come so close to making love the other night. They'd come so close in every way these last weeks, talking, sharing their lives and problems. But once an egg cracked, no sane person thought you could glue the shell back together. How could she possibly believe they really had a second chance?

When she was seventeen, Nate had been her knight in shining armor. When you grew up, the clichés cracked. She didn't want an icon or an idol or a cliché anymore—just a living, breathing man who loved her—but man, this evening sure seemed a tough way to explore the possibilities.

Caitlin was the first petrifying obstacle, knowing what Cait had seen the other night, knowing she didn't want a woman in her father's life. And Nate had coaxed her to come for another reason— because his brothers would be at this birthday party. He wanted her to see his brothers, get to know them, to see if they could gain more understanding of his thief problem.

She'd so willingly agreed to come. She wanted to help him. But, damn. She just couldn't fool herself. This night was a test—to see if she could get along with his daughter. To see if she could fit in his life. And maybe more than anything, a test for herself. She needed to come through for him—the way she'd never had the chance to prove she could fifteen years ago.

Talk, though, was cheap. Her heart thumped like a cowardly puppy's when she climbed out of the car, and then immediately she had to duck back in, because she'd almost forgot the present. Coming up with an appropriate present had been another scary problem. Obviously, she couldn't attend a birthday party without bringing him something, but what to get him? So she'd come up with a book. Not too expensive. Not too cheap. Not too personal, not too impersonal. His love had once been architecture, but to blast him with his old, lost dream seemed cruel. Still, she was trying to think of an interest of his, so she'd gotten a text on feng shui. She thought maybe he'd find it interesting. Or humorous.

Or maybe she was totally stupid and it was the worst idea for a gift any human being could come up with.

She clutched her purse, the wrapped package, and the box of Sander's nougats she'd brought as a hostess gift, but then couldn't seem to move, just stood there studying the house he lived in.

It was big, two stories, white frame, with a fat old maple in the front yard. The house was old— the kind of old with a wraparound porch and lots of character and circular windows over the doors.

The front door stood carelessly open, gaping wide, letting in the cool spring air and letting out the sounds of boisterous conversation and laughter—mostly male.

She stalled again at the sound of the guys, but it was too late to pull a chicken act. Just that quickly, someone must have spotted her, because suddenly there were three hulking-guy shadows jostling in the open doorway.

And then Nate charged down the porch steps toward her—an energy field of virility and vitality and unforgivably sexy eyes. "Thank God you're here. This was supposed to be a little dinner, a little cake. Instead, they got balloons, for God's sake. It's worse than a circus. They're all being obnoxious. Don't leave me."

It wasn't as if she bought into his cry for help— he looked as intimidated as a lion in a den of rabbits—but the damn man forced her to smile. "I just keep thinking that I'm going to be intruding—"

"Wrong. Don't even think about going there. And if you're scared by all the noise, don't waste your time worrying about that, either. My brothers are all animals. Noisy, rude, sick animals—but they don't bite."

"Hey! I'm willing to bite!" one brother said and then chugged ahead of Nate, pulling her into the house. She hadn't met him before, but she saw the slow, lazy grin, the wonderful dark eyes. He was a younger version of Nate, just more slightly built. "I'm Tony. And you're so damn beautiful that I don't care what your na—"

He stopped, giving her enough time to fill in the blank. "Jeanne Claire Cassiday."

"Well, damn. I knew we had a Jeanne coming, but I thought you must be someone else. Nate said

Jeanne was plain, kind of overweight, squinty eyes. We kept looking out the window for an ex-nun type. I'm in love," Tony told his brother.

Nate sighed heavily. "Now you see how I had to develop so much patience, don't you?" To Tony, he said, "Unhand my girl. Coming into this mad-house is traumatic enough without you guys falling all over her before we've even gotten her a drink."

"I'll get you a drink. In fact I'll get you any-thing you want. For the rest of our lives," Tony assured her.

An ounce of that panicked anxiety evaporated. Not all of it, but definitely some. The kid was adorable, wild-haired, bratty, brash . . . but there was a good heart in his eyes. And Tony made out like he was really looking her over . . . but he didn't have half the skill at sizing up a woman that Nate did.

They'd almost made love. She hadn't forgotten it, couldn't forget it, but when Nate looked her over, she felt that memory flush through her, as naked as yesterday. All he did was glance at her, really—yet his gaze gleamed at her like starlight, making her skin warm and her pulse dance. "You're so brave," he said.

Yes. She was. But brownie points for courage didn't seem to make this any easier.

"You didn't have to bring me a present." Typi-

cal of a man, though, he grabbed the present—
and the box of nougats—then shouted to persons
unknown that he was taking a minute to show her
around.

"The present isn't much, Nate, I . . . oh, my."

Most of the voices seemed to come from a
kitchen—or a room that was lit up and wafting
delicious smells from off to the left—but Nate
steered her in the opposite direction. The hall
opened onto an open staircase. Family photographs cluttered most of the wall space, and the
thick, plush carpeting looked fresh-vacuumed—
but battered down by a zillion footprints.

"Caitlin and I live upstairs. A couple years ago,
we refinished it into a separate apartment for us.
When we first moved here, all my brothers and
sisters slept upstairs, and I was the only one sleeping down—because that was the only way I could
birddog anybody trying to break curfew. Now,
though, we all tend to call the downstairs Mom's
house, and the only Donneli kid still keeping a
room here is Tony until he finishes college. We
keep changing things to accommodate changing
needs. I don't want Caitlin alone when I'm working, so we're still with my mom—she's the only
mother Cait's ever known besides—"

He explained more than Jeanne could keep up
with, but his talking gave her a chance to settle
herself and see the place at the same time. His

mother was obviously religious. The room spilling off the east side seemed filled with sturdy, practical furniture, the colors rich and dark, with heavy draperies blocking out the light. Almost every wall had a religious statue or crucifix; almost every table had a lit candle. There was nothing wrong with the decor, but Jeanne was astonished. The place seemed so unlike Nate. She'd have bet the bank he'd like lots of light and airiness and more open space, but who knew?

"It's really beautiful," she said politely.

"It's more crowded than a horse barn—but upstairs, Cait and I had a chance to do things differently. Anyway, this birthday thing—they all made such a fuss that it's mortifying. Try to like them, would you? And I can't keep you hidden much longer; the vultures'll be chomping at the bit to start in on you, so y'all calmed down and ready?"

She had been relatively calmed down—until she walked into the kitchen. The first thing she noticed were the wonderful aromas of veal chops with lemon, spaghetti with mussels, baked fennel, and Italian tomato and bread soup. Clearly his mother regularly fed whole armies. The table had a half dozen leaves and had the look of a treasured family antique. The counters and stove were jammed with pots and bowls. One counter was heaped with presents; another held the infamous birthday cake. Balloons draped the circumference of the gigantic kitchen—the room where obviously everyone lived.

"There's my boy, there's my boy!" His mother bussed him on both cheeks as if she hadn't seen him in weeks. "Finally, you bring Jeanne in here, when you know we've all been waiting to see her . . . so let me look at you. There, aren't you pretty? So. What church do you go to?"

She felt like a bra in a Victoria's Secret window, hopelessly on display.

Impressions of his brothers came in chunks. She'd met Jason at the shop—the accountant who didn't quite have his CPA yet, but who'd been doing the books for Nate for several years now. He had the same dark hair, the same basic Donneli bad-boy looks, but he was the urban version. Slacks with a crease. Italian shoes. Hair done by a stylist. Everything about his appearance seemed to underline how much he didn't like work where he had to get his hands dirty.

She'd seen Daniel more recently in the shop— she'd also met him years ago, when she was dating Nate. Daniel had the Donneli looks, too, but in personality and looks he was the diametric opposite of Jason—his chin was unshaved; his sweatshirt was pushed up to reveal hairy, muscular arms; there was a moodiness underneath the beautiful dark eyes.

Mom Donneli—Maria—looked like a miniature doll next to her sons. She wore tidy slacks and a matching blouse, her long hair darker than midnight and coiled up, out of the cook's way. Her height was diminutive, but her eyes were sharp and cool.

Jeanne tried to take them all in as her plate was mounded—mounded!—with food. His mother was assessing her. She could feel it. She could also sense that no woman ever born was good enough for one of her sons, nor could anyone take as good care of them as she could. "That's so nice, your job, it sounds so interesting. And I didn't get a chance to ask now, your dad and mother—"

"I lost my mother about four years ago."

"Oh, my sweet girl, what a terrible thing. And your father, you are close with your father? Does he happen to be Catholic?"

"Mom, let up with the questions. Let her eat."

Although Nate was sitting next to her, she really didn't want him to intervene or protect her. It didn't matter how nervous she was. This was the first chance she had to really see his family and the family dynamics. She hoped to be able to give him some insights on his thief problem—but more than that, she saw Nate in a whole different way.

All three brothers treated her like a welcome guest, flirting and teasing, going out of their way to charm and make her feel easy . . . but they sure weren't that way with Nate. Apparently showing up for a birthday gig was a family requirement—like the Catholic Church required confession, nothing anyone wanted to do but did because they had to. They joked about Nate's advanced age, his need for Viagra, his developing rheumatism . . . the jokes were funny, but they all had a bite.

When the cake showed up, there was more of the same. They razzed him about what kind of wishes he'd use for his birthday candles—to rule the world? To have everyone finally obey him? To have everyone do things his way? Everyone laughed—including Nate—yet Jeanne felt increasingly unsettled.

Caitlin was allowed to light the candles, igniting a blaze worthy of a smoke alarm. The birthday song was bellowed out while Nate held his head in despair at their godawful singing. No one could possibly eat dessert after that gigantic dinner, yet the men wolfed down more, egged on by Mrs. Donneli—and then came the presents.

On the surface, Jeanne thought the gifts seemed like pretty typical family offerings. His mother bought him a shirt that no one under sixty-five would wear. Daniel got him some kind of electric tool, Tony bought him a CD, and Jason gave him a book on the "inner child" which brought a round of laughs; Jason obviously thought his older brother needed to loosen up.

Jeanne's disquiet grew. Whoever got gifts they really wanted on holidays or birthdays? But every single present seemed to be something the giver wanted, not something Nate wanted or would use.

Caitlin's present was the opposite. She'd obviously saved a ton to buy her dad an expensive book on architecture . . . and when she saw Jeanne's book, their eyes met. Caitlin must have known that her dad had a dream of being an architect. And now she seemed to sense that Jeanne knew something private and personal about her dad, different from the whole rest of the family.

There was no time to dwell on that—no time to dwell on anything. Finally Mrs. Donneli seemed to agree that they might—might—have eaten enough to please her, and the men had obviously sat still all they could stand. It was probably Daniel who first challenged Nate.

"Yeah, you're probably way too old and decrepit to play one-on-one."

Nate was on his feet in a blink. "In your dreams. I could outscore all three of you blindfolded."

"Sure, sure—"

When the boasts and challenges escalated—even before the chairs scraped back—Jeanne looked across the table. Through the whole dinner and cleanup, she'd felt Caitlin's eyes on her like lighthouse beacons on a stormy night.

The child wanted some kind of showdown with

her—and when the men sprinted outside to shoot some hoops, Caitlin stood up, too. "Hey, I could show you the upstairs, if Dad didn't already do it," she said.

"That'd be great," Jeanne responded, and just hoped she'd survive whatever torture the child planned to put her through.

chapter 12

Jeanne's stomach kept flip-flopping as she followed Caitlin upstairs. This was her chance to form a connection to Nate's daughter—maybe her only chance.

Yet she couldn't help but worry that it already might be too late. Cait had very definitely seen that red satin bra the other night. She had every reason to have formed a negative impression. And the girl was chattering easily enough, but Jeanne wasn't fooled into believing Caitlin had so willingly offered her a tour of the house.

Cait wore a baggy sweatshirt and jeans that scuffed the ground, like any other kid her age, but there was attitude in her posture. Determination. Stubbornness. Jeanne strongly suspected that she'd used the excuse of a house tour to get her alone, away from the eyes and ears of the rest of the family.

"So, like, when I was a little kid, all my aunts and uncles slept up here with me," Caitlin informed her. "But then everybody started growing up and moving out, you know? And when Aunt Anne got married a couple years ago, Dad and I decided we'd make the upstairs like our own private house. That way, we could still take care of Grandma. But we could do our own thing. So Dad and I fixed the upstairs together."

"You two did great. It's so different from the downstairs," Jeanne said. It was easy to pour on enthusiasm. The upstairs really was night and day from how Nate's mother had decorated the main floor.

Maybe the second story had originally been a nest of bedrooms, but walls had been taken down to create a large central space that combined a living room and mini kitchen. Unlike the downstairs, everything up here was light and airy. No dark colors. Wooden blinds instead of curtains. A curve-around couch, centered on thick, plush carpeting. There was lots of clutter, but it was living clutter—like books and shoes—rather than doodad-knickknack clutter of any kind.

Beyond the living area were two bedrooms and a study. One peek in Caitlin's room revealed that a princess lived there. The canopy bed was fresh out of a fairy tale. The pink spread matched the pink wallpaper and carpet. White built-in bookcases were jammed with books and stuffed animals and music.

"All the pink was a mistake. I didn't have much judgment when I was ten," Caitlin said with a sigh. "Now that I'm grown up, I gotta get rid of a lot of this stuff. Dad and I are just so busy. It's hard for us to find the time."

"I understand," Jeanne said, and did her best to bite back a smile. Every word Caitlin said established that daughter and dad were an unshakable twosome, no intruders wanted. She got the warning, but she still couldn't help feeling charmed. Cait had so much spirit and spunk, was so much her dad's daughter.

"I know, you probably think the canopy's stupid. I mean, how girly-girl can you get? Especially when I'm going to be a mechanic like my Uncle Daniel. I've already set up a pretty good shop in the garage."

"Personally, I love the canopy. I don't see why you can't be both a girly-girl type and practical, too. I mean, why does that have to be a contradiction? It's just two sides of you, that's all. And that sounds really great, about your having a workshop in the garage."

For a millisecond, Caitlin thawed. "Not to Dad. He says I'm going to college for four years or he'll kill me." She added hastily, "Otherwise, though,

we totally love each other. We don't need anybody else. I mean, we always lived with Grandma
and my aunts and uncles, because we needed to
take care of them and all, but that's because
they're family. And we've got so much family that
we just never seemed to need . . . extra people."

In case Jeanne might have missed the message
before, she got it underlined this time. She was an
outsider. She wasn't needed.

"Now this is Dad's room. He has a study off
from that, but we won't go there." Caitlin took
one step into the bedroom, allowing Jeanne only a
partial snapshot. A gray and cocoa comforter had
been thrown over a giant bed. A wall of closets
concealed clothes and personal belongings. A corner TV was blanketed with dust. The bathroom
had red towels. And that's all she saw before
Caitlin firmly closed the door.

"Dad doesn't like anybody around his private
stuff," she said firmly. "I don't mess with Dad's
space, and he doesn't mess with mine."

"I understand."

"If Dad needs cookies or something, I bake 'em
for him. If he wants to go to the movies, I go with
him. We go out to dinner sometimes, too."

She got it, she got it. Caitlin didn't want any female in her dad's life except for herself.

"See . . . this is the thing." When they reached
the main living area again, Caitlin flopped down
on the curve-around blue couch, one leg hooked

over the arm as if she didn't have a care in the world. "Lots of women chase after my dad. They always have. Even when I was a little kid, I could see it. Some of them were hot for his money. Some liked the cool cars. Some of them are even married." She paused deliberately.

Jeanne understood that she was supposed to respond with shock. "You mean married women come on to your dad?"

"I know. Isn't it terrible? Right in front of me! Sometimes they act like they don't even notice that I'm there. But I *am* there. And that's why I try to protect my dad, you know? They may all think he's cool and all. But they don't really know him. They don't know what's important to him."

Jeanne would have tried to answer, but Caitlin suddenly hunched forward, and serious as a judge, burst out, "Look. I saw you two the other night. Maybe I didn't see anything exactly but I saw enough. So now I'm asking. Are you going to marry my dad, or are you just fooling with him, or what's the story?"

Jeanne had expected a difficult confrontation, and instead felt a heart pull that she'd never anticipated. Maybe Caitlin didn't like her worth beans, but she felt just the opposite. Nate's baby was going to protect her dad come hell or high water—and Jeanne knew perfectly well where she'd inherited that kind of loyalty.

She said carefully, sincerely, "Caitlin, I promise

that I'm not just 'fooling' with your dad. Years ago, I was very much in love with him, and I think he loved me. Then we were split up by some life circumstances, and I don't think either of us expected to ever run into each other again. But now we have. I honestly can't tell you for sure where this is going. Only that I'm glad to have the chance to get to know your dad all over again."

"All right. That's cool. But I need to just say that, like, my dad—he's given up a lot for everybody. He's helped everybody in the whole family. So I don't want him hooked up with some woman who isn't going to be there for him, you know?"

Jeanne opened her mouth to respond, then closed it. Her chest suddenly hurt, a piercing ache that seemed to squeeze her heart and make it hard to breathe. She said, "Yes, I do know. And I'd feel exactly the same way in your shoes."

That honest answer seemed to appease Caitlin, but there was no further chance to talk because Mrs. Donneli called up the stairs, "Caitlin! Quit hogging Jeanne Claire all to yourself! Bring her downstairs so I can visit with you two!"

Caitlin rolled her eyes and hollered back, "Okay, okay, be down in two shakes, Grandma!"

She smiled at Jeanne—the first natural smile she'd won from the girl—and Jeanne wanted to smile back, but the emotional fist squeezing her heart refused to let up. Downstairs, the men were just piling in from outside, boisterously joking with each other, and Nate caught her eye.

She knew he expected her to stay, that they'd planned to find some quiet time together after the party broke up, but when Daniel and Jason stood up, she did, too. She said her thank yous, her goodbyes, her happy birthdays—and of course she could see Nate was confused when she hightailed it for the door. But she still fled.

It was that heart squeeze thing. That panicked, achy feeling just kept getting worse.

She sped through downtown Ann Arbor, making it back home in record time. The sun was just setting when she hurried into the lobby at Oz. The usual mound of messages was waiting for her at the front desk. She scooped them up, but then hustled upstairs before anyone could try talking to her. Once in her apartment, she dropped the messages and mail, pushed off her shoes, and sank in a chair without even turning on a light.

She'd move in a minute. She'd get a grasp on this panicked feeling any minute. It was just . . . Caitlin's voice kept replaying in her mind. *So I don't want him hooked up with some woman who isn't going to be there for him, you know?*

It wasn't a new question—it was the same question she'd already asked herself—but coming from his daughter it reminded Jeanne that more was at stake than just what she needed or wanted.

She loved that man. Maybe she'd never fallen

out of love with him. Maybe all these tumultuous emotions were about a new, yearning-fresh love. It didn't matter. What mattered, initially, was that the reunion announcement had provided an excuse to see each other again. They'd found other excuses since then. But both their lives were too busy and complicated to have excuses work for long.

"Just" loving each other hadn't been enough fifteen years ago. He'd shut her out when he needed help. But the frame on the picture was different now, not just because they were older, but because their choices had changed. Years ago, Nate had had to throw away all his dreams because of his dad's death. Now he was finally coming to a time when he could pursue his life dreams again.

And so could she.

She hadn't been strong enough to stand up for what she needed all those years ago. Nate hadn't just shut her out. She'd shut herself out. Being dumped had hurt like a banshee, but it wasn't rejection she feared now. It was knowing whether she could trust Nate with her underbelly vulnerabilities—and whether a man who never let anyone in could learn to trust her.

It was ten-fifteen that night before Nate could knock on her door. There had been no opportunity to escape the house before that—his brothers had left quickly enough, but his mother needed some time and thanks for putting on the birthday gig, he'd needed a fresh shower, and then obviously he couldn't walk out without touching base with Caitlin.

He'd gotten all the way to his car before realizing he wasn't certain of the address for Oz Enterprises, so then he'd had to look that up. By the time his knuckles were rapping on her apartment door, his mind was spinning nonstop. For one thing, it startled him that he hadn't realized she lived in her father's convention center. Or that he hadn't any idea where she lived.

That seemed impossible. How could he have almost made love with the woman—and brought her into the tortuous, petrifying nest of a Donneli family gathering—without knowing the most elemental details of her life? Of course, fifteen years ago, he'd thought he'd known everything that could possibly matter about Peanut.

But now he wasn't so sure. In fact, right now, he was too rattled to be dead positive of his own name.

He raised his knuckles to pound on the door again when it suddenly pulled open. One look at Jeanne and his throat went dry. She clearly hadn't expected to see him or anyone else that evening, because she'd shed the day's clothes and pulled on a long robe. The robe was a pale oyster color, made of one of those slippery fabrics that whispered over her curves and wouldn't stay tied, satin or silk or something—whatever it was, it had to be a guy who invented the fabric. He liked it. He liked it beyond belief. But just then, damnation, he was trying to keep his head straight and his mind on issues at a far loftier level than below his waist.

"Nate!"

Both her voice and eyes reflected how startled she was to see him—but that didn't necessarily mean she didn't want him there—so before she could object, he started right in. "I know. I should have called. But you took off faster than a bat out of hell, so I figured something had to be wrong. And I couldn't see just calling you if there was some kind of serious problem."

"I'm really sorry you bothered—but honestly, nothing was wrong."

Yeah, sure. She backed up when he pushed in. He closed the door, still looking at how tightly she was knotting the robe, how wounded the eyes, how soft the pale, pale cheeks. "My family's scared the hell out of more than one unprepared visitor before, but I figured I'd talked about them enough that you knew what to expect. It's what Italian families do. Stuff you with food and then pry into your life. I thought I'd warned you—"

"You did warn me. And I loved your daughter, loved your mom. There was no problem—"

Except that she looked all shook up and anxious—and his Peanut simply didn't *do* shook up and anxious. She did poised and able to handle every situation. Especially when she was shook up and anxious.

Christ. He was starting to think like a woman. A scary thought in itself. But the point was, whatever scared her into taking off like that must have been bad.

Without taking his eyes off her, he tried to take in the room peripherally, looking for clues that might help him understand her—but all he really noticed was that he didn't like the place. The room looked elegant and tasteful, like her, and the cream and coral colors were okay. But there was something wrong. He kept trying to pin it down. This wasn't a place she lived in. It was more like a place that she behaved in.

"Well . . . I'm relieved nothing was wrong," he said as he heeled off his shoes, shed his jacket. He sure as hell wasn't leaving. "But since I'm here . . . we were going to meet after the party, remember? Partly because I had to make sure you survived Caitlin, but I already talked to her. She said, 'Maybe you're okay.' Since you don't have a teenager, you might not realize that's an accolade you practically have to die to get if you're an adult over thirty. But that wasn't why I put you through the family ordeal to begin with. I was hoping you'd have some impressions of my brothers."

There now. She was obviously willing to talk about his thief problem. She relaxed—at least for a while. A bottle of red wine showed up from her mini fridge. A lamp got turned on. She sank down on the other side of the couch—not lover-close, but at least not all the way across the room. And she seemed more than willing to leap into a deep, thorough conversation. About his potential thief. Not, for damn sure, about anything to do with the two of them.

"Nate . . . the birthday gifts bothered me."

"Why?"

She lifted a hand in one of those universal woman-speak gestures. "They all gave you things you didn't want. That I'm almost sure they *knew* you didn't want. I mean . . . Tony's young, but he still gave you a CD of his favorite music, rather than yours. Unless you're into alternative—"

"Hate it," Nate admitted. Everywhere he looked, he saw her father's business. A serious heap of financial reports was piled under her reading lamp. Insurance files nested on another lamp table. The TV was on, mutely flashing the stock market numbers, even at this hour. Catering menus were strewn on her ottoman. The walls sported photos of her dad, shaking hands with this bigwig and that bigwig. Nothing was wrong with it all, assuming she loved her work and Oz Enterprises. But nothing implied she was taking any time to have a personal life.

Abruptly it struck Nate how alike they were. It's not that he presumed to understand her. But looking around her place was like looking at his own. This was how he'd lived for years, too—living for family, giving them everything he could, taking no time for his own life. He believed in loyalty, especially to family. So did she.

Lately, it gnawed in his gut that he might have taken loyalty too far. Now he wondered if she had, too.

"The point," Jeanne said, "is that Tony gave you something he wanted. And Daniel gave you a tool that he undoubtedly wanted himself. Then Jason gave you the book about the inner child—that was cute and funny, only not exactly. Because it seemed like criticism of you packaged as a joke."

"Peanut—I told you. My brothers aren't happy with me. They resent me."

"Yeah, you told me you were a dominating, domineering, overbearing bear."

"Which I guess I am. But we are still a family. And they all know how much I gave up for them. Which is why I can't seem to accept that any of them would steal from me." He hunched forward. "You think it's Daniel, don't you?"

She shook her head. "You keep saying Daniel, so I know it's your strongest hunch. But I can't see it. Daniel struck me more as the kind of person who'd punch you in the nose—confront you to your face—rather than do anything behind your back."

Nate frowned thoughtfully. "You're right. About

Daniel being the straightforward type. But I keep coming back to him because . . . well, because I can remember so many things from after my dad died. Like my telling Daniel he had to be home by midnight or I'd ground him for the rest of his life. Like his yelling that he'd hate me until the day I died and I wasn't Dad, so I didn't get to tell him shit."

"Aw, Nate . . ."

He could hear the sympathy in her voice, shook it off. "We were like two rams butting heads, partly because we weren't that far apart in age. I *know* I ordered him around too much. I *know* I came across as a tyrant. I *know* I wasn't the sympathetic older brother they all wanted. But I was mad, too. I was scared, too. Even my mom—she was so busy raising all the kids that she just didn't realize how irresponsible my dad was with money. None of my brothers or sisters realized how much was on my head. They just saw me as being mean."

She hesitated. "I saw some resentment. Like you said. But I also saw the way they were with you, Nate. None of them would have shown up for a birthday gig like that if they didn't care. They all seriously look up to you. They love you—"

"I know that. Really, I know. There's a ton of love in my family. I just don't want to kid myself about how serious the resentments might be. I mean, at least one of them has to be harboring some mighty heavy anger, to be stealing from me."

"I think that's exactly the key," she said thoughtfully. "It just doesn't make sense that this is only about money. There has to be something else. Some kind of frustration or unhappiness that's really festering."

He backed up. "Say what? My thief's stealing money but you don't think it's really about money?"

"I'm just suggesting that I think it's about more. If it were just about money, he could have borrowed from a bank or a friend. Or assuming he was willing to steal, he could have stolen from a store or a friend or an acquaintance. He could have asked anyone in the family for money. Instead he stole from you. He went out of his way to hurt *you*. I just don't think that's accidental."

It's not that he hadn't thought along those same lines, but she made it so much clearer. "That bites," he admitted.

She hesitated again. "I could be totally wrong, Shadow. I'm just giving you an impression—"

"I know. But I think your perception rings true. I'm not sure what to do next—except head back to the drawing board, think harder about which one of my brothers has a rough case against me personally. Then maybe we can talk again?"

A telephone suddenly rang—but the sound didn't emanate from the receiver right next to her on the lamp table. It came from the wall phone by the door, some kind of fancy electronic setup with color-coded lights. When Jeanne saw the blinking blue light, she shot him a glance. He immediately understood it was business. "Go for it. Don't worry about me," he said.

When she hustled to the phone, he stood up and ambled over to her glass doors, glancing down at the night-lit landscaping. Overall, he was just as glad their conversation had been interrupted. He *had* wanted her impressions of his brothers, and he *did* want to think more about that situation—but enough was also enough of his problems.

He still had no idea what had upset her earlier. And he didn't plan on leaving until he found out.

Now, though, without intending to eavesdrop, he still couldn't help overhearing her side of the telephone conversation. There was obviously some kind of security problem regarding a party downstairs.

"Okay," she said finally. "Call me if anything else happens, Carl. And thanks for the heads-up."

"What happened?" Nate asked when she hung up.

Jeanne rolled her eyes, as she curled back up on the couch again. "A guest decided to go swimming wearing his business suit. Carl's the head of night security. He always lets me know if there's a guest problem, who called, what happened, where things stand. He handled it well. The guy's back in his room; everyone's out of the pool, the ruckus is all quieted down. Carl was just filling me in."

"I don't understand. They automatically call you instead of your father when there's a security problem?" He couldn't keep the surprise out of his voice. The errant swimmer hardly sounded like a crisis, but Oz was a huge enterprise. Maybe it was Italian-guy thinking, but he really spurred up at the idea of Jeanne directly having to handle drunks or vandalism or potentially dangerous problems.

She retied the sash of her robe—which refused to stay tied for long—but then she met his eyes. "I guess technically they should call my dad. Security is hardly part of the job description for the events manager. But . . . well, there are things my dad just can't seem to handle. Or doesn't. And somehow they get shifted to me. Normally, I don't mind."

"Believe me, I know how that goes. Family ties are complicated. You get tangled up. Especially if you were brought up to believe that family comes first."

She nodded. "I know you've had it harder than I have. But sometimes it seems as if we both talk exactly the same language. I can do the events manager job, but I never planned on doing this kind of work—just like you never wanted to work in your dad's business. And I never wanted to live here, instead of having my own private place—

just like I'll bet you never wanted to live with family all these years." She added quickly, "I'm not complaining. I love my dad. And right after we lost my mom, he really needed me. I was glad to come through for him. It's just that . . . sometimes I feel bewildered by how differently my life turned out from what I once thought it'd be."

"God. So do I." Again he felt drawn to her the way he never had been with anyone else. No one listened the way Peanut did. No one understood.

He instinctively moved toward her—and then stopped himself. He wanted nothing more than to pull her into his arms, to finish what they'd started the other night. But not with so many emotional hangnails between them. "Jeanne . . . something *did* bother you tonight. You wouldn't have left the house so fast if it hadn't. Are you sure Caitlin or my mother didn't say something to upset you?"

"No. Nothing like that."

He didn't believe her. He knew the Donneli women. But one closed door didn't mean he couldn't try opening another. "I think we've both been avoiding talking about some things—like the other night in the car. And like now, your not feeling comfortable telling me there was a problem. It seems that one minute, we're as close as we used to be. That there's something between us that tugs like two powerful magnets. Something that pulls so strongly I don't want to let it go."

Now it was her turn to lurch to her feet, eyes luminous with emotion—and tension. "Oh, Nate. That's how I feel, too."

He gestured. "I can't make you promises yet."

"I can't make you any, either."

"But something's there."

"Something's there," she agreed softly. Her voice sounded as fragile as a whisper, as honest as risk.

"It's not the past. It's nothing like the past. I thought—when we first met—it was like a déjà vu of the old chemistry? And I remember that chemistry. Remember going crazy with it. Hot for you all the time. High just being with you. Loving every second we were together. But—"

"But," she echoed.

"This is different." He jingled the change in his pocket, giving his hands something new to do. Besides touch her. "This is more. This isn't just a little firecracker chemistry. It's a full forest fire, with a lot more depth and heat."

She swallowed, her eyes on his, luminous and soft. "Yes."

"I don't want to screw it up, Peanut. We lose this chance, for damn sure we'll never get a third one. And when you left so fast tonight—look, I know Caitlin can be a pistol and a half. And I flunked the course in talking to her about the other night. Even in the best of times, she can have a hard stubborn streak—"

"You're kidding. Where on earth would she get a trait like that?"

He started to grin, but then went on seriously again. "I'm just trying to be totally straight with you. I can't say that I'm in an easy position to bring a woman into my life. For a pile of years, that didn't matter to me. I needed to be close to my siblings. My mom would have been stranded alone, and I'd have been stranded without her helping me raise Cait. But—"

"But you're going to have your hands completely full if you try bringing a woman into the house. For damn sure, your mom isn't going to be easy with any woman who happens to be a lapsed Catholic. And Caitlin's used to having you to herself. She's going to be jealous. And protective."

"Um—yeah, she is." For a minute, he was confused. Who was leading this conversation, he or she?

"On your mom—I think she'd warm up over time as long as the woman wasn't trying to take her place. And on Caitlin—well, I didn't have much time with her, Donneli. But enough to realize that I really, really like your daughter—even if the feeling wasn't mutual. I definitely don't have any illusions about that. It'll take a lot more than a conversation or two to win her over. It'll take time. There won't be any hurrying it."

"So . . . Caitlin really didn't scare you off?"

"Nate. We're both adults with full lives. I'd say

we both bring baggage to the situation, but I always hated that term. To me, it implies problems people bring to the next relationship, problems they can't shake. I don't think of your daughter or your mother—or my father—as problems. I think of them as part of our lives. I don't think there are any magic answers for complex people issues . . . but I also have no reason to think we can't put our heads together and come up with ideas to make our lives work . . . if it comes to that."

"If it comes to that," he echoed. In the lamplight, her eyes looked softer than liquid. For that instant, he couldn't seem to breathe. "I have a feeling it could come to that, Peanut. So be warned."

"I'm warned."

"You're not scared off yet?"

"Nope. You?"

"Nope. We have any other immediate crises we need to talk about? Or is the immediate stuff cleared up for now."

"It's cleared up."

His lungs seemed to remember to haul in some air around then. "All right then. I'll be going." It wasn't what he wanted to do. But he kept his hands tight in his pockets as he strode across the room toward her.

The expression on her face—she looked so vulnerable.

He'd hurt her before. Maybe he never had a choice not to, fifteen years ago, but he sure as hell did now. And all their talking, in the quiet lamplit room, was wading into mighty deep waters. They both had damn good reasons to be cautious.

Fifteen years ago, he feared that he couldn't afford Jeanne Claire—and suddenly he realized that he felt just as unsure. She'd gone ahead with her education, with her life . . . where he hadn't. He'd still only finished high school, still got his hands in grease every day. She still could have any classy, high-brow kind of guy she wanted . . . and Nate wasn't about to forget that he still had questions about the other man in her picture.

One way or another, though, he figured they'd both taken all the risks they could afford for one day.

So he bent down, with his hands locked tight in his pockets, and touched his lips to her. It was meant to be a gentle kiss. A good night kiss. A personal, intimate kiss, a kiss that belonged solely to the two of them—but that still, basically, was safe. They weren't going any further. Not this night.

That was the plan.

It just sure as hell didn't work out that way.

chapter 13

Something snapped inside her. She couldn't explain it. Initially, when Nate bent down to kiss her, his lips coasted down and landed, but that was it. He promptly lifted his head. His hands stayed tucked in his jeans pockets. All his body language said that she didn't need to be concerned; he was gonna be a good boy, gonna go home, no making love this night, not to worry anything deep was coming.

But she saw his eyes. There was already something deep and dangerous there. At least deep and dangerous for her.

Before he completely lifted his head, she swung her arms around his neck and lifted up. Her kiss ended his . . . but started another.

She closed her eyes and sank into the feeling, of kissing him, tasting him, wooing him. He went still for at least five full seconds. Well. Maybe only four.

And then his hands swooshed out of his pockets and swept around her, and quicker than trouble, a risky, fretful, dare of a kiss—hers—turned into a maelstrom.

Her fingers slipped down from his neck and started tugging at his shirt.

He was faster. In a single motion he'd loosened the silk tie of her robe. She wasn't wearing anything beneath it because she'd assumed she'd be alone that night. Actually, she'd just padded into the bedroom after a bath and had plucked a nightgown from the drawer when she'd heard the rap on the door, and naturally grabbed the robe fast.

Not as fast as he had it off her, though.

Cool air flushed over her bare skin, yet the look in his eyes kindled heat in every nerve ending. She couldn't remember ever feeling this naked.

She'd been naked with him before, of course. Almost—in the car, the other night. And more than once, when they were seniors in high school. Her mind rousted the memories, replaying them in Technicolor detail. Being naked together on spring-chilled grass at midnight. Naked together on a scratchy stadium blanket by the river. Naked together in a friend's room, one of a zillion moments they'd stolen together, whenever, however they could.

But this was a different kind of naked entirely.

Now she knew what she could lose.

Now she know how much there was to risk.

She'd left his house, after the birthday party, fearing that history was repeating itself. Nate had always been so wonderful, so capable, so driven to achieve. He'd always been full of courage and fearless about taking on anything.

Not her. She'd always been scared of life. People always seemed to judge her on her looks, as if there were nothing under the surface. Maybe that's when she stopped believing in herself, too.

But his kiss. His touch. The warm male smell of him, the rough-tender texture of his hands, the groan in his throat and the way his body tightened for her . . . he made her come alive. He made her feel powerful as a woman, as a lover. He made her believe she could achieve her dreams, be anything she wanted.

A fierce frustration coiled inside her. It was no good—this always wanting, this always having Nate on her heart, in her heart. There was no place left to run. It was past time she put it all on the line. Found out what she was made of. Found out if she had the substance to fight, for once in her life, for something she wanted just for herself.

And she sure as hell had always, always, always wanted him.

"Peanut," he whispered, coming up for air, a question forming in his voice.

"Shut up, Shadow."

"When I came in . . . I'm almost positive I didn't hear the lock click on the door."

"I don't care." Actually she cared tons. The entire staff at Oz Enterprises barged in on her regularly, day and night. No one worried about interrupting her, because they blithely assumed she was alone. On the other hand, when a woman found courage for the first time in her life, it wasn't as if she could just let the moment go.

An unlocked door was too paltry an excuse.

So was a fire.

She kissed him as if there were a fire, though. As if they might have only this moment. As if she'd waited a lifetime for this moment . . . which, damnation, she *had*.

Shamelessly aggressive, she walked him down the hall, past the mirrored wall of closets, kissing him here, there, everywhere her lips could reach. She caught the shapes and shadows of him in the mirror reflections. His rumpled hair. His whiskery jaw. When she finally pulled the shirt over his head, it fell in the bathroom doorway. The bathroom light was still on; she'd never turned it off after her bath. The room still smelled like fragrant steam and toothpaste. Now, though, the light seemed as blaring bright as daylight until they passed by, hustling toward the darker, gentler shadows of her bedroom. She was tugging him. Backwalking him. Even as she reached for the snap of his jeans.

Selfishly she yanked that snap open.

Greedily she reached up, buried her hands in his thick, dark hair, and pulled him down to her mouth for another long, liquid kiss.

Wantonly she took exactly the kind of kiss she wanted from him—hot and wet and deep—and then brazenly demanded another.

When they reached the edge of her bed in the dark, she pushed, and when he fell back, she pounced like the tigress she was. Well . . . maybe she was more an aspiring tigress than the real thing and her frantic heartbeat knew the truth— but just then, just for that moment in time, she was all those things. Greedy and selfish and wanton. And if she was ever going to achieve the level of wicked, shameful badness she intended, obviously it had to be with Nate.

"Hey," he murmured, but she wasn't about to put up with a bunch of backtalk from him. Not now. He'd always been the one to take charge. The go-getter. The cocky one. The sexy one.

But he wasn't so tough when she pounced on him. He sucked in a guttural groan of surprise— and his body hardened tighter than a spring. He hit the mattress at an angle, missing the pillow, but that made it all the easier to layer herself flat on top of him. She was gonna ravish him and ravish him good—assuming the light stayed off and she didn't lose her nerve, didn't start worrying about failing, didn't start thinking that she was never going to win Nate, not this way or any other, because she couldn't even seem to win herself most days.

Those old fears tried to claim her, tried to suck her under, but she refused to let them. Or maybe Nate conspired to make sure those old fears never had a chance to take hold. Her Nate—Nate of the liquid chocolate eyes, Nate of the molded shoulders and the thick, callused hands—had always had a mouth softer than nectar. His hands slid down her bare spine, not fast, not greedily, but as if he were cherishing every inch of her skin, the slope, the feel, the scent. She hadn't quite managed to get his pants off, just opened, and her abdomen pressed against his torso, feeling the coarse hair on his chest, the heat of his body, the swell of his erection against her pelvis.

And suddenly he got chatty.

"Peanut," he whispered, "this is going to be over in a second and a half if we don't at least try to slow down."

"Tough," she said.

"You don't want to talk?"

"No way."

"Call me crazy, but I was thinking you might like some foreplay. Not because it's fun or anything. But just because I'd like to prove that I'm older than seventeen, can even wait—sometimes—three minutes before exploding."

He never used to start long conversations at inappropriate times. She tugged at him. "Forget foreplay. You want foreplay, you can have it tomorrow. Later. Next week. Next year."

"I see," he said.

"I see," she echoed. Even in the shadows, she saw the damn dance in his eyes. He was having a good time. Her lying full-length against him, both of them hotter than lit dynamite. His voice sounded lazier than a mint julep on a hot summer day—but his body was sure pulsing heat and anticipation. And suddenly his voice turned thick and low.

"So . . . are we actually going for broke this time, Jeanne Claire? Risking it all? Throwing all the stakes in the ring?"

"Oh, yeah," she whispered. She could hear the dare in his voice, but there was only one answer she could give him. Her heart was just like her bedroom, everything tidy, everything put away, everything of value out of sight. Her whole life had been tidy for so long, but right now, her whole heart seemed to be naked in front of him, in full view of his eyes, his mouth, his touch.

And damnation, she'd *tried* tidy. She'd tried being what other people wanted her to be. She'd tried doing all the things she was supposed to—and never once felt the thrill she felt with Nate.

Never once felt herself stretch and strain to be more. To want more.

And all she had to do was say yes to get it all back. The wonder. The hunger, the exhilaration. Faster than light, he'd twisted her beneath him. A pillow zoomed to the floor, then another. Outside, a car horn blared. Lights flashed through the closed curtains. Her phone rang. Her phone was always ringing.

He was kissing her so hard and deep she couldn't breathe, couldn't catch her breath . . . and didn't care. He freed her for a second—but only for the time it took to peel off his pants. Then he came back to her, pulling her arms over her head, igniting her senses with the full weight of their bodies together.

She remembered this. The smoking. The heat that poured off the two of them, the intense concentration, the coming up for breath and only seeing his eyes—looking at her, taking her in, treasuring her—before he dipped back down. His tongue laved her breasts, her ribs, her navel, then traveled downward.

Whatever she remembered didn't come close to this. This wasn't a memory. This wasn't a girl in the throes and ecstasy of her first love. This was Nate, a living, breathing, vulnerable man who'd lived life, who knew what sex was, who knew what risk was—coming to her with all of himself.

Her whole body tightened helplessly for his intimate kiss, knees pressing so hard around him that she heard his throaty chuckle . . . but he didn't let up. By the time the first spasm took her over the crest, he lifted up and came to her. His mouth sealed hers with her own taste. His body sealed hers with his claiming. He fit, as no other man could possibly fit, tight, hot, needed more than she needed breath. They both climbed to the next crest, the next pinnacle, eyes open and fierce on each other now. "I love you, Nate," she said helplessly. "So much, so much . . ."

As if the words sabotaged his last hope of control, she felt his body tense in a wild, hot shudder . . . matched by her own. She heard his exultant laugh, then hers. Who could guess there could be joy this huge? That belonged to him. To her. To them.

He crashed in her arms, both of them breathing louder than freight trains, neither able to talk. Neither trying. She closed her eyes, eventually finding the strength to lift her arms in the darkness. She stroked him, treasured him, loved him long into the night.

No matter what, she thought, she'd always have this. There was no way she could imagine regretting this.

Searing heat blasted Nate in the face when he pushed open the door to the outside delivery area. Temperatures had been brain-fry hot since the first of July and refused to let up. This afternoon was the worst yet.

It had been eight weeks, four days, and several hours since he'd had sex—which Nate considered unbelievably unfair. When you got a lover—when you had the most glorious sex in the universe— you were supposed to get more. If that wasn't in the Lovers' Rule Book, it should be. Maybe making love quadrupled all the emotional risks in a relationship, but at least you got to sleep with your girl while you were working out the tough stuff.

Instead she was mad at him. For no reason. He hadn't done one thing wrong! Things were going perfectly! They hadn't even had an argument, for God's sake! She just kept giving him the feeling that he'd let her down.

And since he wasn't getting any, he spent a lot of time replaying the problematic conversations to figure out how the sam hill she could get such a damn fool idea. Right after making love, she'd called that one time, suggested some kind of imbedded program he could put on his computer system to keep track of exactly which family member inputted figures and when. Nothing wrong with that, but he'd moved the conversation along and suddenly she'd said, "Nate, do you even realize that you're shutting me out?"

When he hadn't been. And another time she'd called and started talking about his brothers, asking who had the unhappiest personal life, how did that unhappiness show, stuff like that, trying to get to what motivated one of them to steal. And when he didn't have any answers, she'd said, real gently, real sadly, "I'm not surprised you're shutting me out again."

There was one other time. He'd called her that time. They were getting together, and she'd suddenly asked him if his mother knew she wasn't a practicing Catholic. No one took the lid off *that* cookie jar unless he was prepared to battle about religion until the next millennium, but when he hadn't answered the way Jeanne seemed to want, she'd gone dead silent again.

This was totally crazy. He hadn't been shutting her out. He wasn't being a control freak. A man didn't pawn off his problems on a woman, for God's sake. Not where he grew up. And now that they were close again—or he sure as hell thought sex meant they were getting *damn* close—he wanted time just with her. Intimate time. Private time. Not time about *problems*. What was odd about that? How the hell was that shutting her out?

It wasn't.

Jeanne just seemed to be thinking like a woman. She was confused.

And the more confused she got, the testier he got. Conceivably he was letting a small amount of his testiness show, because people were starting to run full-speed when he entered a room.

Strangers tiptoed around him. His own daughter had started being nice to him. Even so, Nate could have sworn that nothing could make him crabbier today—until he walked outside and his nostrils picked up a godawful stench.

At least the problem temporarily took his mind off Jeanne Claire.

At the far end of the tarmac, the tow vehicle had already unloaded its aromatic treasure. Daniel and Jason were already outside, standing in the full sun. Daniel had his hands on his hips, a short-sleeve T-shirt sticking to his chest and back. Jason never wilted, but even he'd chucked the tie and cuffed up his sleeves for this weather—and was looking green in the gills from the smell.

But then Nate got a look at the car. "Jesus. How in God's name did this happen to her!?"

"One of those cheerful divorce stories," Daniel said dryly. "Husband caught his wife cheating and filed for divorce—but she got the car in the settlement. No proof that he was the one who made this mess, but apparently the car was the love of his life, and if his ex-wife was going to get it, she was going to be sorry."

A bad day—come to think of it, a bad two months—just kept getting worse. Nate listened to Jason fill in more of the details. "Heather's an old friend I went to school with. We used to do all kinds of photography together." Jason hesitated. "Anyway, she called me because she just didn't have a clue what to do—trash it, save it, what. She's no angel, I'm not taking her side, but hell, she was crying buckets. So I just told her, get it towed in here and we'd help her with advice."

Daniel added, "And I backed him up on that—but neither of us knew the car was going to be in this kind of incredible shape until it got here. Which is when we paged you. Damned if I know what to do."

Nate wished he had a clothespin for his nose, but he still circled the car slowly. She was an egg yolk yellow Lamborghini Miura–400. A '65, he guessed, although it wasn't a model he was well familiar with. Low and sleek, busty, no hips. The naked chassis was so breathtaking she could bring a monk to orgasm—at least if the monk was into cars. There'd been tons of things wrong with this model—no a.c., no radio, noisy. But for all its problems, she was a glorious one-of-a-kind star.

Or she had been. Man. The glossy yellow paint had been key-scratched. Tires slashed, glue poured on the windshield. The hot, fragrant perfume attracting flies appeared to be horse manure—which had been dumped inside, filling the elegant leather interior.

"Is the manure the worst?"

"How could there possibly be anything worse?" Daniel said dryly.

"I mean . . . do we know if he dumped anything

else inside—chemicals, acid, anything else besides the manure?"

"They bred and trained racehorses, so I suspect the buckets of shit were meant as a tactful symbolic message for his ex-wife. But I haven't put my hand in there to dig any deeper if that's what you're asking," Daniel said wryly.

Jason started to answer the question, too, but both his older brothers immediately dismissed him. "We know you didn't touch anything, Jase."

Nate kept circling the car. "Does this Heather have insurance?"

"She has money."

"Enough to throw away, no matter what this costs to fix? Because there won't be any way to do this cheaply."

"No limit at all," Jason answered. "The car's the only lover she wants. That's how she puts it. She's through with men."

Nate took care not to ask too many questions. Jeanne had been counseling him not to pry, not to leap in to take charge for his brothers—which was damn near impossible, but he was trying. "All right, well, we can take on the project, but you'll both have to vote yes, because this won't be fun. Thank God the guy was going for maximum humiliation instead of maximum damage. But I don't think it's right to ask one of the employees to take on this manure." Silence from both brothers. "Jason, if you want us to help out this friend of yours—"

"You're saying I have to help clean this up?"

Nate lifted his head. "I'm saying, if we all agree to take on this work, that we all better be willing to pitch in. Either that or be willing to fork over the dollars to hire someone to do this. I don't think it's fair to expect any of the mechanics to do this. It's pretty damn awful work, especially in this heat."

Jason's throat turned red as a brick. "God, I hate this business. And I don't care if you take it on. I just told Heather she could tow it in here, that I'd get your advice. That's all I committed us to."

Nate said, "Fine. But the way I see it, it's your friend, so the decision's on you." That was the other thing Jeanne kept counseling him to do. Quit making decisions for everybody, even when he knew what was best. "There's no question that we can do the job. But I'm not about to force work like this on either of you. So you're either willing or you're not."

Jason said, "The thing is, her ex-husband was a real creep. That's why I wanted to help her to begin with."

Daniel growled, "Which means, yeah, you want us to do it. But you don't want to get your lily white hands dirty yourself."

"I'm not a mechanic. And I never wanted in this business either. You two are the ones who like this work, not me. I just—"

The argument was escalating when Martha's voice boomed on the outside speaker, "Mr. Donneli! Guest in the front lobby!"

The message was in code. Martha used the Mr. tag when she wanted specifically him, and *guest* was another spy code word. It meant that it wasn't a telemarketer or a salesman, but someone he actually needed to handle himself. Which meant that he was saved from a death-by-brothers fist-fight in the sun—at least for the next few minutes.

"Jason, this is really up to you. I don't mind taking on a godforsaken job if it's for someone who matters to you. But you have to be willing to do the work with us." Daniel opened his mouth to offer another two cents, but Nate cut them both short. "Look, let's all just get out of the heat. Cool off. And right now we need this baby pushed in the shade and run under a hose before we can even start to work with her."

"Yeah, well, we both know Jason'll volunteer to do that," Daniel said, which started the two brothers sparring all over again.

Nate hiked inside, thinking that he kept trying to do what Jeanne said—about not always being bossy and domineering, about including the brothers in choices and decisions. But it didn't seem to be doing any good. They both seemed madder at him than ever. Ironically, though, there hadn't been any further incidents of stealing in the last month—but Nate couldn't guess if that was because some circumstance had changed for the thief, or because the thief realized Nate was on to him. Or for the altogether simpler reason that the whole family was just so damn busy that no one had time for stealing or any other kind of shenanigans.

At that precise moment, though, he had to shelve thinking about that problem.

When he strode inside, he sucked in the first welcome blast of air-conditioning—at the same time he spotted the man across the lobby. Nate couldn't see his face until he turned around, but the guy was medium height, with thinning brown hair, dressed in a short-sleeve shirt and saggy slacks. And then he turned.

Right away Nate realized he knew him, but couldn't seem to pin down a name for love or money.

"Arnold Grafton," the man obliged. "You know. From high school. Don't worry about it. Nobody ever recognizes me."

"Of course I did. Right away," Nate lied. "I was just sun blinded for a second, coming in from the outside where it's so bright . . ." He glanced at Martha, who was pelting down the hall toward her office, the traitor. "Somehow I don't think you're here because you're in the market for an antique car . . . ?"

"Actually, no. But I was afraid if I called you first, you might not be willing to see me. It's not as if we were friends years ago. But I just want a few minutes of your time, to talk about the high school reunion."

Oh, hell. What more could go wrong today?

"I promise I won't take more than a few minutes," Arnold repeated.

"Okay. Come on back to my office." He needed another interruption like he needed a hole in the head. "I really can't talk for long." He paused by Martha's office, where she was already installed behind her desk. "Any messages?"

"No, she didn't call."

Martha might be brilliant and unshakably efficient, but the damn woman was a smart-ass.

He motioned Arnold into his office, but his mind had already strayed to Jeanne Claire. Again.

It wasn't as if everything had been wrong between them over the last couple of months. They talked on the phone all the time. They'd stolen some lunches together. They'd done a barbecue with Caitlin.

It was just that whenever they got that pinch closer—seriously closer—Jeanne seemed to pull back. He'd flunked some test he didn't even know he was taking. It wasn't that she expressed anger at him, so much as . . . disappointment.

He couldn't get her back in his life this far, this deep, just to lose her again.

Only, hell, when you made love with a woman and she suddenly became elusive, a guy had to wonder if he'd flunked as a lover. Or if making love had scared the hell out of her.

Either way, he couldn't fix a problem he couldn't even identify. And he knew that summer was her frantically busy season—but damnation, he could have met with the president easier than catching a full two hours alone with Jeanne.

Damn it, was she still seeing that guy? The one who was in the picture before him?

"You got quite a place here," Arnold said.

"Thanks."

"Is that your daughter?" Arnold had wandered over to the wall of pictures of Caitlin.

"Sure is. Caitlin's almost fourteen now. I've been looking into the price of convents—at least until she's thirty. You have any kids?"

"One son. Howie's eight. Best thing that ever happened to me. But being a single parent can be a nightmare."

"You can say that again. Coke, coffee, what's your poison?"

"Actually, an alcoholic drink would be my preference. Except that I don't drink much. You have any ice tea? Like with lemon?"

God save him from the fussbudgets in life. On the other hand, he had few opportunities to get revenge on Martha, so he took advantage by buzzing her. "Martha? If there's a prayer you can come up with ice tea with lemon, could you bring us some? Otherwise, some ice water."

Finally Arnold got around to sitting down and stating his business. "This is the thing, Nate. I want you to be the keynote speaker at the high school reunion. Jeanne Claire said she asked you a couple months ago, and you turned it down."

"I did," Nate confirmed, suddenly feeling itchy.

"Well, it's not like you're under any obligation. But when Jeanne said you didn't want to do it, I searched high and low for someone else. The problem is that there's no one else who even comes close to you, and we're starting to run out of time. The reunion's just around the corner now. And it's not that others haven't made it, but you were a symbol in the class. The guy who started out poor and achieved at every level. The Guy Most Likely to Succeed, hands down. And look at you, this great business you've built up. I mean, why wouldn't you be willing—?"

"Look, Arnold," he started to say, but just as in high school, Arnold was bumbling on.

"You don't have to give a big long talk. A few minutes would do it. Jeanne and Tamara and I settled on a theme. New Dreams. You know how we all had dreams in high school? Only now another fifteen years have passed. We're older, more experienced, more mature. So it's a good time to relook at our lives. The dreams we make now, we have a far better chance of achieving, you know?"

The phone rang, thankfully interrupting this thrilling conversation. When he had a customer in the office, he always used to let Martha answer—but that was B.J. Before Jeanne. Now he grabbed the receiver, just in case it was she.

It took only a barked response to get rid of the telemarketer.

Then he took charge of the conversation. "Arnold, I think you should be the speaker."

Arnold rolled his eyes. "Oh, yeah. That's as likely as a nun doing a striptease."

Nate had to grin. "Come on. I keep hearing you've rich as Croesus, built a multimillion-dollar business from scratch. Why not you?"

"Nate. No one is going to listen to me. I was the class nerd," Arnold reminded him. "They'll come to hear you. They'll listen to anything you tell them. I could talk about where to find a pot of gold—a real pot of gold—and they'd sleep through it. I can't even get Tamara to take me seriously."

"Tamara?"

Arnold shook his head. "Tamara Whitley. You remember her, don't you? Jeanne's good friend? I've been seeing her . . . at least to some extent. I know this sounds nuts, but I think she's afraid of my kid. Howie's nuts for her. But she can't seem to see it."

Nate wanted to hold his head in his hands. It was the middle of a business day. He had an over-flowing workload, two out of three brothers fighting like pit bulls, a daughter free for the summer who kept sneaking into the shop. He had a woman in his life after all these years—the only woman he'd wanted in his life after all these years—who he was petrified he was going to lose.

And Arnold Grafton had shown up like a ghost from the past and for some God unknown reason was telling him about his love life. He didn't know anything about Arnold's love life. Didn't want to know anything. Didn't do male-bonding conversations like this. Yet somehow he heard himself saying, "My daughter can be a real pistol if she thinks I'm interested in someone, too."

"Howie—he's not a pistol. He's crazy about Tamara. And the more I get the two together, the happier they seem . . . but it doesn't seem to help *me*. Not that I'd think she could be seriously interested in me, mind you. But we seemed to be getting closer. And then suddenly, it's like there's this locked door, and I don't know why she locked it."

Phones rang. A noisy argument buzzed past the door. Five o'clock came and went. Office lights started shutting down. Martha announced that she was going home, and that he was going home, too—even though by then, they were on the second pitcher of ice tea.

There was no possibility in the universe that Arnold's love life and his own could ever have anything in common. Nate wasn't a kisser-and-teller, besides. But damned if it wasn't impossibly ironic that both of them were single dads with a kid who was hugely affected by a new woman in their lives. That the kids seemed to be doing fine, but that the new women were terrified of both of them. That they seemed to be hanging out there, risking life, limb, and happiness like lovesick bulls, and unlike when they were eighteen, they didn't have a clue what to do.

"I don't know what happened," Nate grumped. "I knew everything when I was eighteen. I was cocksure about what mattered, what I believed in, what was right and wrong. Now I've got fifteen more years of life on me, and I seem to know absolutely nothing."

"Join the club," Arnold said morosely. "I was the dorky geek of the class. Now I've made several million. Have a golf course outside my back door. Do I know how to talk to a woman any more than I ever did? No. I'm no closer to Tam than I ever was."

Nate *did* know a few things that Arnold didn't. "You have no way to get to first base if you don't swing a bat, Arnie."

Arnold sighed. "I don't want to risk losing the friendship I've finally got with her."

"I understand that. But how can you be sure what she wants if you don't even ask her?"

Arnold fell silent, then looked at him. "Doesn't that apply to you, too?"

"Huh?"

Arnold said patiently, "Are you going after Jeanne, no holds barred? Or are you just advising me to, when you're too scared to take the real risks yourself?"

"That is unbelievably unfair," Nate announced. Who would have thought the untucked Arnold, the dork with no self-esteem who couldn't talk without spitting, would ever turn out so damn aggressive?

And it really sucked that he was right.

Chapter 14

Alien sounds intruded on Jeanne's sleep. A slam.
A thump. Swearing. The overhead light flashed
on in her bedroom, followed by Tamara's voice,
"Man, are you a mess!"

Outside, it was obviously daylight, but with the
blinds and curtains drawn, the bedroom had been
a nice, comforting, gloomy dark. The artificial
light wasn't really the squawk of color so much as
Tamara, dressed for summer in neon green shorts
and tank, and sandals with rhinestone bells that
matched her earrings.

"I made Martha let me in, the old curmudgeon.
You've got the whole place in an uproar. You're
never sick. I'm supposed to talk you into seeing a
doctor."

"No doctor," Jeanne said.

"Yeah, that's what they claimed at the front desk. That you threatened bodily harm to anyone who brought up doctors to you ever again—and I can relate. What do doctors ever do to a woman but put us in stirrups? I brought you chicken soup." Tamara raised the can of Campbell's for inspection. "Which I'm going to make right now."

"Not hungry."

"Yes, you are. Because either you eat, or I'm calling a doc." Tamara shifted her hands, balancing imaginary scales. "Think, which is worse, stirrups or chicken soup. See? It's easy for all of us to make the right decision. We just have to be threatened with the right consequences. Now, you just sit tight and I'll heat up the soup."

Jeanne pushed herself up, then regretted it. Her head hurt. Her fingernails hurt. Her pores hurt. Come to think of it, everything hurt. The fever didn't seem to be as high as last night, but that was like comparing a foot to twelve inches. Her throat felt like a sucked-dry lemon. Her hair . . . her hair, her body, her clothes, her apartment, hadn't been put away or maintained in a day now. Or two? Or three?

Tamara returned to the bedroom moments later, bearing a tray. "Ice water. Soup. Toast. I don't cook this fancy for myself, so you'd better appreciate it."

"I do."

"Now what the hell's going on? You've run yourself right to the ground. When did you turn into such a complete idiot?—and don't even *try* answering questions until you've had at least two spoonfuls of soup."

Holding her head, spooning in the semi-warmed canned soup, Jeanne told her the abridged version—which meant that she left out Nate, because that was too upsetting to talk about. "I've been trying to make some serious, big changes in my life. I mean, I've been repeating certain mistakes for a long time. I finally really saw that. And now I'm getting tougher."

"I can see that," Tamara said dryly. "You look so tough right now a puff of wind could knock you down."

Jeanne sloughed off that comment. A bout of flu didn't change what mattered. She was determined to go after something she needed in her life—which meant leaving Oz. Pursuing something that actually mattered, that she actually wanted to do for a career. Only that meant needing to leave Oz in good shape so she *could* leave.

"Spring and summer's the busiest season here, so I'm always running at crash speed for these weeks." But she'd been cooking. Really bringing in the business. Only then she'd discovered that her dad had taken on several more events below cost. She wouldn't have realized how close they were to a financial crisis until the accountant had cornered her. Absolutely the only way to keep Oz functioning was to fill the conference center to maximum capacity every possible date they could.

"And that's fine," Tamara said impatiently. "Only then why the hell didn't you hire more staff?"

"Because we need every dime. And I was coping okay." At least she'd been okay until three days ago, when the plague had hit.

"Keep sipping that soup," Tamara ordered.

"I am. I am." This stupid virus was just so frustrating. She'd broken date after date with Nate. Cut short call after call. She'd been upset with him, but it had to look to Nate as if she were running away.

The exact opposite was true. Finding him again—loving him—had changed her. Opened her heart to all the risks, all the possibilities. She'd forgotten what it felt like, to believe she had a right to admit her own needs, a right to go after what she wanted and needed in her life. But suddenly the risks seemed inviting instead of just frightening. She wanted to change her job, wanted to change her relationship with her father, wanted to be the woman she'd once dreamed of becoming. And most of all, she wanted love—not any love, not any man, but the kind of love and relationship her heart sensed she could have with Nate.

Unfortunately, making love hadn't eased their differences or made them easier to resolve. Every time a serious issue had come up, Nate had pulled a macho door shut on her. Originally he'd asked for help with this thief, but when she'd probed too deep, he'd backed away from talking about it. When she'd made suggestions, he'd changed the subject. After he'd had a fight with Caitlin, she'd invited a discussion about that, too, but he'd cut her off.

None of the issues had been worth going to war. They were just symbols of things important to both of them. It had taken Jeanne too long to realize that men tended to take care of her, to dismiss her, to not take her seriously. That was a two-way street—since she'd allowed guys to do that for her for years now. But Nate, more than anyone who'd ever been in her life, was a virile, high-powered steamroller personality.

She loved him. But if he was going to shut her out of the serious decisions and problems in his life, this was never going to work. And he had to know—and see—that she was capable of standing up, different from the girl who hadn't been strong enough for him to count on last time.

"You're woolgathering again," Tamara complained. She curled up cross-legged on the bed, supervising every spoonful of soup Jeanne took in. "I didn't just come over to feed you a gourmet get-well meal. I wanted to catch you up on some reunion news."

"I thought almost everything was done," Jeanne started guiltily.

"It is, Ms. Workaholic, thanks to all the piles of work you put in already. But Arnold and I have filled in the blanks in the meantime, so you can stop worrying. Keep eating. And let's get your mind off your troubles. In fact, how about if we talk about sex?"

"Not now."

"I'm not asking about now. I'm thinking about the past. Partly because it's been a month of Sundays since I've had sex and I'm worried about it."

"My God." Jeanne plunked down her spoon. "Are you talking about Arnold? You two have gotten that tight? Arnold and you? Sex?"

"Of course we haven't gotten that tight. He has a kid, I told you. Nobody's going to look at me—who knows my history with pills—and think seriously about my being a mother for his only son. But for one reason or another, I keep mulling the idea of . . . oh. Wait."

After that totally leading statement, Tamara lifted a hand, took off down the hall, and returned moments later with a pint of crème de menthe ice cream and a spoon. One spoon.

"Hey. I get canned soup and you get fancy ice cream?"

"You're sick. I'm not. The point is . . . every woman remembers her first time, right?"

Immediately Jeanne felt a kick in the heart from the memories. "Yes."

Tamara waved the spoon. "Well, not me. I was drunk and high. Oh, I remember the guy—Morrison Fielding, graduated the class ahead of us, hair like a Bristol pad, family who owned that airplane thing?" When Jeanne looked confused, Tam gestured. "It doesn't matter."

"Of course it matters!"

"The point I'm trying to make is that all I remember is . . . waking up later, alone, with a headache the size of an orchestra. The gunk all over the car, all over me. I don't remember him putting it in, what it felt like, whether I wanted him or anything else. It was just something to do when I was high. I didn't care."

"Oh, Tam." Sick or not sick, Jeanne ached for her old friend. "I wish I could give you those years back. For darn sure, the first time wasn't even close to the best. I remember it hurting. But I also remember it being higher than the sun and the moon." Because it was Nate, of course—and because none of her memories of that first time was about body parts fitting together. She remembered the look on his face, when he'd wanted her so badly. The look afterward, when he couldn't talk, just kept stroking her hair, treasuring her with kisses.

"Yeah, well, I was an idiot. I can't take that time in my life back. So my theory is, I've still got the sun and the moon coming to me. The next time I have sex won't be my first—or my dozenth. But sooner I later I want to go for that, you know? The real thing. The sun-and-the-moon thing. Only obviously that can't work with Arnold."

"Wait a minute. How did Arnold get back in this conversation? I thought you said he was positively not in the serious picture?"

"He isn't. I told you. But . . . he does keep asking me out. We keep doing family things with his son—like baseball. And swimming. And croquet. Do you know what croquet is?"

"Um—I think it's that outside game people used to play, like from Victorian times? With a ball and a mallet and little wire thingies?"

"You got it. So—it should go without saying that anything athletic isn't my forte. But Howie got reading about it, so he got interested. One afternoon we spend a glorious three hours skydiving, and the next I'm stuck playing croquet with the two of them. It was so ghastly it made my heart hurt."

Looking at her friend's eyes made Jeanne's heart hurt. Obviously, Tam had it bad. "Quit digressing down side roads. Get back to the point. You're thinking about having sex with Arnold?"

"Sort of. Not sun-and-the-moon sex. But different sex. The kind of sex I'd remember. That's what I was thinking."

"You're killing me, Tam. You just said a minute ago that you two weren't going to get serious—"

"And that's exactly why I'm thinking we should hit the sheets. So he won't be thinking about anything too permanent or steady."

"I see. If you have sex, he'll stop taking you seriously?"

"That's how it worked with every other guy I ever slept with." Tamara peered over the bowl. "I'll be damned. You finished it. See what talking about sex can do for your appetite?"

Jeanne said firmly, "We can keep this light, Tam. But I wish you'd quit it. Making fun of yourself. Thinking you can't have anyone. So you had a drug problem. That doesn't make you a leper."

Tamara leaped off the bed. "That's it. If you're going to start being nice, I'm going to start pushing medicine on you. Think laxatives. Think Vicks VapoRub. Think grape cough syrup."

"Think gag."

"All right, all right. I'll let you go back to bed. But before I go, I have to tell you the big reunion news—Arnold actually got Nate to be our lead speaker."

"Nate *agreed?*"

"Yup. Not willingly, but frankly, he's just like you—pull the we-need-you card and he can't say no. I'll call you tomorrow and give you the details—if you report that you've had two more bowls of soup, at *least*. Hear me?"

Jeanne was smiling when Tamara left . . . feeling both humor and love for her oldest friend. It was beyond ironic that both of them had found men from high school that they'd never imagined seeing again. Never imagined loving.

At least, she'd never imagined having another chance to love Nate.

Her eyes closed on a winsome, willful yearning to see him. Not precisely now—when she looked like hell and felt like death warmed over. But she was finally on the mend. And the impossible stress of the last two months was finally loosening up. And she *needed* to see him, needed to work—with him—on making their twosome work.

There was a reason they hadn't made it the first time. It wasn't because his father died. It was because they couldn't turn to each other when they needed help. They'd had a wonderful puppy love, but not the gut-strong love it took to make a relationship thrive long-term. It wasn't Nate's fault—or hers—that they hadn't been able to count on each other years ago. They'd simply been young.

But now it was fish-or-cut-bait time.

Jeanne had no interest in kicking his butt—but in kicking her own. And that meant she needed to be stronger—not just for him, but for herself. She wasn't the kind of woman who'd politely disappear from his life again.

Big talk for a girl who can barely get out of bed, duckie. Well, it *was* big talk, but she pushed back the covers, thinking a hot shower was the next step in the recovery route. She'd just stood up when the phone rang. Quickly, she grabbed the receiver.

"Honey, can you make dinner tonight?"

Somehow her dad's voice made her heart sink. "Honestly, no, I just can't."

"Just for an hour. I promise. No longer than that. I just want you to hear the deal the Wilburns want us to do—"

"*Dad.* Please, please, don't tell me you've committed to any more events without asking me."

"Of course I didn't, sweetheart. But it would help if you could come to dinner—"

"I just had a bowl of soup. It's the first food I kept down in two days."

Silence. "Princess, I had no idea you were that sick. You should have told me. I'll call a doctor—"

"No. No! Honestly, I'm on the get-well track now; I'm just afraid of pushing it quite yet." Abruptly, she switched subjects. "Dad, what's wrong? Something is. I can hear the stress in your voice."

"Nothing, sweetheart. I just . . . well, I called Donald yesterday. And I have to admit, that was one of the reasons I wanted to talk to you over dinner tonight—"

Donald. He'd left her alone for weeks now. She assumed that he'd finally given up, that he'd finally heard her. Or so she sure hoped. "Exactly why did you call him?" she asked carefully.

"Jeannie . . . I don't think push is going to come to shove, but a few of my stock options didn't come through. You know what the market is. And on the very long chance that we can't make our next loan payments, Donald may be the one person willing to lend us enough to keep us afloat until things turn around. I don't want you thinking about this if you're sick," her dad said hastily. "I just needed you to know that call had taken place. I don't like keeping secrets from you. And if you happened to talk with Donald, I don't want a surprise conversation sprung on you."

"Okay."

"You don't need to do anything about it. I mean that. But something could come up if you talked with him. I wanted you to know what happened ahead of time."

"Okay."

He hung up a few moments later, leaving Jeanne staring at the ceiling. Her dad hadn't asked her to prostitute herself with Donald. He hadn't— and he wouldn't. But she'd have to be stupid not to realize what it all added up to. Her dad was looking for someone to save him from their current financial crisis. He saw an answer in her being nice to Donald. An even better answer if she married Donald.

Jeanne swallowed, hard and fast. Almost five years ago, she'd known exactly what loyalty meant to her. When her dad needed her, she'd jumped to help him. She loved him. As far as she was concerned, that's what family did for each other, cut-and-dried.

At this point, though, she'd been bailing her dad out of financial trouble for almost five years— and no matter what she did, it seemed he could dig himself a bigger hole.

Impatiently she scooped up fresh clothes, padded into the bathroom, and turned on the water as hot as she could stand it. She still loved her dad as much as ever. But did love and loyalty really mean that she owed him the rest of her life? No matter what the sacrifice was to her own needs or her own life?

She stepped under the hot, pulsing spray, thinking it was so ironic that she and Nate were essentially going through some of the same things. Nate was no one's pushover, the way she'd been. But loyalty had led him down roads far, far different from where he'd once wanted to travel.

If both of them didn't take some new risks, demand more from each other, the chance to be together could disappear forever.

She felt as if she were standing on the very tip of an emotional cliff in a high wind. So afraid of losing him. So aware that she could.

That damn Arnold, Tamara fumed. He'd gone off to take a phone call ages ago, leaving her alone with Howie. The eight-year-old was supposed to go to a friend's house for a birthday party—his first sleepover. Only he didn't want to go.

At the moment, he was sitting in the back of his closet—a measure of exactly how much he didn't want to go to the kid's party. And that's when Arnold had deserted her to take the phone. She supposed a multimillionaire did occasionally have to take a business call, but for Pete's sake, he'd acted as if she could just take over and handle the situation.

She didn't have a clue. Not even one.

"You don't like this guy in your class?" She didn't specifically mind lying on the carpet in the doorway to the kid's bedroom closet. It wasn't as if her jeans and red top were going to be ruined or anything. It was just that she had no idea how to fix an eight-year-old's crisis like this.

"Sure, I like him. He's nice. He loaned me his book on snakes and all."

"So . . . why don't you want to go?"

"Because it's stupid."

"Ah."

"I'm happy here. I can read. And play with my

computer. And talk with you and Dad. And have brown sugar toast right before bed. I mean, what's the point?"

"Well, I think the point is that you could be with all the other kids, right?"

"Tam," Howie said, in his old-man voice, the one he used when he was doing his best to show patience with grown-ups. "It's Dad who always wants me to be around other kids. It's because he was a nerd in school. He always felt bad the kids didn't like him. But, see, I'm a nerd and I'm okay with it. Kids like me okay. I have friends. But I just don't like parties and stuff like that, so why do I have to go?"

"Beats me," Tamara muttered, but she didn't say it too loud, because she didn't want to contradict how Arnold wanted to parent his kid. On the other hand, at the rate they were going, she and Howie were going to spend the rest of the night in his closet. "Look, let's wait for your dad to come back to talk about this. But if you come out and sit on the bed, I'll sing a song for you."

"What kind of song?"

"Rock and roll." Desperate women did desperate things. She didn't do music anymore, much less her own, but she didn't want to look like a woman who was clueless around kids when Arnold came back . . . and that's how it was going to look for sure if he found them both still curled up in the kid's closet. Like she couldn't cope. Even with an eight-year-old. More to the point, with the specific eight-year-old who was Arnold's sun and joy.

So she was stuck, that was all. She started in, snapping fingers, moving to the beat, getting into the first bars of "Bucking the Tide."

Almost immediately Arnold scrambled out of the closet. "Hey, I know that song. Dad has the tape."

"Well, good. Then you can sing along with me."

Sing? The kid had a voice like a frog with laryngitis, but wow, for an eight-year-old, could he move. That little butt could bump and grind with the best of them. They kicked up the volume, rocking around the room, climbing on his bed, off his bed, onto the balcony, through his bathroom and back. The big scowl disappeared. The droopy shoulders straightened up.

She'd run through it three times before she finally had to stop for breath. "See, Howie? That's why you want to go to a party with your friends. Yeah, you won't get to be on the computer for a while. But music is something good, you know? It's fun. To dance, to move, to laugh. And it's okay to do that stuff alone, but it's even better with other people."

"I'd rather stay home and sing with you. I love you, Tamara," Howie said. "Can't we sing it one more time?"

And that's when she saw Arnold in the doorway. Damn the man. Double damn the man. She'd been killing herself, trying to make him proud of her for making his son happy, and here he'd been standing there how long?

And then everything went to hell. Howie, the traitor, decided he wanted to go to his friend's party. And then somebody's mother came to pick him up. And then the shrimp not only gave Arnold a good night kiss, but her, too, and then he was gone, chasing out to the car . . . leaving her completely alone with his father.

"Did you hear him? Saying he loved you?" Arnold asked.

"He didn't mean it. It was just something that came out of his mouth because he was having fun singing."

"That's not how it works for Howie. Or for me. 'I love you' doesn't slip out of either of us very easily."

"He was just trying to be nice," Tamara insisted.

"Uh huh." He led her back inside, where he promptly mixed them a fancy drink of lime juice and papaya. His living room overlooked this long, sloped golf-course type of lawn. A diamond-shaped swimming pool gleamed in the summer twilight. Because she'd grown up with money, affluence usually worried rather than impressed her. But she couldn't help feeling drawn to the place, because it was beautiful, quiet, peaceful . . . or it would be, if Arnold weren't right next to her.

"Why don't you play your music anymore?" he asked, as if just dying to get into another tricky subject and completely destroy her peaceful evening.

"I don't know. It just reminds me of everything I did wrong, that's all."

"That was all a long time ago. And listening to you and Howie . . . both of you were just having such a good time." Arnold added, " 'Bucking the Tide' . . . that song is so perfect. It's you. That's who you are. Who I'd like to think my son could be. Someone who'd buck the tide and have the character and courage to go their own way."

"Arn—you've got me completely wrong. I tried to tell you before. I don't have any character. If I had character I'd never have gotten into drugs."

"You figure that how? Rich, poor, old, young, smart, stupid—people get into drugs. It's not about character. It's about a life problem. And you licked it."

"I was lucky."

"You had courage," he corrected her. And then he'd just given her that ghastly papaya drink when he suddenly plucked it out of her hand. Arnold wasn't the kind of guy who could pull off a sophisticated, suave, seductive move like plucking a drink out of a girl's hand. A little juice splashed on his marble tiles. He didn't seem to notice or care.

"Arnold, we need to get some things straight," she said firmly.

"You're damn right we do."

Faster than lightning, she said, "I think we should have sex."

Cool as Clark Gable in his prime, Arnold set down both glasses of papaya juice. Arnold was not cool. Arnold did not do cool. The whole situation was starting to rattle her.

"That's what you've wanted for quite a while, isn't it? Sex?"

"Yup," he said.

"Well, then. Fine." The kid was gone. The house was empty. The curtains were open, but there were no neighbors to see them. She tugged off her cherry red T-shirt, but he didn't even look. She had on her orange and green peekaboo bra. Not even a glance. He just met her eyes square.

"I understand that you don't want a career in music anymore—but not why you've given up something you love so much. I mean, why don't you play for fun? The way you were doing with Howie?"

She felt a burst of hurt. Not a big burst, but definitely a nasty little one. She had damn fine breasts, if she said so herself. Not too big, not too small. Just plain old really nice breasts. Her best feature. Every man she'd ever known had said so—and for years there'd been considerable men who'd had the opportunity to know. And Arnold, for Pete's sake, had lusted after her for all these years. She knew he had. So why wasn't he looking? Or lunging?

"Because," she said.

"Because why."

Hell, she'd had the because-why conversation with his son a hundred times now. "Because when I play 'Bucking the Tide,' it all comes back. The stupid dream I wanted so much. Remembering how it was. The glory. The song that made the charts, that put me on the talk shows, that . . ." She took a breath. "The success that made it so easy to buy any drug I ever wanted. And by that time, I wanted most of them."

Arnold nodded impatiently, as if this were all old news. "That was then. This was now. Why don't you play your music now?"

She clicked the tab on her jeans . . . revealing her navel. "Because," she said.

"Because why?"

Geezle beezle, he was going to drive her right over the edge. "Because, damn it, unlike everybody else, I actually got the dream I wanted so much. I wanted to be a rock star so bad I couldn't stand it when we were in high school. Only then I got it all. And I woke up one morning, in a guy's bed I didn't know, in a house I didn't know, and I felt so sick about myself that I wasn't sure I wanted to live. At all. Ever. Is that what you wanted to hear?" she demanded, furious he'd pulled it out of her . . . and positive that he'd look disgusted when she confessed about the guy.

"Yeah, I wanted you to tell me what you really felt. But you still haven't answered the question. Are you afraid you'll go back to the drugs?"

She hesitated, then said, "Sometimes. Anyone who's had a drug problem would have to be stupid not to be afraid. But most days I'm pretty sure I'd never go back, because I remember it all too damn well. Not just the drugs, but how I hated me. Hated my life. Those memories are a pretty powerful deterrent."

"So," Arnold said. "What's the deal then? If you're not that afraid of drugs anymore, what is it . . . that you're afraid of dreaming anything else? Of wanting anything else like you did the music?"

Since when had Arnold Grafton gotten so perceptive? She didn't think that; she'd never thought that—until he said it. And knew in a blink that it was the truth, the whole truth. It had been fifteen years since she'd admitted wanting anything in her life. Other people, *normal* people, were afraid of not getting their dreams.

She was afraid of getting something she dreamed of and screwing it up again.

Because she could. Screw it up. And she knew it.

Arnold ambled closer to her, by the balcony doors, overlooking all that gorgeous velvet lawn.

She looked out and said, "It's really warm enough for a swim."

He said, "I think you love my son."

Her head whirled around. "Yeah, so? He's a great kid. What's not to love?"

He said, "I think you love me, too."

She said nothing, couldn't.

He said, "I think we should get married. Make some rugrats. A houseful of little nerds who can really sing and wear crazy clothes and are happy."

"Arnold, this is crazy to even talk this way. I'm not going to mess up your life."

He said, "Oh, yes, you are." And then he kissed her. It was a Gable kiss. A Cary Grant/Clark Gable/Humphrey Bogart kiss. His elbow kind of jabbed her near the ear, but that didn't take away from the power of it, the romance of it, the sweeping emotion of it.

It was terrifying to think that Arnold Grafton could be in love with her. That he could know about the drugs, and how she'd lived, and what a screw-up she was, and how afraid she was.

And yet he could still kiss her that way.

She kissed him back, because she was too shook up to think straight. And once she kissed him back—really kissed him, because she was stupid and couldn't think—suddenly they were really bumping elbows and shins in their tussle and hustle to get clothes off. Night fell in violets and thick, sweet blues. Shadows huddled in the doorway. Crickets started up outside, singing their mating calls.

She hadn't made love in ages. Actually, as she discovered sometime later, she'd never made love before.

Later, when they both lay panting like worn-out hounds, sweaty and hot and too exhausted to get up and get pillows—much less have the intelligence to move to a room with beds, he said. "I get it. That you're afraid of the old songs. But I want you to have your music back. And I think we could make new songs, don't you?"

"Arnold, you idiot. If you don't quit pushing me, I'm going to marry you. And then what'll the neighbors say? That you married a has-been rock star instead of a woman who was suitable to be a good mom for your son?"

"Tamara, you idiot. You're so stupid you don't even realize what I've got." He leaned over and kissed her nose—so hard he almost broke it. "But I do. You're mine. We don't have to do dreams anymore. We've got each other."

chapter 15

"Did you have to go to the extent of kidnapping me, Nate?"

"I didn't *have* to. I wanted to," he clarified.

"Well, I think it's only right that the kidnapper should tell the kidnappee where he's taking her."

He grinned. "Hey, I only wish it was Tahiti. But since neither of us could steal more than an hour, the best I could pull off was a surprise getaway."

And none too soon, he thought. She was curled up on the seat next to him, chuckling—and she'd seemed delighted when he'd shown up at Oz Enterprises with a pair of Toys "R" Us handcuffs.

There was no explaining why he'd panicked that morning. He'd called to set up a dinner with her; she couldn't go, and suddenly adrenaline was galloping up and down his veins. He *knew* she'd been swamped. He understood about frantic work seasons. But he also knew they'd had some tense and unsettled conversations that had yet to be resolved. Something in his head—and heart—warned him that the distance between them had just plain gone too far.

"You're being awfully mysterious, Donneli," she complained. She was still twirling the toy handcuffs around a finger—as if she were having a great time and nothing was wrong.

But something was.

She kept smiling and acting totally glad to see him, but then he'd catch her tugging on an earring. She'd joke with him, but then she'd touch her stomach, not as if she were ill, but as if she were struggling with nerves. She looked damn adorable in a red and white summer dress, all perky and crisp, but underneath that perfect makeup, her face was pale and her eyes were strained.

And Nate kept thinking it was a damn good thing he hadn't waited a second longer than this. He'd believed it was important that she see him as understanding—not the kind of guy who'd whine about her busy work schedule or demand that he come before her responsibilities. But now that struck him as horse fodder. He needed time with her. A lifetime. Assuming her feelings for him hadn't disappeared in smoke because they'd been separated so damn long.

It was hardly a good afternoon for a kidnapping. The August day was sweltering hot; smells hung in the air like sticky syrup. He'd wanted to steal off in one of the old, beautiful Rolls, but this just wasn't a day when you could drive anywhere without air-conditioning. So he'd picked a classic Mercedes from the lot, a sweet, sleek, quiet darling, but now, damn, she just seemed too clunky to be a lovers' car. It wouldn't have mattered, except that every detail seemed to shout in Nate's mind as possibly totally mattering.

Damnit. Could he be losing her before he even won her?

She turned to him with another smile. "I love this part of town."

"Yeah, me, too." He saw the smile, but he also saw her tug on that earring again.

The blacktop rolled beneath them. After picking her up, he'd ducked away from downtown and angled through Ann Arbor's old landed neighborhoods—the streets like Austin and Wellinford and Hermitase with all their elegant old houses. After that he crossed the river and aimed up the Huron Parkway.

Jeanne glanced at him, and suddenly his palms turned slick as slides.

She guessed where they were going now.

Eons ago, Ann Arbor had been known for its unique forests of burr oaks. Those forests were long gone, but Nate had grown up with a love of the treasured oaks. The trees had deeply furrowed bark, huge leaves, and shaggy spreading branches. They were so large and shady that they looked as if they were created to conceal lovers in their big old arms.

Jeanne was still looking at him when he turned down a certain lane. He almost missed it— God knew, he hadn't been there in years. There were lots of parks in Ann Arbor, and undoubtedly several with some of those big burr oaks—but not several where he and Peanut had peeled down after a prom and made love on the cool grass at midnight.

When he pulled off the road and they opened the car doors, the heat hit them both like a blast. He'd been stuck wearing a tie because of a morning meeting, but the instant he felt the sultry air, he jettisoned the tie and cuffed up the shirt. She shimmied out of her office jacket just as fast.

"No shoes," he instructed. But he was thinking, *No clothes*. He'd survived years of celibacy, but somehow didn't think he could survive another day without some buck-naked time with Jeanne Claire. And the damn woman had lied to him. She'd claimed to have a little flu—one of her excuses for not being able to see him ten days ago.

But now, without the jacket on her red and white dress, he could see she'd lost weight.

"You look terrific," he said, because she did— but he'd never again believe her when she claimed to be "just a little" sick.

"I've been stuck inside too much. I need some sunshine. In fact, this little getaway couldn't hit me at a more perfect time." She kicked off her red shoes, left them right by the car. Both of them tucked cell phones in pockets, but when he lifted a hand—summer heat or no summer heat—she took his.

A sense of rightness slammed through him, more powerful than even hormones. It was just a palm-to-palm connection, nothing intimate or overtly sexual . . . but the heart of her palm seemed to nest perfectly in his. The smells of leaves and fresh mowed grass and verdant earth chased away the workday pressures. No one else was around. Not in the middle of a Wednesday.

"So much has been going on. I know you've been busy, Peanut. I have, too. But phone calls just aren't cutting it."

"For me, either," she said quietly. She pressed his hand, as if to illustrate how much she meant it, but Nate knew little had been settled between them. Making love never settled things. It upped the stakes. And he couldn't shake the fear that he was closer to losing her than winning her. Both their lives were too complicated for them to see each other on the run and believe that could work.

"I feel like we've both been through a war over the last couple months. I just couldn't seem to get a minute out of the trenches. You haven't had any new experience with your thief, have you?"

"No," he said. "He seems to have gone underground. Which is just as well, since I just plain haven't had time to spend on it." He cleared his throat. "I put in the security system on the computer you suggested."

"Yeah? You didn't seem to like the idea when I brought it up."

"It's not that I didn't like the idea. It's that I didn't like talking to you about nothing but problems. My problems especially." He was hoping that would clear one of the contentious issues between them. Both of them seemed to destress as they wandered barefoot in the silky cool grass. Eventually, though, they both dropped down under the lacy shade of an old oak tree. He leaned up on an elbow, watching her hair shiver in the breeze . . . but he sensed he still had fences to mend from her gentle tone of voice.

"Nate, I don't always want to talk about problems, either. I want to just *be* with you. But I don't want you confusing me with your siblings, either. I don't want to be taken over, taken care of. I won't be another responsibility."

"I never thought of you that way."

"That's because you can't help being a bossy, take-charge type, Donneli." She whisked a handful of grass over his head, her lips curved in a smile. "I'm not asking you to change. Once a bulldozer, always a bulldozer—"

"Hey," he said.

"But I need you to see—to believe—that I'm not on the bulldozee list. We're together on stuff, okay?"

"Okay." Hell, if that was all that was bothering her, he could lower the caretaker volume a couple of notches. In fact, he could prove to her right off that he was seriously listening to her. "I had a problem with Caitlin," he offered.

"Yeah?"

The last time, he'd cut off talking about his pride and joy, thinking he'd scare her off, hearing about life with an impossible teenager. Now, though, he obviously needed to show her that he wouldn't run from sharing a problem. "Cait's summers have been tough for a couple of years. She's bored. She likes to *do* something with her time, but she's still too young to work except for a few baby-sitting jobs, so often enough she ends up at the shop. Everybody sticks up for her. She's got more grease under her fingernails than me. And that's not new—her loving car engines. But we got into this ridiculous fight about my father."

"Your father?"

"Yeah. Out of the blue, Cait said that 'one of my

big problems' is that I never liked my father. I asked what on earth she was talking about. She said that's why I won't let her work as a mechanic—because it's something about my dad."

"Well. Is it?" She was probably going to get that crisp dress all grass-stained, but she still stretched out, close enough to lock fingers with him.

"Damned if I know. I was hoping you could advise me."

She chuckled, one of those throaty woman chuckles that made his pulse thrum. "If you think you're fooling me, Donneli, you need a brain transplant. You want my advice like a hole in the head."

"I do!"

"Yeah, like oaks grow chestnuts." But she smiled at him. Really smiled. "But you *are* trying, aren't you?"

"Yes." It wasn't a joke to him. "Don't give up on me, all right? I admit, I might need some personality rearranging. But if I get where I'm being a jerk, I'll work on it, I swear."

"That's a two-way street."

"No, it's not. You're not a jerk."

She kissed him then. A peck on the neck. Just a little peck, but it was a mightily motivating reward to earn more. "I really *didn't* get what she meant about my dad."

Jeanne looked at him, and then seemed to decide he honestly seemed willing to talk about it. "Well, I think your Caitlin's right. You don't really have that big a sweat with her being so smart mechanically. But inside you've got a fear that if she got into the work, she could turn out like your dad."

He frowned. "So what's weird about that? My dad was lazy to the core. Motivated enough to have six kids—but not motivated enough to put food reliably on the table for them. Motivated to sit and watch football and drink beer, but not motivated enough to set up security for the family if something happened to him."

"So you don't want your daughter to turn out like him."

"Damn right."

"But she's not, is she, Nate? She's just thirteen. And she's not lazy. Not irresponsible. In fact, she seems as committed as you are. Pours on the coals when she wants something, fights with the gloves off."

"Is that how you see me?"

"That's how I see you both."

He said, "Darn kid has a fantastic brain. She's not going to be a mechanic. And that's that."

"Hmm."

"What does that hmm mean?"

"Oh, nothing. Just that someone I know . . . a man . . . has a real hard time when he's forced in a corner. Even if it's a corner he wants to be in. It just grates on him, if he feels trapped into doing something."

"I'm not trapping her into doing anything. I'm trying to trap her into *not* doing one thing. Just one thing. Out of all the careers in the entire universe."

"And if she's fighting you this hard at thirteen, imagine the wars you can have when she's sixteen." She added, "Will the whole world end if you just loosen the controls a wee little bit? Let her do the mechanics thing for now. Let her have her fill of it. As long as she keeps up her grades, why worry this soon? She could well change her mind before she's out of high school. Unless you force her into making this into a cause."

"Quit it," he grumped.

"Quit what?"

"Quit being wise. It's really annoying."

"Oh, thank God. There's my high-handed, domineering, authoritative, dictatorial, bossy lover," she said fervently. "For a minute I thought you were a stranger masquerading as my Nate."

"I'll 'my Nate' you," he murmured. She was grinning, so he knew she was teasing, knew she was okay with him, which was such a relief that his heart took off and soared. She was just lifting a hand to push away a wind-brushed strand of hair when he kissed her. Just a petal-soft kiss. His lips hadn't touched hers in weeks now. He didn't want to fall into her like a randy buck. He wanted to taste, smell, savor.

She took the kiss, added her spin to it, and then remolded it her way. If they both hadn't needed to come up for air, he doubted she'd have suddenly thought of more conversation. "Hey. Did you think you could escape forever not telling me that you agreed to do the reunion speech?"

"Offhand, I can't think of anything less interesting to talk about."

"You'll knock 'em dead," she assured him.

"No, I won't. I shouldn't be doing it. But Arnold got under my skin, twisted everything around so he made out like I had to."

"Nate, do you really still not believe you're a success? Just because you took a different road than the one you first wanted to?"

He lifted his head and frowned thoughtfully. "You know something amazing? That we can talk about high school reunions and speeches and I can still be harder than a hammer. What do you think that means?"

"That you're hopelessly male?"

"I don't think that's it. Because I've never gotten this hot for any other woman." There now. He must have said the right thing, because she promptly lifted up and kissed him . . . a long, lonesome, winsome kiss that turned his heart to smoosh.

One lazy, wicked kiss trailed into another. Maybe she'd forgotten that they had only an hour, that they were in the middle of a workday. They hadn't seen a sign of another body anywhere in the park—but they could. Anyone could play hooky on a somnolent Wednesday afternoon.

"You remembered, Donneli," she whispered.

"Remembered what?"

"That prom night. I had a pale blue dress. I loved that dress. You got me ice blue carnations, a wrist corsage. I had blue shoes. No bra—"

"I remember that part."

"You remember more than that, you bad boy."

He did. She'd gotten mascara in her eye. And the carnation on her wrist got crushed. And she'd lost this little necklace thing, and they had to find it in the moonlight in the grass, and somehow that motivated them to make love all over again.

They tumbled now, into an ardent pool of kisses. But this time, Nate didn't feel as if it were the past catching up to them . . . but more the future coming to meet them. He could see the grown-up enticement in her eyes. He could feel the grown-up promise in his. Need heated between them, sizzled into deep, dark desire. Frustration was a lot more fun when you know how much trouble you could get into.

Every sensation seemed to have her name on it. The scent of her warm, damp throat. The whiskey-hot air compared to her sipping-ice-tea kisses. The ticklish grass and the sun-laced shade, the skirt of her dress riding up, her thigh lifting and then riding him. Her throat released a groan of wanting, a groan of demand. She wanted *him*. Needed *him*.

They could make it—he suddenly knew. They really could have it all. Yeah, they had tons of problems. But they were both smart, both determined, both creative. They could find ways around all the problems; he knew they could.

Her underpants slipped down—assisted by his finger pulling at the miniscule elastic band. She hissed her approval, let him pull them down another inch. She pressed against him, her breasts snugged against his chest, her pelvis teasing against his, rubbing an invitation he couldn't mistake. She was gonna get exactly what she was asking for right here, right in the open, and to hell with—

A cell phone rang. Bleary-eyed, he lifted his head. "Yours or mine?"

She could barely seem to scrape up a whisper. "I don't know. It doesn't matter."

"Doesn't matter to me, either. I only brought mine because I had kind of a crisis meeting this afternoon, but hell. I don't care if the whole place falls apart."

"And I don't care if Oz falls apart, either. I just care about you, Donneli. You. Me. Us."

The cell rang again. He wanted to ignore it, but damn it, he was trying not to be selfish, and she'd

317

hinted that there were some problems with her dad she was trying to work out. "I'm almost sure it's yours. If it's your father—?"

She hesitated.

He kissed her forehead, fast, possessively. "It's okay, Peanut." He knew it was now. They had years to be together.

"I'll just forget it."

"No." Nate finally got it. He could see by the way she suddenly grabbed the phone that he'd been right, and there were worries she just couldn't escape. Kidnapping her had been fun, but not fair if she'd been stuck leaving something serious hanging.

"Hello," she said into the receiver and then went still as stone. "Donald," she said.

Nate felt a stunned slam in his gut. It was the guy. The one who'd been in her life before. The one that he'd known, somehow just *known*, wasn't totally finished business for her.

"No," she said into the receiver, and then started to say something else but was clearly interrupted. She sat up, swallowed, turned her head away from Nate. "Look, I appreciate that, Donald, but I don't see a—"

Again the son of a buck seemed to interrupt her. She turned to him, mouthed, "I promise, I'll be off the phone in a minute."

And she was. But in that minute, he washed a hand over his face, sat up, and then abruptly stood up. In spite of the sultry heat, he suddenly felt ice-cold. He saw the lazy sway of leaves, heard the whisper of summer wind, smelled the sweet grass. He saw the woman he loved, her long elegant neck, her hair blonder than sunlight, the classy bones. The image was already replaying in his head of how she'd yielded in the grass, forgot her dressy clothes, forgot her classy bones, and just gave. From her heart. From her senses.

But for all that had changed in the last fifteen years, he seemed to keep coming heads-up against what hadn't. He'd always known he wasn't in her class. It mattered that he made good money now. Mattered that they came together like fire and smoke. But the bottom line was still, why on earth would she take on a guy with a complicated family from a blue-collar background when it was so easy for her to do much better?

She hung up—almost as quickly as the minute she'd promised him—and turned, looking suddenly confused when she didn't immediately see him. He was there. He'd just charged out of hearing distance so he wouldn't intrude on her conversation.

"We've used up our hour, haven't we? I'll take you back to work," he said cheerfully.

"Hey," she said. Her smile died as she searched his face. "Nate, that was business."

"I figured. But I also figured that was the guy you were involved with, right?"

319

"Yes, it was." She swallowed again. Reached for his arm. He didn't pull back. He just managed to be a half an inch away from her as they hiked toward the car.

"Hell, I'm stuck with more work this afternoon, too. Took me years to get my hands on a Model J Duesenberg, but I finally found one in Belgium, being shipped over—"

She pelted around in front of him, her skin suddenly paler than ice, her eyes miserable. "I have to see him. For my father."

"You don't need to explain. It's none of my business. It's yours."

"I need you to believe me."

"I do. Why the hell wouldn't I?"

She kept looking at him, her chin taking on a stone-stubborn angle. "Nate. I have a problem. Donald has been trying to make that problem more difficult. I'm not seeing him for any personal reasons. Nothing personal is going to happen. There's no chance of that."

"Peanut, I'm not doubting you, not asking, not nothing. What's to be so defensive about?"

"Because I'm looking at your face. And it's like looking at a stranger's. You're angry with me—"

"No, I'm not."

"Well, then you don't trust me—"

"I do trust you."

She looked rattled, shook up. "I swear to God, you're as bullheaded as you ever were. You're obviously upset that I got a call from him." She took a breath. "Possibly I should have told you that I had this problem before. But I knew you'd try to fix it, Nate, and that's why I didn't. I needed to solve it myself. To show you that I could. To show *me* that I could."

"Like I said, I don't know why you're so defensive. I didn't question you—"

Again, she hooked his sleeve. Again, her eyes bored into his face. "Donneli, I need you to listen to me. Do you remember how much you wanted to be an architect? How much that was your dream in high school?"

Of all the irrelevant stuff to bring up. "Of course—"

"And do you know what my dream was?"

The question stopped him dead. It stunned him that he had to answer, "No."

She nodded fiercely. "Because I never told you. I never told you—or anyone else. My whole life, I just kept following what people wanted me to do, wanted me to be. And I've come to believe that's partly why we didn't make it the first time. Because I didn't have the gumption, the character, to hold up my side of things."

"Peanut, that's not true—"

"Yeah, it is. And it's something I'm trying to change, that you can't change for me. You can't take charge and leap in to fix my life. I have to do it. I have to hold my own with tough problems.

And I need you to know that I can, or it just won't work, do you understand? I need to know that you trust me."

Hell, he felt as if he'd fallen into a bed of slivers. She was so fierce, so upset. "I *do* trust you. But if this guy's giving you a problem, that's on me. I love you. That gives me the right—"

"No, it doesn't, Nate. Because that's what you do for everyone. Find their answers. Leap in and take charge. Only it can't be that way for us or it'll never work. I can't let you steamroller me, Donneli. You have to know that you can lean on *me* instead of the other way around. You have to *want* to lean on me. You have to know that I'll do the tough thing, even if I'm afraid—"

"Damnit. You're *afraid* of this guy?"

She answered with a frustrated sound—anger, despair, he didn't know which. But she suddenly pushed to her feet and started walking away.

Panic sliced through him. He'd hurt her again. Not like dumping her that first time, but somehow worse. He got it, that she wanted to handle the son of a bitch by herself. He got it, that she wanted him to trust her. And hell, he did trust her.

But for the first time, he understood that, all this time, she hadn't really been able to trust him. Not at the heart level. Not at the level where she felt she could admit her dreams to him. How could he not know her dreams and claim to love her the way a woman wanted and needed to be loved?

So many people counted on him. How could he have failed the one who really mattered to him more than life?

Hours later, as Jeanne drove to Donald's place, she seemed to hit every traffic jam and red light. Her nerves were razor-rattled, her stomach queasy. Walking away from Nate had been the hardest thing she'd ever done.

Either it worked or it didn't. She wouldn't know until she saw how he responded—but she *did* know that she couldn't lean on him, the way everyone else in his life leaned on him. They had to stand together, an equal partnership, or the relationship would never work—not for her, not for him, not for them. Only, damn. She'd lost him once.

She could hardly bear believing that she could lose him a second time.

But right now, she couldn't cave. She couldn't think about Nate at all, until she found a way to fix the two small, earthquake-sized crises immediately ahead of her. Her dad was second, but Donald very definitely needed to be handled before even another hour passed.

She turned onto the private road, and paused at the security gate to show her ID. Donald owned several places. His town house in Ann Arbor wasn't as luxurious as some of the others, but it was what he called his working house.

She wasn't comfortable, coming to his place—

but there seemed no better choice. If he came to Oz, she wouldn't have the luxury of being able to walk away if she needed to. And although a restaurant was probably the safest type of meeting place, there were things she wouldn't be able to say in public.

At least she'd been here before. Knew what she was getting into—or hoped she did.

"There you are," Donald said warmly, greeting her at the door before she'd even had a chance to knock. "I poured some wine. And I know you said no dinner, but the cook already put in a roast. It's done, but it'll stay on warm until we're both hungry. Come on in."

She didn't want wine or food, but accepted a glass. It was something to occupy her hands. His living room was done in gray—soft dove grays and dark, rich charcoals. She liked it. He had a fascinating oil hung over the couch, a contemporary swirl of satin reds and grays. She liked it, too. Donald used to say that they had good taste in common.

"We need to talk frankly," she said.

He looked at her, her black slacks and black top, the brushed back hair, the earrings. She'd dressed for this encounter carefully. He'd know it. Donald always noticed things like that. "It'd be easier if we had a quiet dinner and relaxed first," he said.

She shook her head. "Not for me."

"Come on, Jeanne. We're hardly enemies. There's no reason to be so stiff around me. We simply have a common problem." He pushed up the knee crease of his slacks, sat down on the couch, and motioned her next to him. She took the chair across from him instead. "Your father is in major financial hot water," he said.

"I know. Although I didn't realize we were at quite such a financial crisis until a few days ago."

"You're outstanding at what you do, Jeanne. I've seen all of the accounting records for every department connected to Oz."

"My dad gave you those records?" she questioned.

"Yes. Because he wanted my financial help. And the only way I'd consider giving it was if I knew exactly what shape the place was in. The first time I met with him, several years ago, I wouldn't have said the place had a prayer. But your efforts—all the business you brought in— really turned that albatross around. You've got a hell of a business mind, sweetheart. A mix of creative and good, solid common sense."

"Thank you."

He added wryly, "But your father can't keep a dollar in his pocket to save his life. He's impossible not to like. He'd give you the shirt off his back. That generous spirit is a wonderful quality . . . but not in business."

"You're not telling me anything I don't know. We'd better move to the point," she said quietly.

"All right. Cards on the table. Oz is going under. Chapter Eleven in a matter of weeks. Frankly, Jeanne, I can't imagine any investor who would willingly sink any more money into it. I'm sorry, but it'd just be crazy. He's a good man, and I don't doubt, a good father. But he's not capable of running a business."

"I know my father," she said quietly. "If that's the only reason you asked me here—to tell me that you're not going to help him—"

He took a long, slow gulp of wine. "It's not. I know how much you love your father. But I'm trying to be straight with you—I can't justify throwing away money, not just out of kindness. At least, not out of kindness to your father. If I were doing something for *you*—now, that'd be a different story."

Suddenly, she couldn't breathe.

"Look, you've had all summer. If you were going to marry this other guy in your life—you had more than enough time to get it done. You haven't, so I have to believe you're not that sure of him." Donald leaned back. "And I was more than willing to wait you out. I know you never felt head-over-heels for me, but I'm too damn old to believe in head-over-heels kind of love. I think we could make a good marriage."

She stood up, feeling her heart pounding like a

detonator. Donald didn't move, just kept talking, slowly, gently.

"I'd have to put some limits on your father, but basically he could keep Oz. He could lose—not at the rate he likes to throw it away—but I can absorb his losses indefinitely. And I'd be glad to, out of loyalty to my wife. For my wife."

Immediately, she started to say something, but he lifted a hand. "Before you say no—and yes, of course I know that's your first inclination, Jeanne. But please, just think. Would this other man save your father?"

"I—"

"Would this other man be willing to throw money indefinitely into a losing enterprise? Guarantee your father's security? Protect your father's pride?" Donald stood up then, too. "I'm a sure thing, Jeanne. Is he?"

She'd tried being nice. She'd tried being tactful. Now she said, "The only answer you have a right to know, Donald, is this one. No. I won't be marrying you. Now or ever. Not if hell froze over. Have a nice life."

When she left his place, she knew this horrendously impossible day wasn't done. She still had to see her father. She had to tell her dad that she was leaving Oz. His "princess" was deserting ship, abandoning him. That's not how it was, but it's how he was going to see it.

God knew, she'd have saved him if she could

have, but reality was that all her loyalty hadn't saved him at all. All she'd ever done was enable him to hang on to a business that wasn't for him. Why had it taken her so long to see it?

She drove into the night, knowing she was facing all kinds of tough dragons this day—dragons she'd once thought she couldn't tackle. But Donald's question still burned in her heart. *I'm a sure thing, Jeanne, is he?*

Because, of course, she wasn't sure of Nate. She had no idea what he'd do from here . . . or if she'd already lost him.

chapter 16

The sound of a rowdy, boisterous poker game echoed up the stairs. His three brothers were playing. Daniel loved to play, loved to gamble, but didn't have any card sense. Tony was a great player but couldn't bluff if his life depended on it. And Jason—from the sound of the yelling—had just won another hand, resulting in a bucket of popcorn being poured over his head.

Even with the confounding, upsetting problem of his thief, Nate had always joined in the family poker games. Tonight, though, he couldn't.

Tonight he was trapped in his upstairs bathroom, facing the mirror, doing war with a ridiculous purple tie. Purple and white were St. Sebastian's school colors, which was why he was stuck wearing the stupid color for the reunion to-night. Unfortunately, the tie wouldn't tie. It just kept hanging there, looking like a drunk rope.

"Dad, sometimes you are so lame." Caitlin came up behind him, stood on tiptoe, and started doing it for him. "Why didn't you just ask for my help?"

"I hate ties."

"Like the whole world doesn't know that."

"Everybody else gets to wear comfortable clothes except for me. I haven't worn a suit since the last time someone died. I thought suits were outlawed. For good reason."

Caitlin finished with the tie, then straightened his shirt collar. She loved this daughter stuff. It was written all over her smug expression. "Look, I know you're worried about the speech, but you're gonna knock 'em dead. Worrying is dumb. They're gonna think you're way cool, because you are."

"Thanks." It was pitiful, a damn thirteen-year-old kid thinking he needed reassurance. But at least she thought the only thing worrying him was the speech.

She stepped out of his way. "So. Are you going to see Jeanne Claire?"

Okay, so maybe he'd misjudged how perceptive his daughter was. Again. "Sure. In fact, since she's on the reunion committee, she's probably already there." As if this question were of no importance to him, he scooped up his keys from the dresser.

"You screwed up with her, didn't you?"

"Screwed up with who?" Since she shadowed him down the stairs and out the back door, she was obviously determined to hound him the entire way to the car. In this case, he'd brought home a '58 Austin-Healey Sprite—cream satin color, round rump, bug eyes. If that car couldn't give a guy confidence, nothing could.

"Screwed up with Jeanne Claire, obviously. Come on, I know you did something. You've been hanging around, doing stuff with me. You've been nice to everybody. So nice you've been starting to scare me. You hurt her feelings or did something really stupid, didn't you?"

This accusation was so unfair that if he'd been willing to tell his daughter about his love life— which he wasn't—he'd have laid it all out. The roses he'd sent. The heart-shaped boxes of chocolates. The thirty-pound tin of peanuts—he really, really thought she'd warm up for that one.

She *had* warmed up.

She'd thanked him. She'd called. She'd talked with him. But in his heart, in his head, he knew damn well this reunion was a crisis point. He'd failed her, by not knowing what her old, secret dream was. By being like everyone else in her life—taking her for granted, taking advantage of her, not looking past that beautiful face to who Jeanne Claire really was.

He'd tried to show he cared, that he loved her. But so far he hadn't found a way to really show that he trusted her, valued her the way she wanted to be valued. And he'd known for days that this reunion might be his last chance.

"Yeah, I did something really stupid," he admitted to his daughter. "On the other hand, the last I knew, you weren't that crazy about my seeing Jeanne Claire to begin with."

Caitlin lovingly stroked the fender of his Austin-Healey. She did love her cars. "Yeah, well, that was before. I like her okay. Everybody else treats me like I'm just a kid. She actually listened to me. But the point is more that it's an ugly thing."

"What is?"

"Your being so miserable. I'm used to you giving orders and yelling and being a royal pain." Caitlin stood back when he climbed into the car. "I don't like it. So fix it with her, okay? Whatever you have to do, do. Tonight. It's the perfect chance."

His thirteen-year-old didn't know *everything*. The reunion wasn't remotely a perfect chance. It was a public spectacle where she had a million things to do and he had to give a speech. The point, though, was that it might be his only chance, his last chance. And the fear of blowing it had his stomach in knots.

God knew why he was speeding when he was scared of getting there. But as the Austin gobbled up the road, lights winked on all over Ann Arbor. The weathermen had forecast frost on the pumpkin for the reunion tonight. It had poured that afternoon, but now a gusty, blustery wind was tossing the leaves, sending flutters of gold and crimson to the ground, an omen of the winter coming.

He turned on the street for St. Sebastian's. Panic immediately started thudding in his stomach.

It amazed him that until this reunion had come up—until Jeanne Claire had popped back into his life—he'd believed he was doing okay. He hadn't been that unhappy with who he was or what he was doing, until he saw her again.

And then, damn it, he'd remembered the man he'd once wanted to be.

He parked the car, patted his jacket pocket to make sure his speech was stashed there, swallowed hard, and headed up the walk. Next door, the high school was all lit up for the kids and their homecoming dance. The reunion group had rented the hall across the road, though, for the obvious reason—they couldn't drink on school premises. The same hall was traditionally used for bingo, potlucks, fund-raisers, and any other school-related event where alcohol might loosen purse strings.

He glanced at the banner hung over the door that read "New Dreams." Man, had she decked the place out. Purple and white balloons bobbed the perimeters of the long room. One counter was set up for food, another for a bar. Sloppy Joes were the fanciest thing on the menu; beer and wine were flowing freely.

He searched the crowded room for Jeanne, but couldn't immediately spot her. Several movie screens back-dropped the revelers. One screen flashed scenes from "their" movies—*Dirty Dancing* and *Die Hard*, *Fatal Attraction* and *Top Gun*. Another screen flashed collages of photographs from their class—some candid, some formal shots from their yearbook. He didn't have to walk two feet before seeing a half dozen of him and Jeanne. A lump started growing in his throat.

Bodies milled everywhere. They'd only had about two hundred fifty in their graduating class, but it looked like they'd all come—with spouses. Weren't people supposed to hate these things? Yet everywhere he turned, there were flushed faces and exuberant chatter. Another screen flashed headlines from "their" time—a group of kids swaying to "We Are the World," a sad picture of seven astronauts lost, a splash of pictures showing the face of an evangelical minister who couldn't keep his pants zipped, economic head-lines discussing Reaganomics.

Still, he couldn't spot Jeanne.

In the background, speakers played a whole range of their songs—"Time of My Life," "Tainted Love," "Never Gonna Give You Up," "Total Eclipse of the Heart." Every song had a memory attached to it. Every single one. Always, a memory involving him and Peanut.

"Nate. Damn, it's you, isn't it? Nate Donneli? Nate, how are you?" A plump butterball of a man with a balding head pumped his hand.

"Just fine. Great to see you," Nate said.

"Hey, Nate—" The woman who suddenly whirled around to greet him had a fluffy bob of blond hair and a grin wider than the Rio Grande.

"Nate Donneli!!"

Everyone recognized him—when he barely knew anyone. The stone in his throat swelled to boulder size. They knew him because he'd been such a big man on the high school campus then. They knew him because they'd expected him to turn into a big man in real life.

Hell, how had he let anyone talk him into this?

The songs, the sights, the flashing movies, the pictures . . . all of it made him feel the fifteen-year-old emotion again—the emotion of hunger. In high school, he'd been so full of want. He'd hun-gered relentlessly for so much. His need to achieve, to succeed, had dominated every minute of his life.

Then, he hadn't realized that the only thing he really needed was Jeanne. Someone who could want him, just as he was. Someone who valued him, without all the constant pressure of expectations.

And then he suddenly saw her across the room.

She still hadn't noticed him, but then she was busier than a one-armed bandit. He walked toward her slowly, not just because of the jammed crowd, but because of the longing that clogged his throat, because he finally seemed to see so many of the things that he'd failed to notice before.

She was wearing a white dressy top with dark purple slacks—the school colors, like she was supposed to—but classed up the way Jeanne classed up everything. Her hair was like sunshine, pulled back from her face, her makeup just so. Just as in high school, crowds gravitated toward her, wanting to be around the darling of the class—the one everyone wanted to be like.

He hadn't understood how it was for her then. Just as now, she greeted everyone and got them talking about themselves. She lifted a hand or cheek, making each person feel special and welcomed, and then eased her way to the next batch of people. In less than five minutes, he saw her flashing her high-kilowatt smile—then zoom to talk to a security man, a moment later zoom behind the counter to talk to the food volunteers, and moments after that she'd zoomed over to the microphone and podium. She was working—but in a way no one saw. Taking care of people—but in a way no one noticed or appreciated.

All these years, people had treated her like the class princess, the fragile blond, the darling. All these years, she'd been the tough cookie who just did and did and did for others.

And just like that, it was done for Nate. He couldn't lose her. No matter what he'd done wrong, there had to be a way to make it right. Somehow, someway, he had to find a way to make it right.

Then, suddenly, her head lifted and she spun around. Their eyes met.

Jeanne saw him. Oh, she'd seen him the instant he entered the room. Her heart leaped like a gamboling colt—all these years, and she still couldn't stop that reaction, couldn't stop her pulse from singing with yearning whenever she was near him.

She'd told herself to give up. After all, how long could a girl bay at the moon before admitting she was behaving like a hapless hound?

But when she was with him, it was never that simple. Especially tonight, he looked unforgettably wonderful, his dark hair such a contrast to his magnetic eyes, the dress jacket making his shoulders look powerfully broad. The white shirt made his ruddy, tanned skin especially striking. Damn the man. Every woman swiveled around when he walked in, no different than they always had.

But she couldn't go over to him, couldn't do anything about anything for a few minutes. Putting on this reunion had turned into a giant project. Tam and Arnold did their share, but they simply didn't know how to organize events the way she did. Par for her course, she stayed behind the scenes—but typical of events like this, a zillion things went wrong every other minute. The problems were all fixable. It's just that someone actually had to fix them.

She raised her hand, giving the signal for the lights to dim and "Bucking the Tide" to shoot through the speakers. Then Tamara leaped on the stage to whistles and applause. Arnold stood just below her, beaming like a hopelessly lovesick calf.

Tam was wearing a purple feather top with white leather slacks. The outfit was typical for Tam, flamboyant and unexpected, but it wasn't shockingingly wild the way her outfits used to be. She'd left her red hair simple, long and flowing, no dye or mousse to spike it up; she was wearing makeup that was on her face instead of in-your-face. And once the song finished, she lifted the microphone from the holder and simply talked.

"They asked me to start our reunion gig with

my 'Bucking the Tide' . . . because that's where we all started, didn't we? At least that's where I did. I desperately wanted to buck the tide. To be different from everyone else. To make my mark on the world. For myself, it wasn't just that I wanted my music . . . but that I wanted so much to *be someone*."

For a rambunctious, noisy crowd, it was amazing how quickly everyone fell silent.

Tamara lifted her hands to them. "It took me earning and throwing away a fortune . . . and two long shots at rehab . . . and fifteen long years. Before I figured out that I already was *someone*. At least to the people who mattered to me."

Jeanne watched her exchange looks with Arnold, and knew darn well the two were aiming for a wedding. Who'd have thought it? That Arnold, of all people, could finally bring Tamara the confidence and peace of heart she'd sought for so long?

Being loved—loving—had so much power.

Or could.

Again, she searched for Nate in the crowd. Again, she spotted him and surged toward him— only to be interrupted again.

"Jeanne Claire! You're just as gorgeous as ever!"

She came through with a smile and shook his hand, but she had to grapple for a name to match the bulldog face. "Buzz," she greeted him, finally recognizing the classmate who'd become a local judge. In school, he'd been insensitive and obnoxious. Poor guy still was.

She just got rid of him when a woman pushed out of the crowd. "Jeanne Claire! I was hoping to run into you!"

"Lara," Jeanne said warmly, yet felt trapped all over again. In the old days, no one could shut Lara Reed up. It seemed she could still talk nonstop, this time about her third marriage, her last boob job, the podiatrist she was currently married to.

Frantically Jeanne's gaze prowled the crowd—not just because she hungered to see Nate now, but because she really needed to. Time was skidding past. Arnold was shuffling onstage, about to make announcements—and right after that Nate was supposed to give his speech.

"Jeanne Claire! I was wondering if I'd run into you!"

Again she pivoted around. Her jaw almost dropped in shock when she recognized Baker Somerfeld. In school, he'd been voted their Best Athlete and really was a maestro jock who'd won a full football scholarship to one of the Big Ten schools. Now, though, he'd grown his Marine haircut into shoulder-length curls, the broad shoulders were encased in a dress, his purse matched his shoes, and the makeup was Elizabeth Arden.

"Nice to see you," she said desperately.

"At least you're willing to talk to me."

"Of course," she said politely, but it wasn't Baker's new lifestyle that shocked her, but the realization of how much these people had once desperately mattered to her. How many dreams they'd hidden inside their deepest selves. How crazy—and ordinary—and lonely they all were.

And then she saw Nate taking the podium. Arnold introduced him. "The guy we all voted Most Likely to Succeed . . . didn't you all wonder what happened to him? Didn't you all wonder about all the things we were so sure of in high school, if they really turned out the way we expected? But In Nate's case, I don't think any of us doubted he was going to turn out to be a total winner . . . and here he is!"

Oh, God, he'd been so shook about this speech. So unwilling to face his old classmates. So sure they'd think he'd failed to live up to anyone's expectations of him. But he had. Damn it, he had, and somehow she'd known from the beginning that was the only mountain between them that she couldn't cross. She couldn't *make* him feel pride in himself. And they didn't have a chance if he couldn't see past that wall—see the real her, see the real Nate Donneli, see the real possibilities that had been denied them before.

"Hell," he started out, obviously flustered by the exuberant applause. When the crowd laughed— and then finally quieted down—he threw up his hands. "You know what? I wrote up this whole fancy speech, but now I think . . . I'm not going to use it. Just being here again—seeing you all again—brought back all the high school memories. Were we dolts or what?"

Again the crowd laughed for him, and her heart swelled. Nate won over people just by being himself, always had. How could he not see it? How wonderful he was?

"Back in high school"—Nate shook his head—"we were always so careful about who we talked to, how we dressed. We worried that everyone would notice if we did anything wrong. We were always afraid that no one would like the real person inside us—so we dressed and acted a certain way, to be more accepted. You remember?"

Nods from everyone.

Nate continued, "We really seemed to believe that if we just behaved in certain ways, we'd succeed at what was important to us. It strikes me as so unbelievable now—that all the dreams we had back then were really about other people. We wanted to do something where other people would think we would be successful, where other people would like us or admire us. I don't know about you all . . . but it seemed to take me fifteen years before I discovered the truth. That the real dream—the only dream that really counts—is having the luxury, the right, to go after what really matters to us."

Nate hesitated, and then went on. "Originally I was afraid to give this speech—because I thought y'all probably didn't want to know that the guy you voted Most Likely to Succeed was just selling used cars for a living." There was another burst of laughter before he could go on. Suddenly his gaze scanned the crowd, searching, searching . . . until he found her. The audience had no reason to understand why there was a moment's silence, but her breath caught. He lifted a hand as if talking only to her, gesturing only to her.

"I think money's great. And to an extent, I think everyone seeks some level of success . . . but it really seems as if the only people who sour on life are those who never gave their dreams a chance. And that has nothing to do with money or success or how fancy your house is. It has to do with taking the artificial smile off. With feeling *safe* inside yourself. With knowing that you're living the life that fits your own skin, your own way . . ."

She never thought he'd get it. That he'd ever really understand those things. But it was as if those concepts suddenly clicked for him, in his mind, in his heart . . . because he said the words looking right at her.

And suddenly he was. Talking. Straight to her. As if there were no one else in the long, crowded hall but the two of them.

"For myself, it took me fifteen years to figure out what I really needed in my life. There's only one person who ever made me feel safe. One person who ever made me afraid—afraid of losing her. I waited fifteen ridiculously long years to ask her to marry me—so long that I'm not willing to wait even another second."

Someone dropped an entire plate of food. Someone else killed the background music system. In a matter of moments, Nate's voice was the only sound in the whole room.

"Jeanne Claire, I loved you in high school and I love you a thousand times more now. I failed you then, not because I didn't love you, but because I was dumb. I'm still dumb, Peanut. I should have known what your dreams were. I should have realized all the times you were thinking of me, of other people, instead of anyone being there for you. But I'd like to change that . . ."

Oh, my God. The damn fool man. The instant he said the word *failed*, she started moving. By the time he said *Peanut*, she was charging for the podium at a dead run.

". . . if you'll consider marrying me, Jeanne Claire, I promise to love you for all of our lives. I promise to trust you, with my heart, with my life. I promise to help you achieve your dreams. In fact, if you'll be my dream catcher, I'll do my damnedest to be yours. I'm asking you, Jeannie, to be my lover. My partner. My wife—"

Before he'd swallowed that last word, she'd thrown her arms around him.

Maybe there was a room full of cheers. Maybe someone loosened all the balloons and let them free.

She saw only Nate's eyes, vulnerable, full of love, focused on hers as if she were the lens of his life. She took another kiss, wrapping her arms securely around him, protecting her strong man the way no one else could—the way no one else even realized he needed protecting. Their lips touched, sealed.

"Yes," she whispered, and then louder, "*Yes.*"

And then, fiercely, at the top of her lungs, "I love you, Nate Donneli!" But then he swiftly pulled her back in his arms—the only place she wanted to be.

chapter 17

It amazed Jeanne how a crowded room of more than three hundred people could so easily seem to fade away. The noise muted, the flashing screens blurred; the smells of sloppy Joes and beer and chips dissipated like smoke. Someone called her name. Someone called his.

She didn't care. She didn't hear any of it. "We have just a few teensy little things to talk about, Donneli. You think you could manage to take me away from all this?"

He grinned, and although there was no escaping the crowd in an instant—in fact, there were rowdy demands to be invited to the wedding—he still managed to bustle her out of there faster than a car chase.

He handed her into the passenger side of the cream Austin-Healey and clipped the door closed. He stole a kiss at the same time he started the engine. "As long as you don't take back that yes, I'll go anywhere you want, do anything you want, and answer anything you want."

"Is this my domineering tyrant of a take-charge Donneli?"

"Yeah, it's me. Just the reformed me. Where we going, boss?"

She chuckled, but she also answered, "Your house."

"MY house? You can't mean that. Peanut, I've got a mom, a daughter, and three brothers playing poker there—"

"We're only going to make a stop," she assured him. "I want you alone, Donneli. All alone, all mine, your mind on nothing else but us. But I think this side trip is a good idea. You just need long enough to talk to Jason. He's your thief, Nate. And as much as I want to concentrate on us—I think it'd be easier for you and him both, if we all got that dragon out in the open and settled."

He promptly stalled the Austin-Healey and had to coax it to start again. "Say what? Jason? Where did you get that idea?"

"From you. From your speech." On the drive to his place, she tried to explain. "You remember when you were talking about the things we all need in life—a place where we can take the artificial smile off. A place where we feel comfortable inside ourselves. You were talking about happiness, the need to live 'a life that fits your own skin' . . . and it just clicked like a light bulb. Jason is the only one who's unhappy that way."

"I don't understand."

Neither did she, exactly. Her mind had been on her and Nate, not Jason or his thief problem or anything else. Yet everything he said had seemed true in so many ways. True for him. For her. For everyone there. It was the essential reason they'd failed each other before. It was the reason they'd come damn close to failing each other this time. "And that's when it hit me. Only one of your brothers is really unhappy in that kind of way. He feels trapped. Unhappy living with his own skin. Unhappy with who he is and what he's doing. Unhappy enough to do something desperate— like betray you."

"But Jason's the one person in the family who's always had access to the books. In a million ways he's always proven I could trust him."

She said quietly, "And I think you still can."

He shot her a confused frown. "Say what? If he stole money from me, betrayed my loyalty? How the hell could I ever trust him again?"

By then, they were already turning onto his street. There was no time to say more. "Just talk to him, okay? Ask him. And then hear out whatever he has to say."

348

He pulled in the drive and glanced at her, clearly confused and wanting to pursue the conversation, but that quickly she saw a face in the window. Even before they climbed out of the car, one of the brothers was pushing open the back screen door.

Jeanne swallowed fast. The guys were obviously in the middle of a poker game, surrounded by the remnants of pizza and nuts. Nate's mom had already gone to sleep, but Caitlin was hunched on a stool, watching the men play, clearly comfortable and happy with her role as her uncles' mascot. Everyone looked surprised to see Nate.

"Hey, we thought you'd be partying at the reunion until the wee hours . . ." And then they spotted Jeanne. "Hey, Jeanne Claire."

Nate honed straight on Jason. "If you could stop the game for a few minutes, I need to talk to you."

"Right now? Are you kidding? For Pete's sake, we're right in the middle of a big pot—"

"Yeah. Right now."

Jason's face suddenly looked punched with white. She knew for sure then. So did Nate. "This won't take that long, Jason," he said quietly. Caitlin popped off the stool, looking worriedly at her dad, which he instinctively responded to. "Everything's fine, Cait. Jason and I just need to talk alone for a couple minutes. Someone get Jeanne Claire a drink, okay?"

When the two men disappeared upstairs, Daniel murmured, "What the hell is going on?"

"Yeah, exactly what's going on here?" Caitlin demanded. "Jeanne, come on, you have to tell us!"

Jeanne squished in a seat between them all, feeling the oddest sense of calm stealing over her. Nate's public and so-romantic proposal had left her reeling—her heart higher than an eagle's wings and her pulse soaring. She wanted to laugh, to sing, to *be* with Nate, right now, alone. Yet . . . being here, in his crowded family kitchen, made something soft and quiet settle inside her.

They were together. Solving a problem. He'd listened to her, trusted her judgment. He'd assumed she could handle his family. And he'd said the words, but this was like the cement coming together, sealing who they were together. And who they could be.

Warming her even more was realizing that the Donnelis had started to naturally treat her as if she belonged with the clan. Tony was pushing a glass into her hand, Caitlin demanding that she take her side, Daniel teasing her. She'd just never expected the huge warmth of acceptance in that lamplit yellow kitchen, yet still she found her gaze bouncing back and forth to the doorway.

Less than ten minutes later, Nate thundered down the stairs and charged into the kitchen. Jason was nowhere in sight. Nate did the family gauntlet at full speed, squeezing Daniel's shoulder, knuckling Tony's arm, then kissing Caitlin with a brusque, "Just go to sleep, sweetheart. I'll see you in the morning." Before Jeanne could catch a good look at his expression, he'd grabbed her hand and aimed for the back door.

"Dad! Wait a minute," Caitlin said. "Where are you going? What happened? What's go—?"

"We'll talk tomorrow," he promised her swiftly. "Right now I need some time with Jeanne Claire. But for the record, Cait . . . when you're eighteen, if you're still determined to be a mechanic, I guess you damn well can be."

"What! What?!"

But Nate was no longer answering questions from his daughter or anyone else. He closed the door, sealing out the cheerful, warm kitchen lights, and letting them out into silent, dark night. A full harvest moon was rising, nestled low in the trees. He didn't seem to notice or care.

"Damn it. You were right." Once he handed her into the passenger side of the Austin-Healey, he ducked down and kissed her once, hard and potently, on the lips. Then snapped the door closed as if he hadn't left her mouth trembling and her hand reaching for him in mid-air.

"We're going to your place. For at least an entire week, I just need you alone. Completely to myself. No more noise or interruptions or complications—hell. Do you know what Jason told me?"

"Tell me." If she couldn't see his expression

clearly in the dark car, it didn't take X-ray vision to figure out Nate was radiating more energy than compressed rocket fuel. The story was going to have to come out.

"He stole the money. He stole all the damn money. But he didn't use any of it. He put it all in a bank account for Caitlin, can you believe that? He never spent a single dime. Never even touched it."

She tried to watch the road, since he seemed completely uninterested in red lights and stop signs.

"He didn't steal it to *steal* it. He stole it because he was angry with me. Damnit, Peanut, you told me. Or that's what you've been trying to tell me for weeks, haven't you?"

"There now. I'll bet you want to stop for that light, huh?" she asked tactfully. Apparently not. Even though she wasn't the practicing Catholic in their twosome, she started praying.

"He cried on me, for God's sake. My own brother." The Austin-Healey zoomed past Ann Arbor's lights, back into the quieter country, right under the romantic harvest moon, past leaves rustling secrets and wet-mirror streets. "My brothers had been telling me the same thing for ages. That I was always pushing them—to get good grades, get their degrees, get them installed in good jobs in the business. I wanted them settled. Safe. I wanted them to be able to support themselves. Was that so damn wrong?"

"No, love."

"But Jason never wanted to be an accountant. That's really what's held him up from getting his formal CPA. He kept postponing the test because he hates the work. Really hates it. And I guess he told me that before . . ." Nate's voice echoed bewilderment. "Okay, I *know* he told me that. But I just never understood the problem the way you did."

Finally he stopped at a light. It happened to be a green light, but at least he stopped. And looked at her. "A hundred years ago, you know how much I wanted to be an architect."

"Yes."

"And of course I couldn't do anything about that, not once Dad died. But Jason said, how the hell could I not understand more than anyone what he was going through? He had a dream, too. He wanted to be a photographer. Even in school, he didn't think he was good enough to make it— not to earn a living at it—but he still wanted a chance to try. Even if he went broke. Even if he failed."

When a man was talking at the speed of bullets, there was no point in trying to answer him. An SUV beeped behind him, though, which at least made him recognize that he'd been braked through both a green and red light. He punched the gas again. "You know what got to me?"

"What?"

"He said he wanted to be like *me*, Jeanne. He wanted to help the family, just like I did. He thought I was a hero for sacrificing so much for the family. He wanted to be the same kind of man. That's what he said. Only he couldn't make the work fit his skin. He hated getting up in the morning. He felt more and more trapped. How could I *not* have seen that I was taking his dream away from him? Me, of all people?"

He pulled up in the front parking lot of Oz Enterprises and braked hard. Both of them surged out of the car. She wanted to answer him, to respond to the anguish in his voice. Yet before she could say anything, he'd pelted around the car and pulled her into his arms. Before she could even breathe, he ducked his head and took her mouth, in a rough-sweet kiss that left her lips tingling and her senses reeling.

"You knew I had it wrong," he said gruffly. "You took my daughter's side about her wanting to be a mechanic. And then you took Jason's side when you defended him earlier—"

"I wasn't defending him for stealing from you, Donneli, how could you think that?" Her heart seemed to be beating in chunks. "Nate, I believe in *you*. I'm on your side. Today, yesterday, tomorrow, always. But being loyal to you can't possibly always mean agreeing with you."

"I know. It took me until tonight to finally get it, and damn it, Peanut, I nearly lost you all over again. You said yes to marrying me, but you still weren't sure if I'd heard you."

She searched his eyes. "You're hearing me now," she whispered. "It wasn't life that separated us before. It was that we didn't know how to be there for each other." A car parked next to them. People piled out, laughing, talking. The sprinkler system turned on, glistening in the moonlight. She saw only him. His eyes, his face. His heart. "I know," she said, "that we were trying to be loyal to our families. And loyalty's a good thing. But we have to be loyal to ourselves, too. That's part of what we didn't understand before."

He started to bend down again—and God knew, she wanted that next kiss—but she interrupted to say, "I need you to know—I not only cut Donald off at the pass, but he won't be calling again. And I sat down with my dad. Told him I loved him, which I sure do, but I won't be working for Oz past the end of this month."

His fingertip trailed the line of her jaw. "That's the stuff you felt you had to do on your own?"

She nodded. "I *knew* I could turn to you, Nate. But I lost you before, because we had the wrong kind of love. We loved the way children do. You assumed I wouldn't be there if you got stuck with a big problem. I assumed I was more important to you than anything in life. Those were children's dreams. That was children's love."

"It's different now."

"Yes. Because I'm not trying to be someone I'm not. The dream I want for you is to be the man you want to be. The best man you can be. On your terms. On our terms."

He started to answer her, and then just seemed to change his mind. He swooped down and kissed her again, instead, the first kiss a slow, sweet promise like the first strains of a love song . . . the second one deeper, darker, softer. More painful. More sweet.

When he finally lifted his head, she was breathing hard and so was he. "And you, Peanut," he said. "We covered what I want. But I've been waiting for fifteen years to hear what you want. And that includes whatever career dream you had that you never told me."

She didn't want to talk. Not anymore. She wanted to be upstairs, in her dark bedroom, buried under the blankets with Nate for the next year—maybe longer.

But even more than that, she wanted him to know unequivocally that she'd never duck from a tough problem again. "Textiles," she said.

"Textiles?"

"Yup. And the reason you don't know is because I never told you. I never told anyone. I just kept trying to be what other people needed from me. But I'm done with that now."

"You're going to get bossy on me?"

"You think you're an authoritarian tyrant? You ain't seen nothing yet," she assured him.

Those dark eyebrows lifted. "Are there any immediate orders you need to give me?"

"Zillions," she said crisply. "I want a Christmas wedding."

"Got it."

"And I want our own place."

"I should think so. You want to buy or build?"

"Whatever we both vote on."

"Hey. Already you're losing some of your take-charge tyrant status," he warned her. "Surely you've got more orders to give me than that."

"I do, I do." She raised both arms around his neck. "I insist—I demand—that you make love with me until the sun comes up."

"Damn, Peanut. I can tell you're going to be real trouble for the next fifty years."

"I'll try. I promise."

He laughed—and kissed her. "And I'll promise right back. Now let's go hide, someplace where I can show you exactly, precisely, and in complete detail how much I love you."

She exuberantly agreed.

ROMANCE HEADLINES

LOVE! PASSION! SEDUCTION!

*Everything you need to know about
Avon's Romance Superleaders*

*Amazing Authors
Unforgettable Books
And a lot of great sex*

MOTHER OF THE BRIDE KEEPS SANITY BUT LOSES HEART TO EX-SPOUSE IN WEDDING GONE AWRY

Once Upon a Wedding
by Kathleen Eagle
September 2003

[Minneapolis, MN] What was Camille thinking? Her determination to make her daughter's wedding a day to remember has gone completely out of control. It's simply too much for one woman to handle! And to make matters somehow worse, Camille's ex-husband, Creed, returns to town, suddenly longing to make up for lost time. Not only does he want to do "the father thing," he's ready, willing, and able to tempt her back into his arms.

"*W*hat are you doing here?"

She regretted the words as soon as they came out of her mouth. It was a rude way to greet the man, even though he had no business messing in her kitchen anymore.

He didn't appear to take offense. He went right on putting cream and sugar in her old "Favorite Teacher" mug. But he'd always taken his coffee straight.

"You haven't had your coffee yet this morning, have you? You still buy the best. I still make the best." He handed her coffee with that same old sloe-eyed, sleepy morning smile. "My daughter lives here."

"Is that how you got in?"

He sipped his own coffee. "She says she's getting married. She's not old enough, is she?"

"How old should she be?"

"Older than my little girl." He boosted himself up the

few inches that it took him to seat himself on the counter. His long legs dangled nearly to the floor. "I always liked Jamie. I thought he was really going to make something of himself. Pick up a couple of instruments, put a band together. He couldn't sing, but he had a good ear."

She let the "make something of himself" jibe sail past her ear.

"How did you get here? I didn't see a strange vehicle in the driveway."

"And you don't see a strange man in your kitchen. You know us both. I'm still driving the same pickup, the one I left here with."

"How old is that thing now?"

"I've lost track. But she had zero miles on her when I got her." He gave his signature wink. "Just like you."

"What a flattering comparison."

"More than you know. That pickup is the only thing I have left that I don't share, but Jordan needed it to haul some stuff." His eyes went soft, as though resting them on her felt good to him. "How've you been?"

"Fine."

"Your mom?"

"Not so fine." She tried to remember what had been going on in her life when she'd last heard from him. "You know she has cancer."

"No, I didn't know. I'm sorry." He wagged his head sadly. "Jordan said she'd moved back, but she didn't say why. How's she doing with it?"

"Jordan, or my mother? Coping, both of them." She took her mothering stance, arms folded. "You haven't given me one straight answer so far. Why are you here, Creed?"

"Jordan called to tell me she was getting married. Actually, she left a message on my new answering machine." He grinned proudly. "I can call from anywhere and check in. So I got this message from her saying she had some news. I was coming into town anyway, so I . . ."

Her undeniable curiosity must have shown, because he was quick to explain. "I've got a gig. Haven't had one here in a long time." His smile seemed almost apologetic. "Yeah, I'm still at it. And, yeah, I still work construction to pay the bills."

"So why are you here," she repeated with exaggerated patience, "in *this house?*"

"Like I said, Jordan called. Talked to her last night. She called again this morning, wanting to use the pickup. She said you were gone with the van."

"That's right," Camille recalled. "She told me she needed it today."

"Said you'd been gone all night." He shrugged diffidently. " 'Cause, we weren't worried."

"I left—"

"I haven't seen the boy yet. What's he like now? Still smart? Still . . ." A trace of the worry he'd disclaimed appeared in his eyes. "I know he's not a boy, and I know I missed my chance to send the bad ones packing and give the good ones fair warning. I left it all to you. He'll treat her right, won't he?"

"I hope so," she said with a sigh. "What am I saying? If he doesn't, she's outta there." Another double take. "*What am I saying?* They'll treat each other right."

"Like partners?"

"They'll make it, Creed."

"They haven't yet?" He gave a nervous laugh. "Just kidding. I don't want to know. I'd have to break his neck, and I don't think that would look too good. A neck brace with a tux." Hunkering down, he propped his elbows on his knees and cradled his coffee between his hands. "She's got her heart set on a fancy wedding, huh?"

"Fancier than ours was, I guess."

"A ten-dollar chapel in Vegas with an Elvis impersonator would be fancier than ours was." His eyes smiled for hers, hauling her into their private memory. "But the wedding night was a different story, wasn't it?"

"It wasn't fancy."

"Neither is heaven."

"Oh?" She raised her brow. "When were *you* last there?"

CURSE MAKES VISCOUNT THE MOST
UNMARRIAGEABLE MAN IN ENGLAND

Who Will Take This Man?
by Jacquie D'Alessandro
October 2003

[London, England] Word is out! Philip Ravensly, Viscount Greybourne, is the victim of a curse, making him completely unmarriagable. Despite all attempts by Meredith Chilton-Grizedale, the Matchmaker of Mayfair, to find him a suitable bride, he remains unwed. Then the viscount begins viewing *her* as a potential mate . . .

$\mathcal{L}$ord Greybourne stepped in front of her. His brown eyes simmered with anger, although there was no mistaking his concern. Reaching out, he gently grasped her shoulders. "I'm sorry you were subjected to such inexcusable rudeness and crude innuendo. Are you all right?"

Meredith simply stared at him for several seconds. Clearly he believed she was distraught due to the duke's remark which cast aspersions upon Lord Greybourne's . . . manliness. Little did Lord Greybourne know that, thanks to her past, very little shocked Meredith. And as for the validity of the duke's claim, she could not fathom that anyone could so much as look at Lord Greybourne and have a doubt regarding his masculinity.

Lowering her hands from her mouth, she swallowed to find her voice. "I'm fine."

"Well, I'm not. I'd have to place myself firmly in the category of 'vastly annoyed.'" His gaze roamed over her face and his hands tightened on her shoulders. "You're not going to faint again, are you?"

"Certainly not." She stepped back, and his hands lowered to his sides. The warm imprint from his palms seeped through her gown, shooting tingles down her arms. "You may place me firmly in the category of 'females who do not succumb to vapors.'"

He cocked a brow. "I happen to know that is not precisely true."

"The episode at St. Paul's was an aberration, I assure you."

While he did not appear entirely convinced, he said, "Glad to hear it."

Clearing her throat, she said, "You came to my defense in a very gentlemanly way. Thank you."

A wry smile lifted one corner of his mouth. "I'm certain you don't mean to sound so surprised."

Indeed, she was surprised—stunned actually—although she had not meant to sound as if she were. But she'd have to reflect upon that later. Right now there were other, bigger issues to contemplate.

Unable to stand still, Meredith paced in front of him. "Unfortunately, with the duke's news, we must now recategorize our situation from 'bad' to 'utterly disastrous.' Your bride is well and truly lost, thus doing away with our plan for you to marry on the twenty-second, and my reputation as a matchmaker is in tatters. And with your father's ill health, time is short." Her mind raced. "There must be a way to somehow turn this situation around. But how?"

"I'm open to suggestions. Even if we are successful in finding the missing piece of stone, my marrying is out of the question without a bride." He shook his head and a humorless sound escaped him. "Between this curse hanging over me, the unflattering story in the newspaper, and the gossip Lord Hedington alluded to circulating about my ability to . . . perform, it seems that the answer to the question posed in today's issue of *The Times* is yes—the cursed viscount *is* the most unmarriageable man in England."

Unmarriageable. The word echoed through Meredith's mind. Damnation, there must be a way—

She abruptly halted her pacing and swung around to

face him. "Unmarriageable," she repeated, her drawn out pronunciation of the word in direct contrast to her runaway thoughts. She stroked her jaw and slowly nodded. "Yes, one might very well christen you The Most Unmarriageable Man in England."

He inclined his head in a mock bow. "A title of dubious honor. And one I'm surprised you sound so . . . enthusiastic about. Perhaps you'd care to share your thoughts?"

"Actually I was thinking you exhibited a moment of brilliance, my lord."

He walked toward her, his gaze never wavering from hers, not stopping until only two feet separated them. Awareness skittered down her spine, and she forced herself to stand her ground when everything inside her urged her to retreat.

"A *moment* of brilliance? In sharp contrast to all my other moments, I suppose. A lovely compliment, although your stunned tone when uttering it took off a bit of the shine. And brilliant though I may be—albeit only for a moment—I'm afraid I'm in the dark as to what I said to inspire you so."

"I think we can agree that Lady Sarah marrying Lord Weycroft places us both in an awkward situation." At his nod, she continued, "Well then, if you are The Most Unmarriageable Man in England, and it seems quite clear you are, the matchmaker who could marry you off would score an incredible coup." She lifted her brows. "If I were successful in such an undertaking, you would gain a wife, and my reputation would be reinstated."

He adjusted his spectacles, clearly pondering her words. "My moment of brilliance clearly remains upon me as I'm following your thought process, and what you've described is a good plan. However, I cannot marry unless I am able to break the curse."

"Which a brilliant man such as yourself will certainly be able to do."

"*If* we are able to locate the missing piece of the Stone of Tears. Assuming we are successful, whom did you have in mind that I would marry?"

Meredith's brow puckered, and she once again commenced pacing. "Hmm. Yes, that is problematic. Yet surely in all of London there must be one unsuperstitious woman willing to be courted by a cursed, gossip-ridden viscount of questionable masculinity who will most likely fill their homes with ancient relics."

"I beg you to cease before all these complimentary words swell my head."

She ignored his dust-dry tone and continued pacing. "Of course, in order to ensure the reinstatement of my reputation, I must match you with just the perfect woman. Not just any woman will do."

"Well, thank goodness for that."

"But who?" She paced, puzzling it over in her mind, then halted and snapped her fingers. "Of course! The perfect woman for The Most Unmarriageable Man in England is The Most Unmarriageable Woman in England!"

"Ah. Yes, she sounds delightful."

Again she ignored him. "I can see the Society pages now—England's Most Unmarriageable Man Weds England's Most Unmarriageable Woman—and praise to Meredith Chilton-Grizedale, the acclaimed Matchmaker of Mayfair, for bringing them together." She pursed her lips and tapped her index finger against her chin. "But who is this Most Unmarriageable Woman?"

He cleared his throat. "Actually, I believe I know."

Meredith halted and turned toward him eagerly. "Excellent. Who?"

"You, Miss Chilton-Grizedale. By the time Society reads tomorrow's edition of *The Times,* *you* will be the Most Unmarriageable Woman in England."

WOMAN MARRIED FOR JUST SIX DISASTROUS HOURS STUNS CITY WITH MURDER CASE INVOLVEMENT

Kill the Competition
by Stephanie Bond
November 2003

[Atlanta, GA] Belinda Hennessey moves to Atlanta to escape all memories of her six-hour marriage. Her new friends are a hoot—they pass time spent in traffic writing an advice book on marriage and men. But the new job is *murder*—literally. When a dead body turns up at the office, Belinda fears for her life. Luckily, she's already acquainted with Officer Wade Alexander . . .

The police cruiser's blue light came on, bathing Belinda's cheeks with condemning heat each time it passed over her face. The officer was male—that she could tell from the span of his shoulders. And he wasn't happy—that she could tell from the way he banged his hand against the steering wheel. Since the cruiser sat at an angle and since her left bumper was imbedded in his right rear fender and since his right signal light still blinked, he apparently had been attempting to change lanes when she'd nailed him.

The officer gestured for her to pull over to the right. When traffic yielded, he pulled away first, eliciting another sickening scrape as their cars disengaged. She followed like a disobedient child, and despite the odd skew of her car and an ominous noise that sounded like *potato potato potato* (probably because she was hungry), managed to pull onto the narrow shoulder behind him. The driver side door of the squad car swung open, and long uniform-clad legs emerged. Belinda swallowed hard.

"Whip up some tears," Libby said.

"What?"

"Hurry, before he gets back here."

"I can't—owww!" She rubbed her fingers over the tender skin on the back of her arm where Libby had pinched the heck out of her. Tears sprang to her eyes, partly from the pain and partly from the awfulness of the situation. She tried to blink away the moisture but wound up overflowing. She was wiping at her eyes when a sharp rap sounded on her window.

"Uh-oh," Carole whispered. "He looks pissed."

An understatement. The officer was scowling, his dark hair hand-ruffled, his shadowed jaw clenched. Belinda zoomed down the window and waited.

"Is everyone okay?" he barked. Bloodshot eyes—maybe gray, maybe blue—blazed from a rocky face.

"Y-yes."

"Then save the tears."

She blinked. "I beg your pardon?"

Libby leaned forward. "My friend is late for an important meeting, Officer."

He eyed Belinda without sympathy. "That makes two of us. I need your driver's license, registration, and proof of insurance, ma'am."

Belinda reached for her purse, which had landed at her feet. "I'm sorry, Officer. I didn't see you."

"Yes, ma'am, these big white cars with sirens really blend."

He glanced at her license, then back at her.

"It's me," she mumbled. The worst driver's license photograph in history—she'd been suffering from the flu, and for some reason, wearing a Mickey Mouse sweatshirt had seemed like a good idea. She was relatively certain that a copy of the humiliating photograph was posted on bulletin boards in DMV break rooms across the state of Ohio.

"I'll be right back."

He circled around to record the numbers on her license plate, then returned to his car, every footfall proclaiming his frustration for inexperienced, un-photogenic female drivers. He used his radio presumably to report her vitals. She'd never been in trouble in her life, but her gut clenched with the absurd notion that some computer glitch might finger her as a lawless fugitive—kidnapper, forger, murderer.

The crunch of gravel signaled the officer's approach. She opened her eyes, but the flat line of his mouth caused the Berry Bonanza with calcium to roil in her stomach.

"Do you live in Cincinnati, Ms. Hennessey?"

"No, I moved here two months ago."

A muscle worked in his jaw as he scribbled on a ticket pad. "I need your address, please."

She recited it as he wrote.

"You were supposed to obtain a Georgia driver's license within thirty days of moving here."

His tone pushed her pulse higher. "I didn't know."

He tore off one, two, three tickets, then thrust them into her hand. "Now you do." He unbuttoned his cuff and began rolling up his sleeve. "I need for you ladies to move to my car, please."

Belinda gaped. "You're hauling us in?"

The officer looked heavenward, then back. "No, ma'am. You have a flat tire and at this time of day, it'll take forever for your road service to get here."

She pressed her lips together, thinking this probably wasn't the best time to say she didn't have a road service. Or a cell phone to *call* a road service.

He nodded toward the cruiser. "You'll be safer in my car than standing on the side of the road."

"I . . . thank you."

He didn't look up. "Yes, ma'am. Will you pop the trunk?"

While the women scrambled out of the car, Belinda released the trunk latch, but the resulting *click* didn't sound right. She opened her door a few inches, then slid out, bracing herself against the traffic wind that threatened to suck her into the path of oncoming cars. The toes of her shoes brushed the uneven edge of the blacktop, and she almost tripped. Her dress clung to her thighs, and her hair

whipped her cheeks. The rush of danger was strangely ex-
hilarating, strangely . . . *alluring*.

Then a large hand clamped onto her shoulder, guiding
her to the back of the car and comparative safety. "That's
a good way to become a statistic," he shouted over the
road noise.

She tilted her head to look into reproachful eyes, and
pain flickered in the back of her neck. Tomorrow she'd be
stiff. "This is very nice of you," she yelled, gesturing as if
she were playing charades.

He simply shrugged, as if to say he would've done the
same for anyone. Dark stubble stained his jaw, and for the
first time she noticed his navy uniform was a bit rumpled.
He frowned and jerked a thumb toward the cruiser. "You
should join your friends, ma'am."

At best, he probably thought she was an airhead. At
worst, a flirt. She pointed. "The trunk release didn't
sound right."

He wedged his fingers into the seam that outlined the
trunk lid, and gave a tug. "I think it's just stuck." Indeed,
on the next tug, the lid sprang open. He twisted to inspect
the latch as he worked the mechanism with his fingers.
"The latch is bent but fixable." He raised the trunk lid and
winced. "I assume the spare tire is underneath all this
stuff."

A sheepish flush crawled over her as she surveyed the
brimming contents. "I'll empty it."

He checked his watch. "I'll help. Anything personal in
here?"

She shook her head in defeat. Nothing that she could
think of, and what did it matter anyway?

But her degradation climbed as he removed item after
item that, in his hands, seemed mundane to the point of
intimate—a ten-pound bag of kitty litter, a twelve-pack of
Diet Pepsi, a pair of old running shoes with curled toes, an
orange Frisbee, a grungy Cincinnati Reds windbreaker, a
Love Songs of the '90s CD, two empty Pringles Potato
Chips canisters (she'd heard a person could do all kinds of

crafty things with them), and two gray plastic crates of reference books she'd been conveying to her cubicle one armload at a time.

Her gaze landed on a tiny blue pillow wedged between the crates, and she cringed. Unwilling to share that particular souvenir of her life, she reached in while he was bent away from her and stuffed it into her shoulder bag.

"I'll get the rest of it," he said.

She nodded and scooted out of the way. "Can I help with—"

"No." He looked up at her, then massaged the bridge of his nose. "No, ma'am. Please."

Glad for the escape, Belinda retreated to the cruiser, picking her way through gravel and mud, steeling herself against the gusts of wind. The girls had crowded into the backseat, so she opened the front passenger door and slid inside, then shut it behind her. The console of the police car was guy-heaven—buttons and lights and gizmos galore. The radio emitted bursts of static. No one said anything for a full thirty seconds.

"How much are the fines?" Carole asked.

She gave up on her hopeless hair and pulled out the three citations signed by—she squinted at the scrawl—Lt. W. Alexander. After adding the numbers in her head, she laid her head back on the headrest. "Two hundred and twenty-five dollars."

"Ooo," they chorused.

Ooo was right.

CLASS REUNION REUNITES "PERFECT" COUPLE CAN LOVE SURVIVE BAD '80s COVER BAND MUSIC?

Where Is He Now?
by Jennifer Greene
December 2003

[Michigan] Teen toasts of the town reunite! Man Most Likely to Succeed Nate Donneli and Most Popular Jeanne Cassiday brace themselves for their class reunion. It's time to discover who still has bad hair, to see who *really* became a doctor . . . and to figure out if they can have another chance at love. It's true that sometimes maturity isn't all it's cracked up to be . . . but sometimes love really is better the second time around . . .

"*Peanut.*"

The sudden masculine voice shocked her like a gunshot . . . but that voice wrapped around her old nickname—the nickname only one man had ever called her—punched her right in the heart and squeezed tight.

It took only a second for her to turn around, but in that second, she saw the round clock with the white face on the far wall. The photographs of old cars—so many they filled one wall like wallpaper. The red leather couch, the red stone counter—furnishings that seemed crazy for a garage, but then, what the sam hill did she know about mechanics and garages? She also saw the pearl-choking Martha drop her aggressive stance in a blink when it finally became obvious that Nate Donneli really did know her.

"Mr. Donneli," Martha said swiftly and sincerely, "I'm terribly sorry if I misunderstood this situation. I was trying to protect you from—"

"I know you were, Martha, and you're a wonderful protector. But the lady thinks she's looking for my father instead of me. That's what the source of the confusion is."

"I see." Martha obviously didn't.

Jeanne didn't either. She was pretty sure she'd get what was going on in a second. Or ten. But she needed a minute to breathe, to gulp in some poise, to lock onto some sense somehow.

Only damn. Temporarily her heart still felt sucker punched. Her pulse started galloping and refused to calm down.

He looked just like he always did. More mature, of course. But those dark, sexy eyes were just as wicked, could still make a girl think, *Oh, yes, please take my virginity; please do anything you want, I don't care.* He still had the cocky, defensive, bad-boy chin. The dark hair, with the one shock on his temple that wouldn't stay brushed. The thin mouth and strong jaw, and shoulders so square you'd think they were huge, when he wasn't that huge. He just had so damn much personality that he seemed big.

He was. So handsome. So in-your-face male. So take-on-all-comers wolf.

And double damn, but he'd called her Peanut.

She hadn't heard the nickname in all these years. Hadn't and didn't want to. But the fact that he even remembered it completely threw her. For God's sake, she'd been over her head, over her heart, over her life in love with him, and believed he'd felt the same way about her. Then suddenly he'd sent that cold note from Princeton: *Life's changed for me. Everything's different. I'm moving on. I don't want to hurt you, but this relationship isn't going any further. You go in with your life, find someone else. I'm never coming back.*

Those weren't the exact words. She didn't remember

the exact words, because it wasn't the words themselves that had devastated her. It was going from one day when she'd believed herself loved, when she'd loved him more than her life, believed she knew him, believed he was The One. Her Prince. The Only Man For Her. To being hurled out of his life after a semester in college because he'd "moved on"—as if that were some kind of explanation. As if real love could die as easily as a mood change.

She'd been stunned. So stunned, she realized now, that it wasn't as simple as being hurt. It rocked her world. And it was from that instant, that time when she'd been knocked flat and crushed, that she'd started down a different road. She'd started making choices she'd never wanted to make. She'd started doing what other people wanted her to do.

It was that letter. His rejection. His dropping her the way he had. That was the catalyst for her losing Jeanne Claire Cassiday. And she'd never found herself since then.

And whatever she'd meant to say, on seeing him again, what came out was "Damnit, Shadow!"

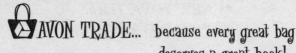